# Sometimes
# When We
# Meet

# Sometimes When We Meet

*Abie Alexander*

AA
BOOKS

First published 2009  Infinity Publishing, PA, USA

**AA Books** ISBNs

| | |
|---|---|
| *Print* | 978-1-946593-41-2 |
| *EPUB* | 978-1-946593-08-5 |
| *AZW3* | 978-1-946593-09-2 |
| *MOBI* | 978-1-946593-10-8 |
| *PDF* | 978-1-946593-11-5 |

Published in the United States of America

This is a work of fiction.  The characters, incidents, and locations described in this work (other than references to historical persons and events or actual places) are the products of the author's imagination and any resemblance to persons, living or dead, or real events or places is purely coincidental.

The opinions expressed by the characters of this work of fiction are not necessarily that of the author.

AA
BOOKS

7919 Mandan Road #103
Greenbelt, Maryland. USA 20770-2828
+1 (301) 335-5632
aa-books@outlook.com
www.abiealexander.com

*To*

*Bruce and Natalie,*

*Cynthia,*

*Dee,*

*and*

*'V'*

*-- dear friends, to whom much is owed.*

*"...a friend that sticketh closer than a brother."*

Proverbs 18:24


*"A stranger is just a friend I haven't met yet."*

Will Rogers

# Contents

## Chapter 1

Jose did not know it then, but that was the last time he would see Carl alive.

The year was 1993. The place Cochin, which has since then been renamed Kochi—not Kochi, on the Pacific coast of Japan, but the other Kochi by the Arabian Sea in Kerala State, South India.

The sweltering equatorial sun caused ripples of heat to rise from the tarmac as Jose, along with the other passengers, stepped out of the terminal to walk to the waiting aircraft. On an impulse, Jose stepped aside from the group to peer back through the glass window. He had to shade his eyes in the blinding sunlight to see Carl, his friend from Sweden, slumped over the airline counter looking disoriented and lost. Jose felt a pang of guilt for having left Carl behind alone. Things had not worked out the way they had hoped. When Jose's firm had asked him unexpectedly to go on a business trip to Bombay (now Mumbai) he and Carl rejoiced because it coincided with Carl's departure to Madras (since renamed Chennai). Jose would not only not have to take a day off from work to see Carl off at the Cochin airport but might even, if he were lucky, be routed via Madras, as the flight to Bombay was usually overbooked with migrant *Malayali* (as the Malayalam speaking residents of the state of Kerala are known) workers headed for the Middle East, and thus get to spend a few more hours in his friend's company.

Jose's wife Leena had insisted on accompanying them in the company car to the Cochin airport to see them both off.

"This will be a nice picnic!" she gushed. "I will make some *appam* and curry for us to have on the way. Carl will like it."

"He may want to keep it simple since he is on a journey," Jose said doubtfully. But he knew better than to try and dissuade his wife. It would take hours of cajoling to restore her good humor, especially because she dotted on Carl.

They had left the tea estate in the hills of Munnar in the wee hours of the morning and the breakneck driving of the tea estate driver had brought them roaring into the sleepy town of Muvattupuzha just as dawn was breaking. As soon as they had crossed the town, they stopped by the river that lent the town its name for breakfast. They sat in the car with the doors open and Leena passed the plates to Carl first and then to Jose and the driver.

"If there is anything I am going to miss when I get back to Stockholm, it will be your cooking, Leena," Carl said.

"I wish you would accept our offer and stay here. Don't go back to Sweden. Instead of living alone in Stockholm, stay with us. Leena and I will take care of you," said Jose.

"There is nothing I would love more, Jose. This, as your tourism department slogan says, is truly God's own country."

"Too much of a hyperbole, that slogan," laughed Jose.

"No. For once I think the copywriters got it right, though I am amused that a Communist government would use God as a marketing gimmick. But this *is* God's own country. There is no other place on earth that can come anywhere close. There is the seashore that runs all along one edge of your state and the hills that are less than an hour from the beach on the other. And then there are the green paddy fields and the unique backwaters with houseboats and catamarans. What more could anyone ask for?"

"Then why are you leaving us?" asked Jose smiling.

"You know perfectly why. I don't think the Indian government will ever let me stay here permanently. And it's not easy to cut myself off for good from Sweden. I have lived in that country for almost forty years now. I'm being selfish, I know, to want to have the best of both worlds. To split the time between Sweden and India."

"As long as you come and visit us every year we will be happy. You should try to obtain special permission to stay here with us on a long-term basis. Staying alone in Sweden is not good for you because of your heart problem," Leena said.

"You must come and see me in Stockholm some time, Leena. Jose has come twice. He is now a seasoned world traveler," Carl said with a smile.

"Well, I couldn't have come either time without your help," said Jose.

"*My* help? You are the one who came and helped *me*. If you hadn't come and kept me company after I was discharged from the hospital, I would be pushing up the daisies by now!"

"Enough of that kind of talk. Let's change the subject. I hope the flight to Bombay is overbooked and they put me on your flight to Madras and then on another flight to Bombay from there. There are more flights to Bombay from Madras than there are from Cochin," said Jose.

"It will be my lucky day to be chaperoned by you from Cochin to Madras and then handed over to Kannan."

"Let's hope it will all work out. We need to get going. We will stop for coffee when we get to Cochin."

The driver threw away the *beedi* he was smoking and got back into the car.

\*\*\*

*They had met for the first time around eleven years earlier. But 'met' is probably not the apt word because it was not a face-to-face meeting. Nor was it a virtual meeting through the medium of interlinked computers because all this happened before the advent of the Internet.*

*The only affordable way to have random personal contacts across international borders in those days was through the medium of amateur radio. Overseas travel was too expensive and pen-friendship through postal mail too slow.*

*Kandathil Kurian Jose, to give his full name, was fascinated by the Western world that he experienced vicariously through books and the Sunday matinee (as it was called and the only time English movies were screened in his hometown of Kottayam).*

*Jose had earned his amateur radio license the hard way. He had traveled all the way to Trivandrum (now the tongue-twister Thiruvananthapuram) by the so-called 'Fast Passenger' bus run by the government-owned transport corporation. The bus ride took four hours each way and the written test itself was three hours on complex radio theory and antiquated regulations. After the written examination came the horrid 'code test'. The sadistic examiner appeared to derive considerable pleasure from tapping out Morse code at nearly twice the fifteen-words-per-minute level that Jose was being examined for.*

*It then took a wait of ten months to find out if he had passed or failed. A folded and stapled sheet of paper stamped 'On India Government Service' arrived in the mail informing him that he was successful. It took another nineteen months for the precious ham license to arrive by registered post from the Ministry of Posts & Telegraphs in New Delhi.*

\*\*\*

Jose turned away from the terminal building. Carl had not seen him from inside the terminal. Leena, not being a passenger, could not enter the airport and she had gone back to the tea estate in Munnar in the hills in the estate car that had brought them all to Cochin. There was nothing left for him to do except join the other passengers hurrying to the Boeing 737 aircraft on the tarmac. Jose always felt a vague unease at goodbyes. As per his custom, this parting was not right. Although, as an Orthodox Christian, he did not believe in the bowing and touching of feet at farewells like the

Hindus did, he still wished he had said his goodbyes to Carl and to his wife Leena in a less abrupt manner. Seeing the throng of passengers, they had taken for granted that Jose would be on the same flight to Madras as Carl. They were caught completely unawares when an Indian Airlines employee came to them with the news that there was one vacant seat on the soon-departing flight to Bombay and Jose would have to be on that flight. Jose left his coffee unfinished and rushed to security without any farewells.

"That is the way the cookie crumbles," Carl had said philosophically as Jose picked his bag up to leave.

Jose regretted that he had not said his goodbyes before leaving Munnar. Even in the four-hour car ride, they had avoided any mention of parting.

"I wish I had thanked Carl for making this trip in spite of his ill-health. I wish I had thanked him again for his generosity," thought Jose. "Hope Kannan takes good care of him in Madras and puts him on the flight to Sweden healthier than when he arrived."

When he reached his seat, he discovered that all the overhead compartments were full and he had to stow his bag beneath the seat in front of him. It was a full flight. The bulk of the passengers were menial labor headed for the 'Gulf', the term commonly used for the Persian Gulf area. It was the lack of employment opportunities, due in part to the aggressive trade unionism of the Communists, that drove hordes of young *Malayalis* to mortgage their ancestral land and travel far distances in search of work and fortune.

The aircraft hurtled down the runway that ended just a few hundred feet from the edge of the water and was airborne over the Arabian Sea. As the plane slowly climbed into the gray clouds, the outside turned dark and the plane shuddered violently. Jose reflexively gripped the armrests. In spite of his own fears, he turned to look at the passenger across the aisle. The man sat petrified, sweat pouring down his creased forehead. The plane lurched again, more heavily than before. Then it hit an air pocket and seemed to fall vertically. There was a clicking sound and then the oxygen mask above the scared passenger dropped down, dangling six inches from his face. It must have been a malfunction of some sort because none of the other masks deployed. But for the frightened passenger it seemed to be the end of the world. A wordless scream seemed to emanate from his lips as tears joined the sweat dribbling down his face.

In another minute the plane had climbed above the rain clouds and it was as calm as calm could be. The emotionally exhausted passenger fell back in his seat out of sheer relief and closed his eyes. Jose smiled.

***

*Jose's joy had known no bounds when the ham radio license arrived. He had had no inkling when it would come. Like most government permissions in developing countries, there was no indication whether it would take months or years. He had begun work on building a transmitter immediately after he received the notice of passing the tests. But he had decided that the antenna could wait. The transmitter construction was no easy job. He was not a fan of do-it-yourself electronics ('home-brew' in ham parlance) but he could not afford the cost of an imported Japanese transceiver. So, he had modified an old valve radio to receive Morse code and single-sideband transmissions. He hoped the self-constructed transmitter would help him communicate with the world.*

*He loved the call sign the government had allotted him – VU2KKJ, the initials of his name. When he said it aloud phonetically, it had a nice ring to it. "Victor Uniform Two Kilo Kilo Juliet". He repeated it over and over reveling in his new unique identifier in the international radio world. After years of passively listening to general broadcast and ham radio transmissions, he would now be able to transmit on his own from the comfort of his home and communicate with fellow amateur radio operators all over the world. Jose was thrilled.*

*Within an hour of receiving the license, Jose measured out ordinary insulated electrical wire and made a crude dipole antenna. But he needed the help of Koshy, the telephone department's pole-climber, to shinny up two coconut trees in the yard to suspend the wire dipole about thirty-five feet above the ground.*

*"Isn't this a little too high for hanging clothes out to dry?" asked Koshy sarcastically when he had climbed down.*

*When Jose connected his homebrew transmitter he was in business.*

*Jose tapped out a general call in Morse code to any listening station: "CQ CQ CQ de VU2KKJ …". His first contact was with VU2RCH in the north-eastern state of Assam. His heart pounded with excitement as he tapped out his name and location and exchanged signal reports with Ranjit, the other ham. He was so excited he needed to take a break when they ended the contact. He entered the details into his logbook and marveled at the power of radio. He had just made contact with another ham more than a thousand miles away using just a piece of wire and a few watts of power. He was euphoric.*

*A little later the same afternoon he made contacts with other Indian hams from Madras, Bombay, Delhi, and Hyderabad.*

*He realized after tuning and retuning the transmitter that the home-brew transmitter was not stable enough for voice communication on single-sideband and he could only operate on Morse code. The initial contacts were not easy, due in equal parts to his nervousness about being 'on the air' and to the instability of the transmitter he had built. Over the next few days, Jose's proficiency in Morse code rapidly increased and he was pounding away on the brass key whenever he had some time to spare.*

*But this was still months before he met Carl.*

***

After the flight landed in Bombay he took a pre-paid taxi from the airport straight to the hotel in Cuffe Parade where his office had booked him a room. To his utter consternation, he discovered that the hotel was overbooked and there were no rooms available. The taxi had already left by then. He had to wait for almost an hour before another taxi arrived with a guest. It was only on the third try that he found a hotel that had a vacant room. By then it was past the closing time of the office at the tea estate. "Contacting them will have to wait until tomorrow afternoon," he decided, because his meeting with the importer of tea from Russia was at nine o'clock in the morning and his office would open only at ten. This was before cellphones arrived a decade later and revolutionized communications in India. The unreliable and expensive landline was the sole means of telephonic contact at that time.

Jose was more concerned about Leena and Carl than he was about informing the office of his whereabouts. He wondered how Carl was faring in Madras. He hoped Carl had got a seat with enough legroom and that Kannan had met him on arrival at the airport instead of turning up late as he had done on previous occasions.

He tried calling their home phone to tell Leena of his safe arrival. But the call would not go through.

Wearily he walked out to the Iranian restaurant he had noticed on the way in and had mutton *biryani* for dinner. On his way back, he tried again to call Leena from another PCO (public call office) but all he got was a busy tone at the other end.

***

Carl meanwhile was frustrated, angry, and close to a physical breakdown. His flight to Madras was delayed but, as was typical, there were no announcements. An hour passed before infuriated passengers were served coffee and a slice each of fruitcake. Another hour and a half of waiting followed before departure was finally announced. Carl felt weak from exhaustion. The sweating had dehydrated him. He was afraid he would have another heart attack like the one he had had on arrival from Sweden. His throat had dried up and he imagined pain radiating to his neck and arms. He wished he were back in Stockholm, in the midst of his stamps and coins and just a phone call away from efficient medical care.

To make matters worse, the flight turned out to be a nightmare. The seats were so crammed together that there was not enough leg space. The cabin crew were unsympathetic. "You should travel business class if you cannot fit into these seats," they suggested unhelpfully. In the waning light, the plane flew into a thunderstorm and the turbulence was so intense that several passengers were sick. The pilot did not seem to be in any hurry to get out of the thunder and lightning.

And, to top it all, when he landed in Madras, Kannan was nowhere to be found.

*** 

*It was the kindness and generosity of Japanese hams that put Jose in the big league. And if it weren't for them he probably would never have met Carl.*

*Jose's love affair with Japanese hams started with his very first radio contact, or QSO in ham jargon, with an overseas ham, who turned out to be from Onomichi city in Hiroshima prefecture in Japan. JA4DOB, Kono-san, an English schoolteacher, was the quintessential amateur radio operator – polite, precise and friendly. From then on there was no looking back. In a short period of six months, he had made over a thousand Japanese contacts.*

*Japanese hams wanted him to operate not just code but also voice and with more output power. Teru-san, JM2HBO from Komaki city in Aichi prefecture, bought him a Yaesu-Musen transceiver and Hide-san, JG5UNQ from Kochi city in Kochi prefecture, carried it to India on a visit. Another ham, Yujiro-san, JF6WCP from Nagasaki prefecture, sent him a factory-made beam antenna and rotor.*

The new equipment opened up a whole new world to Jose. Soon he was chatting away with hams from Japan, Russia, England, East and West Germany, Finland—and even the USA—when conditions were right. Morse code was rarely used after that.

It took only a half-hour to dismantle his station at Kottayam when he was selected as a management trainee at the tea estate in Munnar. But getting the new location registered on his license took almost six months, thanks to the bureaucratic red tape at the government offices in New Delhi.

The tea plantation turned out to be a ham radio enthusiast's paradise – acres and acres of tea shrubs and no electrical interference. The new site was just as close to the equator as the previous location and the elevation of the foothills added a punch to his signal.

After a day of managing the office and driving around the tea plantation, there was no better way for Jose to relax than to sit down and connect to the rest of the world through the medium of radio, while his colleagues drank and plotted ways to seduce young tea-pickers.

It was one such evening as he sipped his coffee and twiddled the radio dial that he met Carl.

He had just made a general CQ call for any station to respond when he heard a faint response through the static.

"VU2KKJ this is Sugar Mike Five Bravo Foxtrot Echo."

Jose wasn't sure he had heard right. It was not often that he heard a call from Sweden.

*"Would you give me your call again, please? Did you say, Sugar Mike? Are you calling from Sweden? This is Victor Uniform Two Kilo Kilo Juliet."*

*"Roger! VU2KKJ this is SM5BFE – Sugar Mike Five Big Fat Elephant! The handle is Carl. The location is Stockholm, the capital of Sweden."*

*Neither of them knew it then, but that was the beginning of a lifelong friendship that would end only with the death of one of them.*

\*\*\*

Kannan arrived at last but did not seem to think he was late.

"How do you do, Mr. Carl? I am so glad you have come."

He had on a brightly colored yellow and brown shirt, navy blue trousers, and a pair of white tennis shoes, looking every bit a gaudy Tamil film star.

"I wish I were half as glad," replied Carl wearily. "Where were you? My plane landed ages ago."

"I called the airport and they told me your plane was late and the baggage service is also very slow here," replied Kannan unperturbed.

Carl realized there was no point arguing. Punctuality was not one of Kannan's strong points.

"Just take me to my hotel. I am tired. I need some rest," Carl said resignedly.

"I have arranged an *autorickshaw* for you," said Kannan.

"*What?*" shouted Carl unable to contain his exasperation. "Why didn't you hire a taxi like everybody else? Who travels in a tiny three-wheeler from an airport?"

"I thought you liked *autos*," Kannan defensively.

"I like *autorickshaws* for traveling around the city. Not from an airport with heavy baggage!"

Kannan took charge of the baggage trolley. When they reached the curb, he said to Carl, "Please wait here while I get the *auto*."

The *autorickshaw*, the ubiquitous black and yellow three-wheeler with open sides (a modified scooter really), arrived a short while later. It did not look as if the *autorickshaw* could contain the two of them and the large suitcase. In the end, Carl shared the rear seat with his suitcase while Kannan perched on the edge of the driver's seat in front, holding the driver around his waist with his left arm while clutching the rim of the roof with his right.

The three-wheeler sputtered to life when the driver cranked the engine by tugging on a metal rod.

Carl invariably hired these vehicles for getting around Indian cities. They were cheap and could navigate the chaotic Indian traffic better than a taxi.

"I have arranged with the driver to pick you up every day for sightseeing. His name is Muthu. He understands English."

As if on cue the driver grinned at him through the broken rearview mirror and said, "Yess, saar! My name is Muthu!"

Muthu and his three-wheeler *auto* were to play a fateful role in the events that were to unfold.

***

*Jose and Carl exchanged names, signal reports and locations like all ham stations do when they make a contact. But when Jose gave his location as*

Kerala, Carl asked pointedly, "Where exactly in Kerala?"

"Central Kerala," was Jose's reply.

"What is the name of your town in central Kerala?" persisted Carl.

"You won't find it on any map in Sweden," said Jose.

"I am sure it is there on mine!" answered Carl. "You see, I have been to your state and I have a map of Kerala on my wall."

"Really?" Jose couldn't believe what he was hearing.

"Yes. And I have been there not once but several times," said Carl with a chuckle.

"I would never have imagined!" said a surprised Jose. "I am transmitting from a tea estate at a place called Munnar in the hills. This is close to a lake called Periyar Lake."

"I have been there too!" said Carl, laughing at the astonishment of his friend. "Lovely wildlife sanctuary you have there called Periyar. It also goes by the name of Thekkady. One of India's finest. So many elephants!"

"I am completely floored," was all Jose could say.

"I also know that Kerala was the first province in the world to elect a Communist government to power. That happened in the first general elections in the '50s. Your state has the highest literacy rate in India. Higher even than some Western nations."

"You do know a lot about my state. Surprised would be an understatement."

Unlike other random radio contacts that usually never occur again, Jose and Carl agreed to meet a second time the following weekend.

"The fifteen meter-band works best," Jose said.

"Let's meet on Saturday and again on Sunday," Carl suggested.

The time they set was twelve o'clock Greenwich Mean Time, the standard time used by amateurs worldwide. This would be five thirty in the evening in India and two in the afternoon in Stockholm in summer.

In the middle of their second contact, the following Saturday Jose noticed that Carl was pronouncing his name Spanish style.

"That's not how my name is pronounced, Carl," protested Jose gently.

"Not as in 'no way José'?" asked Carl.

"No! I am not Spanish," Jose said. "My name is not pronounced like José Feliciano's. My name is spelt as in Joseph without the last two letters. J-O-S-E- and is pronounced with a 'j' as in Japan and with the last 'e' silent. It rhymes with 'nose'."

"I got it. I'm sorry," Carl said.

"No, that's OK. You don't need to apologize."

"Carl is not my first name either really. My name is Alain Carlson. I prefer Carl to my first name which I don't really like."

They talked about Carl's experiences on a houseboat on the backwaters during his last visit to Kerala.

"Have you been to Europe or America?" asked Carl.

"No, that is something I cannot afford on my meager salary. Radio contacts are good enough for me. When's your next visit to India?"

"I have been coming every other winter for the past ten years. The cold here is brutal. I cannot bear it anymore. I am getting old. When I am in India I stay three to four weeks depending on how well my stocks have done and then I head back to Sweden."

"I envy you!" Jose said.

Thus, was set a schedule that they kept week after week till Jose was compelled to give up the hobby and except, of course, when they were visiting each other or were otherwise engaged.

## Chapter 2

Jose's first trip to Sweden had happened nine years earlier in the year1984. Delhi was scorching hot that day in June when Jose arrived in the nation's capital from distant Kerala.

While it was peaceful in South India, trouble had been brewing for some years in the North Indian state of Punjab. This state, which had seen more prosperity than any other Indian state, was in the throes of a revolt. Separatists were waging an increasingly overt war against the Indian government for the creation of an independent Khalistan nation. Sant Jarnail Singh Bhindranwale, their leader, was sowing the seeds of dissension openly and with impunity.

For a person from near the equator to find the weather unbearably hot, it had to be truly hot. And at fifty degrees on the Centigrade scale, it was sizzling. "How fitting that the name of the Centigrade scale is being changed to Celsius," thought Jose as he stood on the sidewalk waiting to catch an *autorickshaw*. He had just remembered that Celsius was a Swedish scientist and it was to Sweden that he would soon be headed if he could get the tickets and a visa.

"How much would fifty degrees Celsius be on the Fahrenheit scale?" wondered Jose idly as he tried to keep his mind off the uncomfortable wait in the blinding sun.

He had arrived after a three-day journey by train from Cochin; first to Madras on the smoke-spewing, steam engine driven Madras Mail and from there by the diesel-electric Grand Trunk Express all the way to Delhi. He did not mind the discomfort of the crowded sleeper coach with no air-conditioning. He knew he had to save every rupee he could for the plane ticket to Sweden. He slept only fitfully during the three nights on the train. It was not the rocking of the train and the noise of vendors and passengers that kept him awake but the excitement of his first trip overseas and the fear of having his belongings stolen.

*** 

The day before his departure from the tea estate his colleagues had thrown him a farewell party. His peers were a motley lot.

There was Asokan Nair, the trainee overseer. He was the black sheep of his family. His job was to supervise the foremen of the estate who managed the tea-pickers, the majority of them being *Adivasi* women who belonged to the old untouchable class. Their pariah status did not deter the sexually repressed Asokan from flirting with the young girls and making every effort, so far unsuccessful, to seduce the more susceptible of them. The girls did not succumb to his overtures because older women had warned them of the wiles of 'bourgeois' managers. Asokan had one other distinguishing habit. Though a Hindu, he had no compunctions about eating beef. He also drank like a fish.

Hariharan Iyer, the Brahmin, was the trainee-engineer in the factory. Hari, as he liked to be called, was a math wizard and had won the university's gold medal for the highest marks in mechanical engineering. His distinguishing feature was the parallel lines he painted on his forehead every morning with white ash, as is customary for devout upper-caste Hindus. He had started out as an ascetic but was slowly being drawn into the decadent lifestyle of tea garden managers. He was introduced to alcohol soon after he got to the tea estate. After a disastrous initiation, he had taken to booze like a duck takes to water.

Rounding off their group was Chandy Thomas, a born-again Pentecostal Christian, who was the trainee tea-taster. This job suited him well because he was not only a teetotaler but also a non-smoker. On account of his religious convictions, he also abjured almost everything worldly, including movies, as evil. He confined himself to his work with single-minded dedication. Chandy's tea-tasting consisted of delicately sniffing the light brew, then sipping it and swirling it around in his mouth before drawing it to the back of the throat and up to the olfactory nerve. He would then spit it delicately into a bowl that the peon held out. Finally, Chandy would daintily dab his mouth with a thin white cotton towel and make his pronouncement on the quality of the tea he had just tasted.

There could not have been a more disparate group. But they considered themselves immensely lucky to have been chosen as management trainees from a veritable sea of applicants. On their first day at work the personnel manager, puffing on his trademark cheroot, had told them that they had been carefully handpicked (he repeated 'handpicked' to make sure that the allusion to tea-leaf plucking was not lost on the listeners). Jose was relieved that he did not have to remain unemployed for very long. By the time his undergraduate results had been published five months after the written examination, the selection process in the tea estate had also been complete. This was not the job he had yearned for. The coveted government administrative cadre was his ambitious goal. But he was happy that he had got this job without having to pay an exorbitant bribe that would have kept him indebted for many years.

Jose did not remember much of what transpired that evening. His thoughts were on the first foreign trip that he would soon be undertaking.

Asokan had a worn-out copy of *Playboy* that he was trying to get Chandy to take a look at. Chandy steadfastly refused.

"A look will not kill you," taunted Asokan.

Chandy shook his head. "I think it will harm me more than you think. It will wound my soul," he said.

"What will you do when you get married? You won't look at your wife?" Asokan persisted.

"I don't want to talk about it. I consider marriage sacred."

"OK, holy man, have it your way. Pass me the beef."

Chandy handed over the stainless-steel plate with the roast beef.

"Asokan, since Chandy doesn't want the *Playboy*, I will take it," piped up Hari, "I will return it to you tomorrow."

Asokan lit a cigarette and blew rings as he studied Jose.

"You are the lucky one. Next week you will be looking at the real thing in Sweden while Hari and myself are looking at these pictures," said Asokan. Hari laughed uproariously and Asokan himself joined in.

"That's not the reason I am going to Stockholm," Jose said defensively. "I am going to attend the amateur radio conference."

"That's what you keep telling us. Who knows what your real intentions are!" laughed Asokan stroking his slick oily hair.

"I don't even know if I will get a visa."

"Carry all your certificates and the letter from the company. You will get it," Chandy said encouragingly.

"Kurup!" shouted Asokan, "Bring some banana chips for Hari *sar*. Don't you know he doesn't eat meat?"

"And some water for me," added Chandy.

A little later Kurup, the servant, scooted in carrying a plate of fried banana chips and a glass of water.

"Are you taking any chips with you to Sweden?" asked Hari. "You know this is unique to Kerala. Even in North India, you won't get this."

"I don't know if I should take it or not. It is a long trip. It might get spoiled. And I don't even know if my friend Carl likes it that much."

"Here, have some more whiskey," offered Asokan.

"No, thanks. I have had two pegs already. I don't want to board the train to Madras with a hangover tomorrow."

"This rum is good," Hari said, pouring himself another drink. "*Old Monk* is the best rum in the world."

"You can keep your *Old Monk.* What I need is a young nun!" guffawed Asokan.

"Please don't say indecent things," protested Chandy.

"What is indecent about this? It is only a pun. Anyway you Pentecostals are enemies of the Catholics. Why are you defending them now?"

"Cool it," said Jose. "Listen Asokan, I would advise you to leave the *Adivasi* women alone. The personnel manager told me that the recently set up Communist labor unions are very assertive and are flexing their muscles for a showdown. The instigators are pushing for violence against manipulative and oppressive managers. They view us as the ruling class that is harassing them. There is trouble brewing in the workers' sections of almost all tea estates, including ours."

"I don't care. What can those illiterate louts do to me? It is the privilege of rulers to treat their subjects like scum. Jose, tell me have you ever seen a naked woman?" asked Asokan.

"Is there no other subject in the world that interests you? Does it always have to be sex, sex, sex?" Jose was clearly irritated.

"Why don't you answer my question?" persisted Asokan, his words were slurred from the whiskey.

"If you insist – the answer is no," replied Jose.

"Twenty-nine years old and haven't see the naked female form yet!" Asokan laughed derisively. "You are going to Sweden, the world's capital of blue movies. Be sure to watch a few porn movies while you are there – if you can't get the real stuff."

Hari, half-drunk already, found the advice funny and laughed uncontrollably.

"This is too much. I must go," Chandy said. "I will see you tomorrow morning before you leave."

"I will leave too. Must finish my packing and get some sleep. I have a three-day train journey ahead of me."

"Two leaves and a bud! That is all we need to know. Ripe for the picking! Two leaves and a bud! That is the whole story of tea," ranted Asokan drunkenly.

The next morning only Chandy was there to see him off on the bus to Cochin. Asokan and Hari were nowhere to be seen and Jose guessed that they were sleeping off their hangover.

***

It had all started very innocuously about four months earlier.

*Jose's skill in ham radio had increased rapidly in the year and a half he had been at the tea estate. He added another two thousand Japanese ham stations to his logbook. He had under his belt a little over a thousand European stations as well. But by far the most frequent contact was with Carl. Although they had initially agreed to meet only on weekends they had a brief chat almost every day. Sweden being four hours and thirty minutes behind India,*

Carl hurried home from his translation jobs to catch Jose before he shut his station down for the night.

In the middle of one of their long radio conversations, Carl popped a question to Jose out of the blue.

"Do you want to come to Sweden?"

There was a pause at the other end.

"Now how is that linked to the topic we were discussing, which was the tropical monsoon?"

"No direct connection except that the European Amateur Radio conference will be held in Stockholm this year just about the time the monsoon will be hitting the coastline of Kerala!"

"Carl, I think you keep forgetting my situation. I am in only the second year of my first job. A foreign trip is simply not possible in the short-term," replied Jose.

"My question was not whether you were planning on participating in the conference but whether you would like to come to Sweden?"

"That is only a – what's the word for it? – hypothetical question?"

"Answer it all the same," persisted Carl.

"Of course, I would like to come to Sweden! But what is the probability of that happening?"

"It is higher than you think," answered Carl.

"Really? Are the organizers handing out free tickets to Indian hams to attend?" joked Jose.

"No, I don't think they can afford that kind of expense though they certainly would like hams from all over the world to participate," responded Carl.

"*The hotel costs for five days and the return air ticket together will cost a fortune.*"

"*But who is suggesting that you stay in an expensive hotel? I just realized that Hotel Domus, the conference venue, is right in the city, well connected by bus and the underground. And I have a guest room.*"

"Wow! This is most unexpected!" exclaimed Jose excitedly. "You mean you are inviting me to stay with you?"

"*Wait! There's more. My stocks did so well on the stock exchange that I received something like a windfall.*"

"*Congratulations, Carl! You can use the extra cash for your next trip to India.*"

"*Well, I have set aside enough for that. And I still have three thousand Swedish kronor left over. This won't cover the full cost of a return air ticket but it will cover some of it. I want to give this to you so you can come for the conference,*" said Carl.

"*That is very kind of you. But how can you give me so much money? You don't even know me.*"

"*I have known you for almost two years now and though we haven't met I have a pretty good estimate of who you are.*"

"*I am still reluctant to accept money from you. There is nothing I can give in return,*" Jose said hesitantly.

"*I am the one who benefits more – I will have the pleasure of your company for a week without having to travel all the way to India. I would like you to accept it.*"

"Thank you, Carl. You are very generous. All right, I accept it gratefully and with much happiness."

"Good! I will wire you the money tomorrow."

"But I don't have a passport!"

"Well, go get one pronto!"

Jose did not lose any time. He walked over to the house of the marketing manager the same night and got his verbal approval for a day's casual leave the next day. The next morning, he caught the first bus to the state capital Trivandrum and, after a hectic day of filling up forms and getting certificates attested, he submitted his passport application under the fast-track scheme to the Regional Passport Commissioner.

Even the fast-track route took a month and a half. First came a uniformed police constable for verification and then a detective in mufti from the criminal investigation department. Jose paid bribes of a hundred rupees to each of them to move the file along.

The money that Carl wired took two whole weeks, much to Carl's impatience, to be credited to Jose's bank account and it lay there till the passport arrived one morning by registered post.

In the meantime, they had come to the understanding that Jose should stay for a minimum of two weeks instead of just one week.

***

In the searing heat of Delhi, Jose directed the *autorickshaw* to Connaught Place, to an Indian travel agency called Gita Travels. He hoped that they would be more accommodating towards a greenhorn traveler like him than an international travel agency. "How did the street get its Irish name? Must be our colonial heritage," wondered Jose as he got out of the *autorickshaw*. When he entered the cool, air-conditioned office he was overwhelmed by its elegance and upscale ambience. He walked diffidently to the chic lady in a stylish sari.

"Do you book plane tickets?" asked Jose clearing his throat nervously.

The woman looked him up and down with a haughty air.

"We do. But we don't do it for everybody," she said arrogantly with her nose in the air.

Even if English wasn't his first language Jose saw the snub in the sneering words and his ears burned with shame.

"Sorry," he stammered in confusion before stepping back out on the hot pavement.

"This trip is not going to be easy," he thought as he weighed his options between going to a fly-by-night shop or to an established travel agent. Finally, he decided to go to Thomas Cook. "Their fees might be high but at least they won't cheat me out of my money because I don't speak Hindi," reasoned Jose.

His move paid off. The middle-aged agent at Thomas Cook spoke fluent English and was most helpful. He did not seem to mind that this was Jose's first trip overseas.

"When do you have to be in Stockholm?" he asked.

"The conference starts on the 8th," replied Jose.

"That gives us just three days."

"I don't mind if I get there a day late—if it cannot be helped."

"Do you want to travel by the cheapest means or do you have a lot of money?" the agent smiled as he asked.

"I have no idea how much the ticket will cost. But I cannot afford expensive travel," Jose replied dispiritedly.

"OK, not to worry. Let me see if something can be done." He then pulled out the heavy book with airline schedules (again, this was before the days of the Internet) and expertly thumbed through the pages making notes on a pad in front of him. Finally, he looked up.

"SAS flies direct to Stockholm but their weekly flight was yesterday. The only way you can get there is by flying to a European city like Frankfurt, London or Amsterdam and then catching another flight to Stockholm."

"I can do that," Jose jumped in excitedly.

"But there is a catch."

"What is the catch?" Jose asked.

"The cost would be nearly twice that of the direct flight from here on SAS. Flights within Europe are very, very expensive," said the travel agent.

"Then I may have to forget my plans and go back to Kerala."

"Not so fast! There is one other option. There is a Lufthansa flight to Frankfurt tomorrow night which will get you into West Germany. From there you can travel by train to Stockholm and be there before the conference starts."

"*Really?*" Jose cried excitedly.

"Yes. And the total cost will be only slightly more than the direct flight to Stockholm," beamed the agent.

"I cannot believe it! Traveling by train is better. I can see more of Europe!"

"I will block a seat for you right away. But you need to run to the Embassy of West Germany and get a visa for West Germany. You don't need a visa for Sweden."

"Thanks a million!" said Jose.

He caught the first *auto* he could find and rushed to the West German Embassy located at Chanakyapuri near Nyaya Marg. But, unfortunately for him, the consular section had just closed their receiving counter for the day.

"The planets are working against me," thought Jose and then he corrected himself, "I don't believe in that astrology claptrap of the Hindus."

He went back to Thomas Cook.

The agent was sympathetic. "They usually take a day for issuing the visa and return your passport the next day, but if you go early in the morning and be the first in the line and explain the situation to the visa officer, things might work out for you. Show them the conference invitation. If you have a ticket it might help."

"What happens if – God forbid – they don't issue me a visa? Can I cancel the ticket?"

"You can but there will be a small penalty," said the agent.

"You know what, I will buy that ticket now!" Jose said after a minute's thought. "Whatever it takes, I am going to be on that plane!" he said with determination.

"When will you be returning?" asked the agent.

"Exactly two weeks after the date of arrival."

"You had better convert your money also today. You may not get enough time for this tomorrow. I can give you currency notes and traveler's checks in dollars."

"Can you give me Deutsche marks or Swedish kronor?" asked Jose.

"Sorry. We deal only in dollars here. You can convert dollars to marks or kronor after you get to Europe."

Jose got two hundred dollars in currency notes and three hundred dollars in traveler's checks.

This was the first time he had seen a hundred-dollar bill. After he got back to his cramped hotel room at Paharganj he examined the note closely. He marveled at the value of this small sheet of paper. The thick wad of Indian money that he had been carrying on his person had shrunk to just two currency notes and three traveler's checks, all of which fit unobtrusively in his wallet.

***

The next morning Jose rushed to the West German Embassy with his passport, ticket, money, and papers in hand.

Nervously he explained his predicament to the visa officer.

"Have you had any radio contact with hams in our Embassy?" asked the visa officer looking up from the invitation to the ham radio conference.

"No, I didn't know there were hams in the Embassy," said Jose surprised.

"There are. And why are you traveling by train instead of catching a connecting flight?"

"Sir, airfares are too expensive ..." Jose stammered apologetically.

After leafing through the rest of the papers the visa officer looked up again.

"Normally we issue visa only the next day but since you are traveling on the Lufthansa flight tonight, I will make an exception. You can come and collect your passport from the Embassy at four o'clock this evening."

Jose's joy knew no bounds. After profusely thanking the visa officer, Jose rushed back to Thomas Cook.

"You had better get some rest before the journey tonight. See you don't get sunstroke running about in the hot sun. You have turned as black as coal in two days. Drink lots of water to prevent dehydration," advised the travel agent.

"I will do everything you say!" said Jose with a smile.

"Here is a small gift for you," said the travel agent handing over an elongated leather wallet. "This will hold your passport, air ticket, traveler's checks and foreign currency all in one place."

Jose thought the shiny red leather ticket holder was beautiful.

"Thank you very much. Without your help I would not be making this trip," said Jose fervently as he shook the travel agent's hand.

When he had reached the door, the agent called out, "Remember, the railway station in Frankfurt is close to the airport. There is one other thing. Buy a jacket. You will need it."

On the way back to the hotel, Jose stopped at the Karol Bagh market and bought a second-hand navy-blue jacket. The Bhutia vendor looked at him as if he was crazy buying a jacket in the hot summer. When he reached his hotel room in Paharganj he straightaway drank two carafes of iced water. With all the excitement, he had forgotten how unbearably hot it was. He took a shower and washed his sweat-soaked clothes. Then he pulled the blinds down and tried to sleep, pressing the pillow over his head to drown out the noisy whirring of the fan and the traffic outside.

But try as he might, Jose could not sleep. When he shut his eyes, he saw visions of Germany and Sweden and, for some strange reason, Lapland. In the *autorickshaw* headed for the West German Embassy, he remembered that he had studied about Lapland in the fifth grade.

The passport was ready at the delivery counter. During the ride back to the hotel in the *autorickshaw,* Jose opened the passport several times to look fondly at the West German visa. His name, painstakingly handwritten, on the visa sticker, looked strangely alien in the foreign hand. He gently caressed the national emblem of *Bundesrepublik Deutschland* and smiled.

\*\*\*

Jose reached the Delhi International airport (to be later renamed the Indira Gandhi International airport after her assassination) a full five hours before departure. It felt only slightly cooler inside and the milling crowds gave it the impression of being a railway station rather than an international airport. After checking through security, sleep finally caught up with Jose and he slept soundly as he sat waiting for his flight to be announced.

When he boarded Lufthansa LH-661 at 1:15 AM, the atmosphere was decidedly different. There was already a touch of foreignness – the blonde air hostesses and the spick and span interior.

"Are you Jana ... Janar ... dhan ... Acha ... Acharya?" one of the airhostesses asked the distinguished looking gentleman sitting in the row ahead.

"Yes, that is me," the man responded.

"Sorry, your names are so difficult to pronounce," she said apologetically.

"Your names are equally difficult for us, madam," came the prompt riposte.

The air hostess blushed scarlet. "Sorry, I did not mean it that way. I apologize."

Jose had an aisle seat. The longhaired young man in the seat next to him leaned forward talked animatedly to a redhead in the middle seat across the aisle. Having listened to Radio Nederland on short-wave radio, Jose guessed that they were speaking in Dutch. Jose pushed back in his seat so they could talk to each other. The young man was apologetic.

"Sorry! She's my girlfriend. We spent two months in India. We are going back," the longhaired guy explained.

"No problem," replied Jose. "Would you like to sit together? I can change seats with your girlfriend."

The young man looked surprised. "But you have an aisle seat!"

"It is not that important. It is only for a few hours," said Jose.

"This is very surprising. Thank you! Very friendly! Very friendly!" repeated the young man shaking his head.

Jose moved to the middle seat, nodding to the smiling redhead as they crossed each other.

Soon they were airborne. Jose was surprised when dinner was served on reaching cruising height. "It is 2:00 a.m. and almost morning!" he said to himself. This was his introduction to Western cuisine. There was no rice! But he thoroughly enjoyed the delicate aroma and flavor of the meal and cleaned his plate out completely. He noticed that the Indian gentleman next to him had hardly touched anything.

"I don't like this foreign food," he complained.

"That is too bad. The food is actually very good," Jose replied. Inside he wondered, "Why is he going abroad then if he hates foreign things?"

After the trays were cleared the movie came on. It was *Gorky Park* with William Hurt and Lee Marvin. Much as he wanted to watch the film (it would be at least two years before this movie came to his town), the exhaustion of the last five days, coupled with the immense relief of actually having accomplished the near-impossible, brought sleep on almost immediately and Jose slept the sleep of death as the aircraft winged its way through the night to Frankfurt.

When he awoke, after what only seemed a short while, breakfast was being served. Jose enjoyed the omelet, bacon, and sausage. The man next to him went hungry again pushing his tray away in disgust much to the amusement of Jose.

As the Boeing 747 descended, Jose looked out of the window and was stunned to see the dark woods and the speeding orderly traffic on the motorways, a far cry from the teeming chaos and mayhem of Indian roads. Everything looked so neat and perfect. He had never seen anything like it before.

As the plane touched down he remembered that he only had a little over two hours to get to the rail station, purchase the ticket to Stockholm, and get on board the train.

He watched with amusement as the Indian passengers pushed and jostled and created a minor nuisance while the Westerners waited patiently for their turn to disembark.

## Chapter 3

The official at Passport Control eyed him suspiciously.

"Why are you in Germany?" he asked in a gruff voice.

Jose fished out his ticket and itinerary from the Thomas Cook ticket holder.

"I am traveling to Stockholm to attend a radio conference," explained Jose.

The official wordlessly stamped the visa and pushed the passport back to him.

Jose rushed to the baggage claim area. He looked around at the throng of people and could not believe that a single aircraft had carried so many people and so much heavy luggage all the way from India. His bag took forever to appear on the conveyor belt.

After a quick stop at the restroom, Jose hurried to the railway station. Downward pointing arrows led him from the second level. Here he came up against the escalator for the first time in his life. He had never seen a moving staircase before. He was scared he might fall down and make a fool of himself. Nervously he balanced his heavy bag and stepped onto the moving step. He was about midway when he heard a high-pitched scream of terror and saw a woman lying on the ground at the foot of the opposite escalator with the heel of her shoe caught between the moving steps.

"*Hilfe! Helfen sie mir!*" she shouted in terror. The machine kept pulling her back even as she clawed the floor. A bystander charged in and pressed the emergency stop button bringing the escalator to a halt. All this happened in only a few seconds. Watching transfixed, Jose forgot to mind his own step and nearly fell down himself when his step reached the bottom. He felt some consolation that he had navigated this unscathed while the lady who probably had used elevators all her life was not so lucky.

From there he followed the exit signs and was soon outside. He looked around but could not locate anything that looked, even remotely, like a railway station – or at least like the railway stations of India. He looked at his watch. It had taken him almost an hour to get through immigration and to collect his baggage. He wondered anxiously whether he would be able to make it to the train in time. He walked up and down the sidewalk lugging the heavy suitcase looking for the train station. He could neither hear any cacophony nor see any swarming multitudes that he associated with Indian railway stations. He looked around puzzled for some indication of a railway line. There was none.

Finally, he took courage and accosted a man hurrying out of the airport.

"Excuse me, sir, do you know where the railway station is?"

The man only snorted disdainfully and quickened his pace.

Jose tried again but with no success. This time the answer was polite but in German. He guessed from the body language and from what the man said that he did not understand English. Or did not want to speak in English. Jose had thought that all Westerners spoke and understood English. He realized now how wrong he was. Resignedly he turned back to the airport. He decided to try his luck one more time. The tall older gentleman reading the newspaper was more helpful.

"Excuse me, sir, can you tell me the way to the railway station?" asked Jose.

"Entschuldigung! Excuse me, mine English ... ist not very goot. What did you say?" he asked in a heavily accented voice.

"The railway station?" replied Jose.

The man shook his head.

"Railway ... rail ... train," tried Jose desperately.

"Ah! The train! Die Bahnhof!" exclaimed the gentleman. "It is below," he said pointing his finger to the ground.

"Is he out of his mind or is he making fun of me?" wondered Jose.

Sensing Jose's incomprehension the man repeated, "It is below ... underground ..."

Then it registered. "That was why the directions pointed downward! The train station was actually under the airport!" Jose thought excitedly.

Jose profusely thanked the gentleman before hastening back inside the airport. His helper beamed back in happiness, glad that he was able to help.

Jose had only read about underground trains but had never seen one. All trains in India ran overground. He would never have guessed that there would be a train station beneath an airport. He was amazed.

Jose took the elevator down but discovered that this was the local train station or the S-Bahnhof. The helpful employee directed him to the third level where he said the Fernbahnhof or the long-distance train station was.

When he, at last, reached the station he was surprised at the tranquility of the place and the very few people who were there. He marveled at the technological ingenuity of the Germans; not one, but two train stations within the same premises as the airport – and at two different levels. He said to himself that none of his friends would believe him when he told them of this on his return.

Jose had one more thing to do before he could purchase the train ticket to Stockholm. He had to convert the dollars he carried into Deutsche marks. Luckily for him, there was a Commerzbank foreign exchange bureau at hand and he changed three hundred dollars.

In less than twenty-five minutes Jose not only had a ticket to Stockholm but he was also on board the Kommodore [IC-670] that had just arrived from Basel on the way to Hamburg. At 9:23 a.m. (the exact time the reservation clerk had written down on his Ihre Reiseverbindungen slip) the train noiselessly pulled out and quickly gathered momentum. Jose was amazed at the punctuality. The train had departed at the precise, scheduled time—not a minute sooner or later. Jose had never experienced this level of precision on Indian railways. Delays of even a day or even two were not uncommon on Indian trains. The only time trains ran on time in India was during the 'Emergency' when Indira Gandhi, the then Prime Minister, briefly flirted with totalitarianism. Jose's wonderment soon reached new heights as he gazed out of the window at the picture-postcard landscape that was sliding by. It all seemed a dream. The anxiety of the past two hours had again drained him. The total relief of having overcome all the obstacles so far and of finally being on the last leg of his journey to meet Carl caused Jose to lose his battle against sleep. Try as he might he just could not stay awake.

He awoke briefly when the train pulled into Fulda an hour later and then promptly went back to sleep. He knew the other passengers were watching him but there was nothing he could do to stay awake. When he awoke again the train was pulling into Göttingen. He pulled out the train schedule called Ihr Zug-Begleiter and was amazed that the train was still punctual to the very minute. Jose recalled that Göttingen was the site of the famous university. The passengers in his vicinity detrained and a middle-aged lady with a scarf tied around her head, carrying a wicker basket, got on board. Jose surreptitiously looked around for the sleeping berths but could not locate any. On Indian trains, the berths could be lowered during the day and people slept on them as the trains slowly wound their way around the arid tracts of central India. Obviously, the German system was different. Since he had paid for a sleeping berth he figured the berth would be provided at the appropriate time.

When a uniformed vendor brought food around Jose bought a bratwurst and bread and a packet of potato chips. When he opened the packet he was caught in two minds. On an Indian train, the custom would be to share one's food with fellow travelers. Even if the offer was not always accepted, it would be discourteous not to make it. He was unsure of the custom in Germany. Since there were only the two of them, Jose decided to risk it. He rose and held out the opened packet of chips to the lady.

To his great relief, she did not take offense. Instead, she smiled and declined with a friendly gesture.

"Thank you," she said in a clear tone. "But I have enough food here," she added pointing to the wicker basket.

"Are you sure?" Jose persisted.

"Yes, thank you," she replied.

Jose devoured the bratwurst and the bread. He had not had anything since the breakfast on the plane. He munched on the chips as he watched the astonishingly beautiful scenery flit by.

"Is this your first trip to West Germany?" the lady asked gently.

"Yes," he replied. "I arrived this morning from India."

"From India!" the woman gushed. "I have heard so much about your great country."

"Your country is many times greater than mine," Jose gallantly replied.

"We have a history of great sorrow and shame. During the Second World War, we killed millions of people and our own country was divided into two. The Berlin Wall keeps our nation apart," she said dejectedly.

"Every country has something to be ashamed of," Jose replied as he looked around surreptitiously for the waste bin. "We have the Hindu-Muslim killings at the time of our Independence to be ashamed of. The current poverty, disease, and injustice are also nothing to be proud of."

"You can drop the rubbish there," she said pointing to the covered receptacle below the window, which to Jose had not looked like a waste bin.

"Thank you for your help!"

Train passengers in India just threw garbage out of the window but Jose knew that was not the way it was done here in Germany.

"I am going to see my sister," the lady said.

"Where does she live? In Hamburg?" asked Jose.

"How I wish she did! She lives in East Germany." Then the tears came and Jose realized how deep the hurt was.

"Can she not come and visit you here?" Jose asked.

"No, the East German guards would shoot her dead if she tried to escape. It is like a prison. My sister is ill and there is nothing I can do. I meet her every three months and carry ham and sausages and cheese for her," she said dabbing at her eyes with a handkerchief.

"I am sorry." Jose couldn't think of anything else to say.

In her eyes, he saw the pain of war and separation and a trace of envy, he thought, for his own situation.

"Someday, the wall will be broken and we will be one nation again," the lady said with resolute hope.

He did not then realize how prophetic those words would turn out to be. Before he made the next trip to see Carl, the Wall, however, implausible and far-fetched its destruction might have seemed earlier, would come crashing down and there would again be only one reunified Germany.

"Here, have a banana," the lady offered, taking out a bunch from the basket.

Jose wanted to refuse but sensed that she would be happier if he accepted it.

"Thank you, you are very kind. I hope your sister gets well again soon."

"You are welcome. Thank you for your wishes. You are a nice young man. Enjoy your trip."

Jose fell asleep again. The train was pulling into Hannover when he woke again.

"I need to change trains here. Goodbye! Auf wiedersehen!" said the lady as she moved to the door.

"Goodbye! God bless you!" Jose said.

Jose walked over to the Schaffner and inquired about the sleeping berth. He looked at Jose's ticket and explained that the berth would be available in the evening on the train from Hamburg and not during the day. On the way back to his seat, he stopped at the toilet. This one was different from the toilet on the plane and the one at the airport. Try as he might he could not figure out how to operate the flush. He felt a pang of guilt later when he saw the Schaffner operate a half-hidden pedal near the base of the commode.

Jose slept again. He was making up for all the lost sleep. Half-awake and half-asleep he thought he saw ships and large boats pass over the train. He knew that roads and railway tracks crossed each other but he had never heard of canals crossing over a railway track. "I must be dreaming," he thought. He was not.

The Kommodore pulled into Hamburg on the dot at 14:04. Jose got down and went to confirm the platform number of the next train. This was the gleaming Merkur [IC-102] bound for Copenhagen and the train was to leave in ten minutes. He was told the ferry crossing at Puttgarden would be at 16:22.

Jose forced himself to stay awake. He did not want to fall asleep and be left behind when the train reached the ferry.

Two uniformed men politely demanded to see his passport. Jose realized that this was because they would soon be crossing the international border into Denmark. He hoped they would affix an impressive stamp in his passport, something on the lines of the German visa, as proof of visiting Denmark. To his disappointment, he found a tiny oblong imprint with the words 'Rigspolitiet, Denmark' and the date.

Jose was somewhat puzzled when he noticed that the other passengers were not making any moves to disembark from the train to board the waiting ferry. He expected a second train to be waiting on the other side of the crossing. As the train slowed, Jose took down his bag and waited to be told to disembark. The train stopped for a few minutes and then to his utter astonishment slowly rolled onto the ferry, with the passengers still on the train.

Jose was dumbfounded. He had never imagined a ferry taking on a whole train. Once the train was on the ferry, the passengers got down and Jose's amazement increased still further. There was not just the train, but also a great many trucks and cars on the deck of the ferry.

And a whole new world awaited Jose below deck. The *Theodorheuss* (for that was the name of the ferry) had the biggest restaurant Jose had ever seen and next to it was a duty-free shop with a variety of wines, liquors, chocolates, and perfumes and all kinds of electronic gadgets. The glitz and the glamor were stupendous. As he walked around the shop in a daze, there was a loud crash as a bottle of wine fell from the hands of a customer near the counter. One of the female employees rushed over with a mop and a bucket to clean up the mess.

"Sorry, it slipped from my hands. I will pay," the culprit said contritely to the employee as she swabbed the floor.

Jose did not want to break anything in his nervousness. He had just enough money for the expenses of travel and the conference. He quickly exited the duty-free shop and moved to the restaurant. All the tables seemed to have been taken and he did not know the rules of etiquette in a situation like this. He decided to go hungry and was about to turn back when he saw a distinguished looking man beckoning him. Jose looked behind to make sure the man was not trying to attract the attention of someone else. The man smiled and jabbed his finger at him and motioned Jose over. Jose walked shyly up to his table.

"Excuse me, sir. Were you calling me?" asked Jose hesitantly.

"Yes. I thought you were looking for a table. You may join me if you like. As you can see I am dining alone," said the stranger smiling disarmingly.

"Thank you. That is kind of you. I will join you," said Jose, grateful for the company, pulling out a chair.

"My name is Hans Jacobsen. I am from Copenhagen. And you are?"

"My name is Kurian Jose. You can call me Jose. That is my given name."

Just then the waiter came to take their orders. While Hans, who appeared to know what he wanted, was placing his order, Jose quickly scanned the menu on the table. There was nothing he recognized. The waiter appeared to be speaking to the gentleman in German.

"And what will you have?" asked the waiter in English, turning to Jose. For a moment, Jose was nonplussed. He was at a loss for words. The names on the menu were not only hard to pronounce but he also had no clue what they were.

Jose thought quickly. "I will have the same," he said closing the menu and handing it to the waiter.

"Anything to drink? Some wine perhaps?"

"No, thank you. Just water will do."

Jose had no idea what he had just ordered and, worse still, how much it cost. He hoped the stranger whose order he had copied did not have fancy or expensive tastes.

"Is this your first visit to Scandinavia?" asked Hans.

"Yes. Actually, it is my first trip out of my country."

"Ah! And you are from?"

"From India. From South India, actually."

"Are you visiting friends or relatives in Denmark?"

"Neither. I am going through to Stockholm. I am attending a conference of amateur radio operators," Jose said.

The waiter brought the food then. Jose was relieved to find that it smelled good and looked very edible.

"Gesegnete Mahlzeit! Guten Appetit! Bon appetit!" Hans said.

"Same to you," replied Jose and began to eat. The generous serving looked huge but Jose was hungry and he polished off the whole plate silently, completely oblivious of Hans who made as if to make small talk but then thought the better of it when he saw how intent Jose was on the food.

When the waiter brought the bill Jose anxiously reached for his wallet hoping it would not be anything too high.

But Hans would have none of it.

"I'll take care of it. Consider it a welcome treat," said Hans. Then sensing Jose's confusion, he added, "This is your first visit to my country, Denmark. And you are my guest."

"Thank you from the bottom of my heart," said Jose earnestly much to the amusement of Hans who laughed lightly as he laid out the money on the table.

Soon they boarded the train again as the ferry neared Rødby. After the ferry docked, the train slowly rolled off on to the tracks on solid ground, and about two hours later they were pulling into Copenhagen. Jose never saw his benefactor Hans again.

Jose marveled at the fact that in less than a day he was not only thousands of miles from India but had also traveled through the heart of West Germany and was now in the land of Hans Christian Andersen. All the things he had seen and experienced since deplaning at Frankfurt would seem farfetched and fanciful to his friends back on the tea estate in Munnar. "This is a fairy tale straight out of Hans Christian!" he told himself.

There was a two-hour wait for the train to Stockholm. When he boarded the train the conductor was in the process of lowering the sleeping berths using a small tool. Jose could not help but admire the ingenuity and orderliness of the system. He went to the toilet and quickly changed into pajamas for the night. On Indian railways, he recalled, people would change their clothes right at their seats even in mixed company.

As he slept he thought the train went on another ferry but he was too tired to get up and find out. Much later he awoke and watched towns with lyrical names like Jönköping, Linköping, Nyköping, and Norrköping slip by as the train wound its way to Stockholm.

## Chapter 4

At 7:05 the next morning the train rolled into Stockholm Central. Jose had had a shave and was ready and eager to meet his ham radio friend Carl.

But when he got off the train he felt diffident. He knew he had to call Carl to tell him he was here. The only thing Carl knew about his itinerary was the letter Jose had posted before he left Kerala for Delhi. But that was prior to booking his tickets and getting his visa. Jose was not even sure that that letter had reached Carl.

Jose looked around the platform but did not see a telephone. He guessed that the phone would be some kind of automatic contraption instead of the public call offices in India that had a waiting attendant to collect the payment. Jose felt shy about asking for assistance for something as basic as using the telephone. That was when he saw a young man of African descent get down from the train.

"Hello! Do you live in Stockholm?" asked Jose.

"Yes," came the guarded answer.

"I need some help to get to my friend's house," said Jose.

"Where does he live?"

Jose fished out the slip of paper he had kept within his passport.

"Jungfrugatan," said Jose.

"I don't know where that place is."

"My name is Jose. Care for something to eat?"

"OK. My name is Kassa. I'm from Ethiopia. Are you from India?"

"Yes, that is correct. I'm from South India and this is my first trip abroad."

There was a small coffee booth nearby. Jose ordered two muffins and coffees.

"Why did you order for me?" asked Kassa puzzled.

"I thought you wanted to eat something," said Jose confused.

"I don't drink coffee but I'll take the muffin," Kassa said.

According to Indian custom, it was the giver – not the receiver – who decided what the treat was. He felt foolish that he had thrown his money away for something that the other did not appreciate. It was not his custom to spurn hospitality.

"OK. I need the extra cup of coffee," said Jose. "Do you know from where I can call my friend?"

"That I can help you with," Kassa said seriously. "I will show you when we get to the exit."

At least it is not a complete waste, thought Jose as he sipped the strong black coffee.

Carl picked the phone up on the second ring when Jose made the call with help from Kassa.

"Hello! Can I speak to Carl?"

The unknown accent caused a brief pause at the other end. "This is Carl speaking. Who is calling?"

"It is me, Jose," Jose replied excitedly.

"*Who?*" asked Carl.

"This is Jose. Kurian Jose. Victor Uniform Two Kilo Kilo Juliet."

"*Jose!* Is that you? Where are you? Are you calling from Delhi?"

"No. I am in Stockholm!"

"*What?*" Carl was incredulous. "When did you get here?"

"Just one hour ago. I came by train from Frankfurt. I am at the Stockholm railway station," said Jose, his excitement rising again.

"Really! Stay right there. I will come and get you."

"What do you look like? How will I recognize you?" asked Jose.

"You don't need to worry. I will find *you*," said Carl laughing.

It took a moment to sink in. Then Jose realized that with his jet-black hair and brown skin, Carl would have no problem at all in locating him in a largely Scandinavian crowd.

"Stay right there in the meet and greet area and I will come and get you."

For the next thirty minutes, Jose wandered around looking at the posters on the wall while keeping an eye out for anyone who fit his mental image of Carl. When he felt a light tap on his shoulder and his name called out softly—almost whispered— Jose whirled around to find himself looking up at a tall and, it seemed to Jose, gigantic man. But no words came out as he stared open-mouthed at the bespectacled, silver-haired Carl.

"Welcome to Stockholm!" said Carl warmly and crushed Jose in a bear hug. "What a pleasant surprise! To tell you the truth I never thought you would make it here in time."

"You are big!" Jose exclaimed as he extricated himself.

"It is not for nothing that I chose Big Fat Elephant for my call sign phonetics!" laughed Carl. "But we need to rush. You don't want to be late for the conference. Do you need any help with the luggage?"

"No, thank you. I think I can manage," replied Jose.

When they came out of the station, Jose looked around and asked, "Where's your car?"

"Who said I had a car?" laughed Carl heartily. "I am not rich."

"Sorry. I thought all Westerners owned cars."

"Don't be sorry. I don't have any need for owning a car here. The public transport system is excellent and cheap."

Jose thought the big red city bus was beautiful but he was startled by the sound the hydraulic doors made as they closed. He had not seen any buses with doors in India and certainly not buses with doors that closed on their own. The bigger difference was the sparse number of passengers in the bus. He counted sixteen and reckoned that in India there would be at least eighty people squashed in tight and hanging out the door in a bus half the size.

***

On reaching Junfrugatan Carl punched in the code (no keys! another surprise for Jose) to let themselves in while Jose stared awestruck at the stately dome of the church at the end of the street and the neatly parked cars on either side with not a human being in sight. Once they were inside the building, Jose lugged the suitcase up to the second floor.

"We need to hurry for the conference," Carl said.

"I need to have a bath first," Jose said.

"OK. Just have a quick shower," suggested Carl.

But Jose needed Carl's help to figure out how the shower controls worked. The hot shower was a luxury as Jose washed away the caked sweat and grime he had carried from the broiling heat of Delhi.

"Did you turn the geyser on before you came to the station?" asked Jose as they left the apartment.

"Geyser? You mean the water heater?"

"Yes."

"I don't have one. Hot and cold water are piped in," explained Carl.

"Round the clock? Twenty-four hours a day?"

"Yes, of course. I know what you are thinking. In India, only the rich can afford piped water supply in their homes. I have got used to being provided warm water in buckets for bathing when I am in India. But when I am back in Sweden I tend to forget how the rest of the world lives."

"I will need to change some money for paying the conference fees," Jose said.

"There is a Sparbanken branch at the corner."

Jose was surprised when he got seven kronor to the dollar. This was about three times as much as the Deutsch mark exchange rate and was only about a third less than the Indian rupee rate, at a little over eleven.

\*\*\*

The foyer of Domus Hotel was a jostling crowd of amateur radio enthusiasts.

"I am already registered. You need to get in that line there to register," Carl said.

The queue (as Jose would call it) moved pretty quickly and he filled out the form and paid the two hundred sixty kronor registration fee.

"All the way from India! How wonderful!" gushed the young lady as she filled out the nametag with VU2KKJ in big bold letters with a black marker.

Jose looked around for Carl but could not find him. For the first time since he had left India, he felt alone and out of place.

The hams stood around in small groups animatedly discussing in languages that Jose had heard only on short-wave radio before. Idly he started connecting the countries to the call sign prefixes on the nametags. SM-Sweden, OH-Finland, LA-Norway, G4-England, FR-France, DL-West Germany …

Then it was time for the conference to begin. The various countries represented were acknowledged by having the participants stand up as their countries were announced. Jose was the lone ham from the South Asian subcontinent and received a vigorous ovation. The only others from Asia were a bunch of Japanese hams and a couple from Singapore. The breakout sessions found Jose and Carl in different groups. Jose joined the discussion on sunspot activity and radio propagation while Carl was with the Scandinavian group. But at lunch, they sat at the same table.

"We will get out the moment the last session ends. The rest will be getting together in groups at nearby bars and drinking till the early morning. I am sure you are tired and want to go home."

"I think so. The sunspot discussions were fascinating. But I am beginning to feel a little tired with the lack of regular sleep."

"The exhibition booths open tomorrow. Then on Wednesday night there is the smörgåsbord and the cruise on the Stockholm archipelago."

"What is a smörgåsbord? Is it some kind of a board game?"

"No!" laughed Carl. "It is a Swedish institution. A smörgåsbord is a vast buffet with a large variety of selections. People generally overeat. You will find out for yourself on Wednesday."

*** 

They were back in Carl's apartment before 6:00 p.m.

"Would you like to wash up and change into something comfortable while I fix us something to eat?" asked Carl.

"OK. That would be nice."

The shower was alluring and irresistible. Jose had his second shower of the day and a second shave as well before slipping into his nightclothes. When he returned, Carl had the TV on and was watching the evening news on TV1.

"Are you turning in already?" asked Carl surprised looking at Jose's pajamas and bare feet.

"No I just changed into something comfortable," replied Jose uneasily wondering if he had done something wrong.

"Don't worry. I thought you were tired and wanted to sleep early. We change into nightclothes only just before getting into bed. People also wear socks around the house. But no worries! You can be barefoot if you like for all I care. Just relax and enjoy yourself."

"Are you sure it is OK?"

"Absolutely! What would you like to drink? Some wine or whiskey may be?"

"I think I will have some wine. I have never had wine before," said Jose.

"Never had wine before? I know it is very expensive in India. I am not going to ask you then to choose between the French and the Italian. The French wine is already open and I will pour you a glass."

Carl raised his glass. "To my honored guest from across the ocean. *Skål!*"

Jose, unsure how to respond, just stuck to, "Cheers!" and took a sip of the wine.

"Skål is the standard Swedish toast," Carl said as he turned off the TV. "I can't believe you are actually here. I thought it was a long shot. Glad, you pulled it off."

"I am myself not sure how I did it," smiled Jose.

"How are you feeling?" asked Carl.

"I feel like I have died and gone to heaven. Everything I have seen since I got off the plane in Frankfurt has been unbelievable. Sometimes I wonder if I am dreaming."

"I can understand the feeling of unreality. Each time I go to India I feel the same way myself."

"But it must be the opposite. For me, it is pleasant disbelief. For you, it would be the opposite. Shock?" suggested Jose.

"Not necessarily. If that were true, I would not be coming back year after year. I would be a masochist to continue to do that!"

Jose laughed.

"I love Kerala. The green paddy fields, the clean beaches and the quiet backwaters," Carl continued.

"Thank you. I am very fortunate I was born there."

"The only thing I haven't got my head around is your language. It is more difficult than even Finnish, which is considered the most difficult language to learn."

"It is actually very easy. By the way, Malayalam – the name of my language – is a palindromic word."

"Meaning?"

"It reads the same backwards and forwards. Like radar," Jose explained.

"Gee! I never realized that!" exclaimed Carl. "Let's have dinner first and then we can sit and talk and get to know each other."

Jose wondered if it was not too early for dinner. In India dinnertime was generally around nine o'clock, and in some regions as late as eleven o'clock. The dinner on the ferry was early but he had thought that was due to the short ferry crossing. Carl laid out the table with great care humming a tune. He also lit a candle and turned down the light.

"What's the candle for?" asked Jose.

"It is a special welcome for a special guest," said Carl.

"In India, we use candles at meal time only when there is the likelihood of a power failure."

"Ha, ha!" Carl laughed heartily. "I remember there was a blackout almost every night in Madras. We don't have those here – not in recent memory," said Carl shaking his head. "About the food. I love cooking. The food that you will have while you are here with me in Stockholm will be very, very different from the food you are used to in Kerala. But I hope you will like it. I hope you will be game for everything that I cook." Carl looked at Jose thoughtfully. "You eat beef, don't you?"

"Carl, I told you I am an Orthodox Christian. Of course, I eat beef."

"Just checking! I know even Hindus eat beef in Kerala. What I have cooked for you today is pasta, Swedish meatballs, and pineapple upside cake."

"I haven't had any of those things before."

Jose was unsure about how to proceed.

"Help yourself," prompted Carl.

"Thank you," said Jose. In India, it would have been unthinkable for guests to serve themselves; that was always the prerogative of the host.

"Feel at home. Enjoy the food! I know everyone eats with the fingers in India. Hope you are OK with the fork and spoon."

"I will be fine. I have used them before. Though not every day."

The meal was a silent affair. Jose watched Carl for clues on table etiquette and Carl glanced at Jose from time to time to see if he was enjoying the food.

"Do you miss rice?" asked Carl.

"In India, a meal is not a meal without rice – at least in South India. But I'm enjoying this food. It is new for me but it is really good."

Jose helped Carl clear the table.

"Just dump them in the sink," said Carl.

"May I wash the dishes?" asked Jose.

"But we haven't finished our dinner yet! You forgot there's dessert," Carl said smiling.

"Sorry! I am not used to Western-style meals. We don't have a dessert at the end of our meal."

After the pineapple upside down cake, Jose washed the dishes. But he needed some help from Carl. Jose was surprised by the faucet and spout that could be swung out of the way, the rubber gloves, the long-handled brush and, most of all, the scalding hot water available on tap.

"At home, we wash dishes with our bare hands and a piece of coconut husk as a scrubber. This is luxury!"

"It is a chore. I hate washing dishes. I let them pile up and clear them all in one go in the dishwasher," said Carl.

The dishwasher was a big surprise for Jose when Carl explained how it worked. Carl also demonstrated how the washing machine and the spin dryer in the bathroom worked.

"This is amazing! You have a machine for washing clothes and another for washing dishes!"

From the kitchen, they moved to the living room. Jose wandered around the room looking at the mementos and curios on the wall.

"Almost everything is from India. There are a few from the Soviet Republic of Armenia and from the island of Cyprus, two of my favorite places – after India," said Carl.

"What is that cloth covered box on the wall for?"

"That is the electric meter," laughed Carl. "The textile covering it is from Gujarat. The macramé on the door is from the same state. The batiks are from Sri Lanka and South India. The tie-and-dye piece is from Tamil Nadu. The artifacts and objets d'art in this room are all from India. There's more in my study. The black obsidian cross is from Edjmiadzin, the headquarters of the Armenian Orthodox church."

"Which reminds me. I forgot to give you a few things I brought for you."

"You needn't have brought anything, Jose. Your presence here is its own reward."

Jose returned with three garishly wrapped packages.

Carl held his hands together in the traditional Indian gesture and said, "*Namaste!*" before receiving the gifts.

"*Namaste,*" responded Jose, smiling appreciatively.

Carl tore open the first packet to reveal a *Kathakali* mask.

"Wow! This is amazing! I have attended a *Kathakali* performance on each of my visits to Kerala. It is one of the highest art forms – a dance-drama on par with the stylized *Kabuki* of Japan. You know what the two have in common?"

"No. What?" Jose was curious.

"There are no female actors in either *Kathakali* or *Kabuki*. Male actors play the female roles too."

"Really? I knew that about *Kathakali* but did not know the same was true of *Kabuki*."

"There is another reason why this *Kathakali* mask is appropriate. I will tell you after the conference is over," Carl said with an impish smile.

"Banana chips!" exclaimed Carl as he opened the second package. "This is something I fell in love with. But I will make something else for you with bananas. Not chips. Again, you will have to wait a few days."

"I wonder what's in the last one?" Carl said as he unwrapped the heaviest of the three packages. "This is beautiful!" Carl said softly as he took out the carving of an elephant.

"It is handmade," said Jose. "Smell it," he urged Carl.

"Let me guess. Sandalwood?"

"Yes! You really know a lot about Kerala and India!"

"My favorite animal is the elephant. I think in a previous life I must have been one! Matches my girth and size," winked Carl.

"Have you heard about reincarnation?"

"Of course, Hinduism is one of the faiths that I am keenly interested in and actively studying," Carl said.

"So, you are not a Christian?" asked Jose surprised.

"No, I am not. I lost my faith forty years ago, but that is a story for another time. Some more wine?"

"No, thank you. I am not sleepy but I think I should go to bed. This must be jetlag kicking in."

"Well, goodnight then! And see you in the morning!"

"Thank you for everything, Carl. I am so happy to be here. This is all a dream. Goodnight!"

Jose went to his room, shut the door and lay down. But sleep would not come. There was too much light coming in from the direction of the window. Jose went to see if it was a streetlight that was the cause of the problem. When he pulled the curtain aside he saw to his surprise that there appeared to be bright sunshine outside. He looked at his watch. It was close to midnight. He wondered for a moment if he had set the time wrong and it was already morning. And then the realization came that this was the extended daylight of the northern latitudes in summer. "The land of the midnight sun!" he recalled his geography lesson in school. He wondered if there would at least be a short period of real darkness before the new day broke.

"I feel like a chicken in a poultry farm under artificial light," said Jose to himself as he pressed the pillow over his head in a vain effort to shut out the light.

## Chapter 5

Jose woke up early, though he knew it was early only by looking at his watch. The light at the window seemed as bright as when he had gone to bed. He tiptoed to the bathroom and ran through the morning ablutions. He was excited about the first full day in Stockholm.

He found Carl in the living room reading the morning newspaper and sipping a gigantic cup of coffee. The TV was on the Swedish news channel.

"Good morning, Carl!" Jose said self-consciously.

"*God morgon!*" responded Carl. "The sleeper awakes!"

"Am I late?" asked Jose hesitantly.

"No, you are not. I was just kidding. We have plenty of time. But look what has been happening in your country while you were asleep. Looks like you fled in the nick of time," said Carl handing the newspaper over.

Jose saw that the newspaper was in Swedish and was called the *Dagens Nyheter*. It had on the front page a hazy picture of the Golden Temple of Amritsar surrounded by Indian soldiers. The whole first page appeared to be about India. The names

'Indira Gandhi', 'Punjab', 'Bhindranwale', 'Operation Blue Star' and 'Khalistan' recurred frequently.

"What happened?" asked Jose alarmed.

"The day after you left India, your Prime Minister Indira Gandhi ordered the Indian army into the Golden Temple of the Sikhs—called Harimandir—at Amritsar. The assault was code-named 'Operation Blue Star'. The insurgents holed up inside surrendered yesterday after a fierce battle. The rebel leader ... I cannot pronounce his name ... was killed. More than a hundred Indian soldiers were killed and an unknown number of Khalistani rebels, probably several hundred. The temple has been badly damaged," Carl explained reading from the newspaper.

"My God! There will be a revolution in my country. Half the armed forces are Sikhs from the Punjab. They will revolt. How will I go back?"

"Whoa! Not so fast! Don't panic. You still have two weeks left. Things will return to normalcy by then. How do you like your eggs?"

The breakfast of orange juice, toast, butter, marmalade, fried eggs, and bacon was completely different from the *idli-sambar* or *appam* and curry that he was used to. Coffee was the lone common factor and even that tasted different. It tasted more bitter to Jose's tongue than even some *Ayurvedic* concoction.

When they were out on the street Jose inquired about the church at the far end of Jungfrugatan.

"That is the Hedvig Eleonora Kyrka. Maybe we can visit it some time."

They walked to Östermalmstorg and caught the bus to the conference venue.

***

The day passed quickly. Jose was more relaxed than the previous day and made more friends. The best part of the day was the manufacturer's exhibition that opened after lunch. Jose visited the stalls of all the big names in the business – Kenwood, ICOM, and Yaesu-Musen. He could not take his eyes off the state-of-the-art transceivers. He envied the hams in the Western world who could afford to buy these beautiful radios off the shelf. Just the base prices of these wonderful machines were outside the reach of Third World hams. But when crippling import duties of two hundred percent or more, and the prohibitive airfreight, were added, the cost rose to astronomical levels. He was thrilled with the keepsakes the Yaesu-Musen representative gave him – a logbook, a wall map of the world and a red cap with the distinctive Yaesu logo.

Jose was chosen to participate in a panel discussion on the state of amateur radio around the world. He was terribly nervous at the start about speaking in public in English. But when the discussion started, he discovered that the other participants from non-English speaking countries like Norway, Belgium, France, Finland, Spain, Poland, and Czechoslovakia had even greater difficulty than he did with spoken English and he relaxed. Jose seized the opportunity to highlight the ingenuity of Indian hams in rewiring surplus army radios left behind by the Allied forces after World War II and sold as junk in the city of Agra, not far from the Taj Mahal.

\*\*\*

"We are eating out this evening," announced Carl as they left the conference in the evening.

"Won't it be expensive?" asked Jose.

"You haven't forgotten the deal we made, have you? You don't have to worry about any of your expenses while in Stockholm. I thought we had agreed on that!"

"You are very kind," responded Jose simply.

"Don't say that. I am the one who is getting the better bargain here. It is a luxury for me to have someone to talk to and eat out with. And even at home, I am not alone while you are here. I am blessed! Let's go to a Greek restaurant today."

Carl helped Jose with the menu and they ordered *dolma, kleftiko,* and *stifado.*

"I still cannot get over the fact that you are actually here. You are the first visitor I have had from India," Carl said.

Jose merely smiled.

"But why didn't you phone me from Delhi to let me know you got your visa and were coming?" Carl asked.

"I was busy running around getting the visa and the tickets. But the main reason was that it is not easy to phone overseas from India. It is expensive too. Moreover, I knew you were here."

Carl laughed. "What if I had gone out of town? That was one big gamble that you took."

Jose realized the enormity of the risk he had run. If Carl had not been in town he would have had no place to stay.

"It is just my inexperience. By Indian standards your invitation was sufficient. But I see your point."

When they reached home after dinner Jose wanted to listen to the BBC for news about what was happening in India. Carl fetched his Sony digital short-wave receiver from his bedroom and they listened together to the news. There were conflicting reports on the number of casualties in the attack on the Golden Temple. Official Indian reports placed the number at four hundred while Khalistan sources claimed over four thousand had been killed. The Indian government downplayed the death of over a hundred of its soldiers. Jose was relieved to learn that there was no major upheaval in the country as a result of the army's assault on the Amritsar temple.

"Carl, in spite of all the news about the Punjab, I am feeling really sleepy. I think my body clock is adjusting to local time," said Jose.

"That's a good sign. Tomorrow is the last day of the conference. I need to go back to work the day after. But we will have more time to talk and to see the sights of the city once the conference is over."

***

The highlight of the last day of the radio conference was the cruise and the smörgåsbord.

Carl had some unexpected news during the lunch break.

"I received a message from my office a short while ago. There's some urgent translation that needs to be done. The principals are Americans and they insist that the Swedish version be delivered tonight."

"But we have the cruise tonight," reminded Jose.

"Yeah, I know. But unfortunately, I won't be able to make it. But you go ahead. I will get someone to drop you home afterward."

The cruise passes were distributed after lunch. Jose smiled at the title. It read - 'Smörgåsboarding Card'. "What an ingenious pun!" he thought. His serial number was 130. The last discussion on the sunspot cycle was tedious and technical. Jose could not wait for the cruise to start.

The participants were transported to the quay at Nybroplan in two coaches. The vessel was bigger than he had imagined. The organizers had to shout to make themselves heard above the noise. The smörgåsbord itself was wonderful to behold. On five long tables placed end to end at the center of the deck were stacked the most alluring array of gastronomical delights Jose had ever seen.

"Welcome! We are pleased to welcome you aboard the *MS Victoria*! Our cruise will take approximately three hours. You can watch the beautiful sights of Stockholm from the boat while enjoying our traditional smörgåsbord, of which we are very, very proud. The Swedish custom is to take small portions and return several times to the smörgåsbord for second and third – or even fourth – helpings."

He might as well have been talking to a room full of starving savages.

"The trick is to get your free beer first, leave it at your table and then rush back to the smörgåsbord. That way you will have both your hands free," suggested the ham from Kiel helpfully.

Jose marveled at the mad rush for food, totally unheeding the pleas of the announcer. It was like the desperation of the displaced poor in a Third World country during a flood or a drought. Jose watched fellow participants, their plates piled high with food, carefully wend their way back to their tables. He was amazed at how quickly free food had stripped away the veneer of decorum and social restraint from the citizens of affluent nations. The platters were all quickly emptied much to the chagrin of the Swedish hosts. There was no relaxed sampling of the fare or orderly return trips to the table for replenishing. It was all rolled into one big, gargantuan meal.

Jose could not figure out what some of the dishes were made of but he enjoyed almost all of it, especially the baked herring, 'Jansson's Temptation', gravlax and the Swedish meatballs.

Then, after the meal, a mesmerized Jose watched the brightly lit city of Stockholm, and its inverted reflection in the water, slip by as the boat slid unhurriedly through the placid, dark waters of the archipelago.

\*\*\*

After the cruise, Arne, a Swedish ham, dropped Jose off at Jungfrugatan. Jose was surprised to find Carl not working but watching TV.

"I had a flash of inspiration and the translation flowed beautifully. It was over in half the time I had thought it would take. I got back to the apartment after handing in the typed manuscript at the office. Did you enjoy the cruise?"

"The cruise was wonderful," Jose responded. But his attention was quickly drawn to the program on the television and he watched it with the same absorption that Carl did. Jose found the sitcom funny and laughed aloud.

"What is the name of this funny drama?" asked Jose when it ended.

"It's called *Cheers*. In the *Röster I Radio-TV*, which is the weekly TV Guide, the show is titled *Skål*, which, as you already know, is the Swedish equivalent of 'cheers'. Do you get to watch this show in India?"

"I don't have a TV set, Carl. Actually, television hasn't come to my town yet. It is available only in big cities like Delhi and Bombay. You'll be surprised. I haven't watched TV before. This is the first time," Jose admitted a trifle shamefacedly.

"I'm sorry. I should have remembered. I watched Indian national television only in Delhi and Madras on my last visit. I think it's called Doordarshan, isn't it? This is the first time you are watching TV? And that too an American sitcom? Yet you laugh at all the right places!" said a surprised Carl.

"I try not to miss the Sunday matinees of Hollywood movies back home. That is the only chance I get to watch English films. Not many people come to watch them. Which is why they screen them only on Sundays at 11:00 a.m. Hindi films from Bollywood or the local Malayalam movies are more popular," explained Jose. "But I have fallen in love with *Cheers*. It is funny and intelligent. Also, very elegant and cerebral. The waitress who loves poetry is beautiful."

Carl laughed. "Her name is Shelley Long. How about a drink?"

"I won't say no. I am tired."

"Here is an American whiskey you've probably never heard of before," said Carl holding up the bottle. "Jack Daniel's," he pronounced the name with dramatic reverence and added, "Old No.7 brand sour mash whiskey from Tennessee."

"I like a good whiskey and I hope this is one."

"On the rocks or neat?" asked Carl.

"What?"

"Would you like your whiskey on ice or straight?"

"Sorry, never tried whiskey with ice. Just plain water," said Jose embarrassedly. "Refrigerators are not yet very common in India. I don't have one. But I am not used to drinking whiskey straight. I think I will try it on the rocks."

After taking a sip Jose swirled the drink and said in measured tones, "This whiskey is good! I think I like it better than the Scotch whiskeys I have had."

Carl was delighted. "Any friend of Jack Daniel's is a friend of mine!"

They watched a replay of Mats Wilander's Wimbledon match and then watched a Swedish program on polka dancing.

"How was the work you did today? Was the translation difficult?" asked Jose.

"No, I'm blessed to be doing what I really love. Translating is not difficult for me now. In the beginning, while I was still learning Swedish, it was. But not now."

"*Learning* Swedish? But you are a Swede, aren't you?" asked Jose incredulously.

"I am now – but a naturalized one. I was originally an American," Carl replied with an enigmatic smile.

"I don't understand. I always thought you were Swedish. You have a Swedish surname – Carlson."

"That's true. There are settlers from all parts of Europe in the United States. My forbears were from Sweden. I was a third generation American when I came to Sweden to live here. I've been here almost forty years now."

Jose looked at him disbelievingly, "I never imagined you were anything else other than a Swede."

"I was a Swede when we met," laughed Carl.

"Why did you leave America?" asked Jose.

"That is a long story for another time. I came here after the Second World War."

"I am very surprised. That explains your fluency in English, though you don't have a typical American accent," said Jose.

"It's been a long time. Thirty-nine years and four months to be precise. I never went back," said Carl wistfully.

"Where is your family?" blurted out Jose.

Carl smiled wanly and took a large gulp of whiskey. "That's an even longer story for a much later time. Care for another?"

"OK. Just one more."

Their conversation floundered after that while Carl flipped the channels.

"I have something neat planned for you tomorrow. This will be in the afternoon. I need to go to the office in the morning," said Carl.

"I would like to see more of this beautiful city. That will be nice."

A short while later Jose retired to his room for the night.

***

After breakfast the next morning Carl left for work and Jose was all alone. He washed the dishes and cleaned the sink. He thumbed through the *Dagens Nyheter* newspaper but could not understand a word. He felt like reading a book but the books were all in Carl's bedroom and he did not want to trespass on Carl's private space. For want of anything better to do, Jose switched on the TV and surfed the channels looking for something in English or Hindi. There were none. At this time of the day the programming was in Swedish. But he chanced upon a channel that sent his pulse racing. It was something he had never seen before on TV or in real life – strip poker. Jose was flabbergasted to see the woman who lost her hand casually remove her top and sit bare-breasted. He could not believe this was being broadcast in broad daylight. Jose was transfixed by the lush body of the semi-naked woman but quickly switched off the TV in confusion before she began to discard more of her clothing.

He decided to take a walk by himself to cool off.

Since he did not have a map, he took with him a piece of blank paper on which to note the street names and the turns he took so he could find his way back to the Jungfrugatan apartment. As he was leaving, a man in a gray jacket entered the building and smilingly accosted him with what sounded like "Hey, hey!" Jose was puzzled why the man had addressed him in such a rude fashion, as 'hey!' was a crude way of drawing the attention of a menial in India. It was only when another passerby repeated it on the street that realization dawned on Jose. It was not 'hey!' but 'hej', the Swedish equivalent of 'hello' or 'hi' and there was nothing rude about it! From then on, he returned the greeting, though a trifle self-consciously the first time. He had to consciously delink the insulting past associations of the sound in his head.

The immediate vicinity of Jungfrugatan had become rather familiar territory for Jose from the morning trips to the conference venue on previous days. He started out confidently along Linnégatan and turned left on Nybrogatan towards Östermalmstorg. Jose marveled at the cleanliness of the streets and the aesthetic style of the buildings. He straightaway recognized the repeating motif of yellow and blue, the colors of the Swedish flag. Why, there were even yellow and blue petunias hanging from windowsills!

Glancing to his right to confirm that no vehicles were coming, he stepped out onto the pavement to cross the road but the screeching of brakes and the blaring of horns to his left caused him to jump back hastily to the safety of the sidewalk. His confusion turned to acute discomfiture when he realized that pedestrians on both sides of the road had stopped to turn and glare at him disapprovingly. He hastily abandoned any thoughts of crossing the street and continued ahead on the same side of the road. Jose was quick to figure out what had happened. Vehicles here were driven on the right side of the road – not on the left, as in India. Out of habit ingrained from childhood, he had looked to his right before crossing, forgetting that he should instead have looked in the opposite direction first. "Look to the left and then to the right," he castigated himself. "Left. Right. Left. Right."

When he reached the next intersection, he saw a female pedestrian press a button on a post by the side of the road and, sure enough, after a short wait, the traffic lights turned red and vehicles in either direction stopped. Not only that, the pedestrian indicator turned green, accompanied by the tinkling of bells. "What an ingenious system, pushing a button to cross the street safely!" he thought. "And traffic lights even for people!" He remembered that there were no traffic lights in his hometown of Kottayam or in any of the other small towns of India. Instead, there were khaki-clad policemen at intersections with their shrill whistles, directing traffic with flailing arms. Traffic lights were in operation only in metropolises like Delhi, Bombay, and Madras. He vowed that from then on, he would wait till he got to a pedestrian crossing and not dash across the street, as was his wont in India.

It was such a pleasant day under a clear blue sky that Jose could have walked all day. The most amazing thing to him was that the physical exertion merely warmed his body but did not cause him to sweat copiously as it did in the scalding heat of India. He could not believe that only three days ago, he had been roasting in the searing heat of fifty degrees Celsius. The best part of it all was the sunlight, which did not blind him like the tropical sun, and the colors seemed so much richer and deeper. He could have walked for hours, but he decided to return to the apartment for fear of wandering too far and losing his way.

It was near Östermalmstorg that Jose saw the jogger. She wore a yellow T-shirt, the briefest of navy blue shorts, white socks, and white running shoes. Blonde, flaxen hair covered her head like a halo and her burnished limbs shone golden in the sunlight as she came running towards him. To Jose, she was the veritable apparition of an angel or a Norse goddess. He stared mesmerized at her as she came towards him, his eyes instinctively going to her teeny shorts. She blushed scarlet but smiled as she passed him. Jose was embarrassed that she had noticed his look. "Is she real?" wondered Jose as he walked home.

***

Carl returned earlier than Jose had expected.

"I hope you have not been starving," said Carl.

"No, I had some bread with butter and jam."

"Good! But you could have made yourself a ham sandwich."

"I wasn't sure if it required cooking," replied Jose.

"I will teach you all about Western food before you go back," said Carl laughing good-naturedly. "But we're going to a swell place this afternoon."

That turned out to be the Vasa Museet or the Vasa Museum. Jose felt proud to be walking along Strandvägen beside the big and burly Carl, who, for his part, gave the impression that *he* enjoyed Jose's presence in Sweden more than Jose himself did. The story of the seventeenth-century man-of-war that had sunk even before it left the harbor on its maiden voyage and its subsequent salvage from the seabed more than three centuries later captivated Jose. He wandered around the museum looking at the exhibits and reading all descriptions beside them.

"Did you enjoy it?" asked Carl as they left.

"Very much," replied Jose enthusiastically. "I am amazed at how well the articles in the ship have been preserved and how carefully they have been restored. I could not believe they were three hundred and fifty years old. The guided tour of the seventeenth-century ship was fantastic!"

"I have another treat for you. I'm going to cook something very special tonight. Is there any meat you don't eat?"

"Remember Carl, I eat everything," replied Jose.

"I guess you already told me that. Just checking!"

On the way home, they stopped at the butcher's and Carl bought a kilogram of rabbit meat, which the butcher cut according to Carl's directions.

Carl's rabbit stew was a big hit with Jose who more than assuaged the ravenous hunger he had been nursing all day.

"This is the first time I have eaten rabbit meat and I like it. You are an excellent cook!" Jose said.

"Thank you. Cooking is a skill I picked up in my state of single blessedness."

After chocolate mousse cheesecake, they sat in the living room and chatted, sipping Jack Daniel's. Carl smiled amusedly, peering over his glasses, when Jose narrated his adventures of the morning, especially the misunderstanding of the 'hej' greeting and how he had nearly been run over in Östermalmstorg.

"Adjusting to Western life is not easy. Even something as mundane as toilet paper can cause problems. I had trouble finding TP in Kerala on my first visit. The bigger challenge for many Indians is food. They are so accustomed to spicy food that they find Western food bland and inedible," said Carl.

"On the contrary! I find the food delicious!"

"You are different. You are the most flexible guest I have had. But I did not think you would be going out on your own today."

"Oh, I thoroughly enjoyed my explorations of the neighborhood. I would like to walk around by myself again whenever you are busy."

"You are quick to pick up life-skills. I will take some time off from work this coming week to show you around. There are a few places I would like you to see. Uppsala, for instance. We might even take the ferry to Helsinki."

"That would be nice. Isn't Uppsala the University where Celsius, the inventor of the centigrade scale, was a professor? Asked Jose.

"Yes, that's right! How did you know?" asked Carl surprised.

"I think it was in our physics textbook in school. By a coincidence, I remembered Celsius while in Delhi. The temperature was fifty degrees Celsius that day."

"*Fifty* degrees?" asked Carl surprised. "That must be about a hundred and ten on the Fahrenheit scale."

"It is actually a little bit higher than that. It is one hundred and twenty-two."

"That must have been hot. I don't remember the temperature going above forty degrees Celsius when I was in Kerala. Madras was a little hotter than that, though."

"Yes, that's true. Kerala is not as hot as Madras. But the humidity makes it seem almost as bad."

"At my age, I much prefer the heat of India to the bone-chilling cold of Sweden."

"How old are you, Carl?" asked Jose suddenly.

"I am ancient. I turned sixty-three in April. And you?"

"I am twenty-nine. You are old enough to be my father!" exclaimed Jose.

"I wish you wouldn't think of me as a father figure. I was hoping we could be just friends. But I know that may be difficult for you because of the Asian respect for age."

"Well, I will try to treat you as a friend and ... what's the right word? ... contemporary. It is amazing how we met. I still cannot believe that it was a random radio contact that brought us together. And now, after traveling thousands of kilometers, I am in Sweden. In your house!"

"Amazing, isn't it? I am glad you are here."

"I wonder what's happening in India?" said Jose.

Carl switched the TV off and tuned into the BBC on the short-wave radio. The news was the same – the killing of Sant Jarnail Singh Bhindranwale, the damage to the Golden Temple, and the loss of lives on both sides. It was clear that the army actions had further alienated the Sikh community. Indira

Gandhi had proved yet again how ruthless she could be.

"I need a stiff peg," Jose said.

"That's quite British, you know," said Carl rising and pouring out a generous measure of Jack Daniel's.

"I've been listening too much to the BBC."

They must have had a few more rounds when Carl looked quizzically at Jose and asked, "When do you plan on getting married? Will it be an arranged marriage like most marriages are in India?"

"I think so. I think it will be an arranged marriage. I don't want to break social conventions and upset my uncle. But I will get to see the girl and decide if I like her or not," said Jose.

"But you won't get to court her or anything, will you?"

"No, that won't happen. Our family is quite conservative." Then he added pensively, "If my parents were alive, I would have felt much better. Ever since they passed away I have had to depend on my uncle and he does not always look out for my interests."

"Will you get a big dowry? I've been told the bride's family has to pay a large sum of money to the groom's family."

"It is a social custom that has been distorted," Jose's words were beginning to slur.

"If I am not being too personal, do you have a secret girlfriend?" asked Carl with his head tilted to one side, sizing Jose up.

"No, I do not have a girlfriend. Our culture does not give us the freedom to have girlfriends."

"Any boyfriends?" asked Carl winking.

Jose thought he had not heard right. He tried to clear his head of the intoxication that was beginning to set in. "What?" he asked, trying to focus his eyes on Carl.

"Do you have any inclination for persons of your own gender?" asked Carl emboldened by Jose's tipsy state.

When realization struck him, Jose cringed back in horror, waving his hands. "No, no ... never!" he managed to croak. "Never even heard of it."

"Homosexuality may be hidden but it exists in every society," Carl stated.

Jose's head was reeling. This was becoming uncomfortable. He made as if to rise.

"Maybe. But I have no knowledge of it. Nobody talks about it," Jose.

Then came the coup de grâce.

"I am gay," Carl announced softly with a sardonic smile.

Jose's world came crashing down. His head spun. "Was that why Carl invited me to Stockholm?" he wondered. He did not know what to say. Alarmed and confused, he rose from the sofa and fled to his room, calling out a hasty "Goodnight!" to Carl.

## Chapter 6

When Jose came to the kitchen the next morning, he found Carl in his dressing gown sipping coffee and reading the day's *Dagens Nyheter*.

"Good morning, Carl," said Jose a trifle hesitantly.

"Top of the morning, young man!" Carl responded expansively as if nothing had happened the previous night. "Do you have a hangover?"

"A little. It is very mild. A little coffee will clear it."

"Your breakfast is ready and waiting."

When Jose turned the cover plate over he found fried eggs, hash browns, and sausage links.

"This is wonderful. Thank you!"

"You are welcome. Help yourself to coffee," said Carl pushing the coffee pot towards Jose.

As Jose made himself a cup of coffee, he noticed that Carl had kept the newspaper down and was watching him intently with disapproval writ large on his face.

"What am I doing wrong?" asked Jose puzzled.

"You dipped the sugar spoon in the coffee."

"No, Carl, I am stirring the coffee with my own spoon," protested Jose.

"Look in the pot. You will see wet clumps of sugar. You have been doing this from the first day."

Jose looked in the pot. Carl was right. There were brownish bunches of wet sugar sticking together.

"I am sorry. I didn't mean to. It must be the steam from the coffee condensing on the spoon. Or I may have unknowingly touched the surface of the coffee with the spoon. Sorry."

"No worries. Just giving you some feedback."

"Thanks, Carl. I will be more careful in future," said Jose apologetically. Inwardly he wondered if this had anything to do with the incident of the previous night.

"Don't worry about it. Just get on with your breakfast," said Carl. "Looks like things are calm in India."

"I am relieved. I was almost certain there would be widespread violence in Punjab."

"I need to go to the office again this morning. Another urgent order for translation. I will be back by noon."

"Please give me some books from your library to read," requested Jose.

"Have you read R. K. Narayan?" asked Carl.

"No, but I have heard of him."

"Read *Swami and Friends* or *The Guide*. Narayan deserved to win the Nobel Prize."

"I didn't know he was that good," said Jose.

"Graham Greene was a friend of his. *He* didn't get the Nobel Prize either."

Before he left, Carl brought out a pile of books from his bedroom and left them on the center table.

After breakfast, Jose wondered what he should do. He quickly ruled out reading. Sitting indoors reading seemed such a waste of time after all the trouble he had gone through to get to Sweden. Suddenly he remembered the strip poker on TV. He turned the television on with great anticipation and flipped channels. Sure enough, it was there. There were two women today, a blonde and a brunette, both naked to the waist. "They must have lost their bets early," he thought. Guiltily he turned the TV off and walked around the room. He then decided that being outdoors was the safer option and left the apartment after a quick shower.

***

Jose took a different route this time. He headed out towards Nybroplan and then turned towards Strandvägen. As he walked along the strand, Jose was truly enamored of the blue skies and the deep blue waters with the boats and the seagulls bobbing gently. He crossed the bridge to Nordiska Museet and sat on a bench outside, watching the people come and go. "The Swedes are all so beautiful and so elegantly dressed," Jose said to himself. Just then a horse-drawn carriage rolled by and Jose was transported back in time to bygone days. He remembered that Carl would be back by noon and though there was still more than an hour left, he decided to get back to the apartment.

Jose did not see the young lady when he stepped into the hall from the stairway. He was about to insert the key in the door when he noticed the motionless form beside the door across the hall. She stood unmoving with her hands held together and her back against the wall. Jose stared speechless at the blonde haired young woman who looked back at him expressionless, wide-open, blue eyes.

Jose finally found his voice. "I'm sorry. I didn't see you."

The young woman only smiled faintly.

"Can I help you?" Jose tried again.

"No, thank you, I'm fine. I'm here for an interview at eleven o'clock in this apartment," she replied.

"It is already twenty past."

"I know. I will wait," she responded.

Then Jose said without thinking, "Would you like to come in and sit down while you wait?" The moment the words left his mouth, he knew that he had said the wrong thing.

The lady blushed and involuntarily pressed herself further back against the wall.

"No, thanks. I will just wait here," she replied guardedly with a trace of suspicion.

Jose wondered for a moment if he should explain that he had made the offer with no ulterior motive but then decided against it as he might only end up digging himself deeper in the hole. In desperation, he clawed at the front door and rushed inside with a nervous wave to the lady. Once inside, he leaned back against the hastily shut door and reprimanded himself for his foolishness. He had just exposed his complete lack of experience in dealing with the opposite sex.

"Would any sane woman accept an invitation to be alone indoors with a strange man – and that too a foreigner? What will she think of me?" he asked himself.

He slapped his forehead in despair and then looked out through the peephole. She was still there, exactly as she was when he left her. To Jose, she was the perfect angel with her neatly combed golden hair, blue eyes, and demure demeanor, as she waited patiently. Jose dragged himself away from the peephole and set about changing his clothes. After taking off his shirt and vest he wrapped a towel around his waist as he removed his trousers. The pile of books that Carl had left for him attracted his attention and he picked up *A Farewell to Arms*. There were also *The Grapes of Wrath*, *As I Lay Dying* and, of course, Narayan's *Swami and Friends* and *The Guide*. Jose thumbed through the books oblivious of his state of undress.

About ten minutes later he remembered the girl outside the door. *Swami and Friends* in hand, Jose strode to the front door and squinted through the peephole. The lady was no longer there. He strained his eyes to the left and to the right to catch a glimpse of her but to no avail. He felt a sense of disappointment. The angel had vanished. Dejectedly he turned around to go back to reading. But the optimistic side of him obstinately clung to the hope that she had not left, that she was still there.

He took a few steps in the direction of his room but stopped abruptly. He had to conclusively prove or disprove her presence. Wheeling around, he marched to the door and opened it a tad. She was not at the original location. Jose opened the door wider and took half a step outside for a better look.

She was still there! Jose was thrilled. She had only moved to the other side of the door. But now that he was face to face with her, his shyness returned and he was tongue-tied.

She looked at him incredulously and her right hand flew involuntarily to her mouth. Jose wondered for a moment why she was reacting like that. Then looking down he realized, with surprise and shame, his own semi-nudity and lunged back into the apartment with an anguished moan.

If he had been embarrassed earlier, he was absolutely mortified now. The sheer weight of his disgrace caused him to sink to the floor, holding his head in his hands. Then slowly raising himself he changed his clothes and switched on the TV. He could not bring himself to watch strip poker anymore. Instead, he watched *The French Connection* with English subtitles.

\*\*\*

The surprise that Carl had for Jose was an Indian music performance at the Musikmuseet on Sibyllegatan.

"Do you ever dress Indian?" asked Carl.

"I have worn a white *mundu*. That is a white cotton or linen garment tied like a sarong tied around the waist."

"I know what a *mundu* is. You keep forgetting I have been to Kerala many times. I tried wearing one once. But they didn't have anything my size. The largest *mundu* they had couldn't cover me decently.

When I pulled it in one direction to cover one part, I exposed another part of me. In the end, I gave up."

"And it is difficult to keep it tied securely around one's waist. It keeps slipping off," added Jose laughing.

"I would like you to wear an Indian *kurta* this afternoon," said Carl with a knowing smile.

"I have never worn one before. That is a North Indian dress," protested Jose.

"Nobody here in Stockholm knows the difference between South India and North India. Just wear it. You will know why when we get there," said Carl.

"Where are we going?" asked Jose.

"That's a secret!" laughed Carl.

Jose took his shirt off and slipped on the *kurta*. Though he felt awkward in the collarless garment he decided to play along.

When they reached Musikmuseet Jose realized why Carl had pressed him to wear the *kurta*. The evening's performance was a violin recital in the classical music tradition of South India by the maestro Prof. K. Gopalakrishnan. The accompanist on *mridangam* was Shankar Rao.

Jose had never cared for Carnatic music, the classical music of South India. But Carl and the Swedish audience lapped it up. The maestro reveled in the generous applause and performed an encore.

Jose was uneasy throughout the performance for another reason. The maestro Prof. Gopalakrishnan seemed to have eyes only for him, the lone Indian in the audience.

"Lovely, wasn't it?" asked Carl rhetorically as they left the auditorium.

"To be honest, Carl, this is the first time in my life that I have attended a South Indian classical music concert. Ironically, I had to travel all the way to Stockholm for this – and wear a *kurta* to boot!" laughed Jose amused by the incongruity of it all.

"The music is difficult to understand. It is quite unlike Western classical music. But I still like it. It brings India to me here in Sweden. It makes me feel as if I am back in India. When I listen to cassette tapes of Indian music it's all I can do to keep myself from running out and getting on a plane to India," said Carl.

"Quite frankly, Carl, I don't find anything musical in what we listened to just now. But thanks all the same, for the experience. And this *kurta* is a little too tight under the arms."

"I am disappointed. I thought you would be a lover of Indian classical music."

"Maybe if I were a Hindu Brahmin I would be a fan. Orthodox Christianity and Indian classical music somehow do not go together."

\*\*\*

The next morning after breakfast they caught bus number 47 for Skansen. The trip turned out to be a turning point. Jose fell in love with Skansen right away.

"This is absolutely brilliant!" he gushed.

"I'm glad you like it so much. Hazelius would have been pleased!" said Carl.

"Hazelius? Who is Hazelius?" asked Jose.

"Artur Hazelius. The guy who created Skansen. Way back in 1891."

"He must have been a genius. This is what I like about you Swedes. You cherish your history and preserve it. Whether it is the Vasa ship or old buildings."

"*Your* history goes back much longer than ours," Carl said.

"That may be true but we do not conserve our past. We destroy them – whether they be buildings, old writings, or ancient artifacts," lamented Jose.

They caught the little train from Sollidsplatån and took a ride around Skansen. And then they walked to Marknadsgatan to view the old wooden church of Seglora. The zoo did not interest Jose except for the reindeer. But the old trades of the blacksmith and the glass blower fascinated Jose.

"Jose, I am going to present you a special souvenir to show how much I appreciate your coming to visit me."

"Carl, I am the one who owes you presents," said Jose.

"I'll have none of that. You already gave me your presents. Now it is my turn."

Carl spoke in Swedish to the glassblower who took the long blower and dipped it into molten glass. He then blew out a glowing red bulb and shaped it by twirling it around before finally dipping it in water, producing a hissing sound. When the product was taken out and fitted with a copper cap, Jose gasped in wonderment. The result was a beautiful bottle with annealing streaks.

Carl paid the artisan and then presented the bottle ceremoniously to Jose.

"Thank you for being my friend. You don't know how much your visit means to me," Carl said with emotion.

Jose was taken aback. His thoughts went back to Carl's confession of being gay. But Carl was quick to dispel Jose's fears.

"No, not that. I meant only friendship – nothing more, nothing less."

"I reciprocate that," said Jose visibly relieved. "You have no idea how much you have changed my life. You have opened up a whole new world for me."

They celebrated their bond of friendship with a typical Swedish lunch at the Solliden restaurant.

"The women in traditional costumes look like angels," Jose said looking at a red-cheeked, blonde young woman in an eighteenth-century costume.

"I see that you are quite attracted to Swedish girls," Carl said laughing.

"I cannot help it. They are so beautiful!"

***

The next morning after Carl had left for work Jose decided to explore the city on foot again. This time he decided to walk up to Skeppsholmen. After reaching the Grand Hotel on Södra Blasiholmshamnen he took a wrong turn and ended up on Strömbron instead of Skeppsholmsbron. But Jose did not mind. He walked down Skeppsbron to Kungliga Slottet, the Royal Palace, and then traced his way back to Kungsträdgården. Here he sat down on a bench to overcome his tiredness and to enjoy the novelty of being in Sweden. His thoughts went back to the incidents of the day before. He was too ashamed to tell Carl of his ludicrous encounter with the young woman in the hall. He wondered what it would be like to have a Swedish girlfriend but quickly banished the thought as being too preposterous. After checking the map, he figured out that he was not far from Skeppsholmen. But he decided to leave it for another day and returned home on foot via Nybroplan.

He had just stepped into the building after punching in the entry code when, to his total surprise, he came face to face with the young woman of the gaffe incident. He was absolutely tongue-tied and his ears burned with embarrassment at the memory. But she seemed not to remember.

"Hej! Hello!" she said with a pleasant smile.

"Hello!" replied Jose. "Sorry about the other day," he quickly added.

"There's nothing to it. Don't … mention it," she said searching for words.

Jose remembered the interview. "Did you get the job?"

She smiled broadly. "You remember! Yes, I got the job. There was some confusion about the time that day. The lady thought the interview was an hour later."

"Congratulations! What kind of work do you do?" asked Jose.

"I am a trainee interior designer." Then she added, holding out her hand, "My name is Inga."

"Glad to meet you … Inga! My name is Jose." As he took her alabaster hand in his, a shiver passed through his frame. His eyes were riveted on her blue eyes.

"Where are you from Jose? Do you work here in Stockholm?" she asked.

"No, I am here for a conference. It is over. I go back to India in a week. I am staying here with a friend."

"Female?" asked Inga with a mischievous smile.

"No!" Jose hastily replied, shaking his head in violent negation. "Male ... man ... we are only friends. We met through ham radio."

Inga laughed her eyes crinkling and dimples appearing on both cheeks. "You are a funny man. And you are the first Indian I have met."

"And you are first Swedish lady I have met. Actually, you are also the first young woman from anywhere that I have talked to—excepting for classmates, of course. Ingrid Bergman is my favorite actress."

"My first name actually is Ingrid," Inga said with a smile. "The full name is Ingrid Gustafsson."

"I am so happy to meet you. My full name is Kandathil Kurian Jose."

"That is too difficult for me to repeat. I will call you just Jose."

"That will be fine, Inga. Will you come again?"

"Of course! I have to come to this building every day. Remember, I have a job now."

"Can I meet you again?" asked Jose, hoping against hope.

"Yes. I will be happy to meet you too. My work gets over by twelve noon. I work only four hours. See you in the hall. I must go now. Hej, hej!"

And with that, she was gone.

Jose climbed the stairs in a happy daze, unable to get the fetching figure in the green dress out of his mind.

***

"I have another surprise for you today," announced Carl after he got home.

"Where are we going today? Are we taking the cruise ship to Helsinki?" asked Jose excitedly.

"No, unfortunately not. We may not be able to do that on this trip. You will have to come back another time."

"What is the surprise then?"

"There is something I want to show you. It is in my small study off the bedroom."

Coffee mug in hand Jose followed Carl, curious to see what he had to show. There, on a white, wooden shelf were what, at first glance, appeared to be photo albums, neatly stacked. Carl smiled mysteriously and motioned for the coffee cup to be placed at a safe distance. He then picked out one album and held it open for Jose to see.

Jose's mouth opened in wonder when he saw postage stamps of the old kingdoms of Travancore and Cochin.

"These are pre-independence stamps! They cost a fortune!" exclaimed Jose.

"Yes, I knew you would be surprised to see them," said a smiling Carl.

"I am so happy to see old stamps from my state. These kingdoms existed before the state of Kerala was formed in 1956. Actually, Kerala State was initially called the State of Travancore-Cochin."

"Yes, I know. I have been collecting stamps of old Indian kingdoms and of India for more than twenty years. My collection of the stamps of the kingdoms of Jaipur, Bikaner, and Patiala are even more valuable. I stumbled upon some very rare stamps at a street vendor's shop in Jaipur."

"I never expected to see old stamps from my state so far away in Sweden," said Jose shaking his head.

"That is something unique that you do," said Carl cocking his head to one side.

"What?" asked Jose puzzled.

"The shaking of your head. That stands out. You wobble your head like a dancer all the time. That is something most Indians do. I noticed that on my visits India."

Jose was embarrassed. "Yes, it is a cultural trait. Everybody does it." Then changing the subject Jose asked, "These collections must be worth millions?"

"I am not sure if they will add up to that much. But some of the stamps are worth a few thousand dollars each. Someday I will prepare an estimate using the Stanley Gibbons catalog to see how much my collection is worth."

"I like the way you keep them – in transparent plastic sheets," Jose said appreciatively.

"I don't even touch them. I use tweezers."

"How do you find the time for so many hobbies? Ham radio, philately ... music. I am sure there are more."

"I also write songs. Jazz songs. But to answer your question. I live alone and life can get incredibly lonely sometimes. Hobbies preserve my sanity."

He spontaneously put an arm around Jose's shoulder, but Jose stiffened in alarm.

Later in the afternoon, they went to Stortorget.

"This is Stockholm's oldest square. It may be hard to believe that more than one hundred people were beheaded here once."

"That cannot be true surely. You are joking. Swedes seem so gentle and delicate as to be incapable of murder and evil. You are making that up," said a skeptical Jose.

"No. It really happened in the sixteenth century. This was the square for public punishment."

"That is very hard to believe. I cannot imagine a people as beautiful and genteel as the Swedes would do anything as cruel as public executions and floggings."

Carl laughed. "You are looking at modern Sweden. The Sweden of olden days was a martial nation frequently at war with their neighbors. Obviously, things have changed a lot since then. Much water under the bridge – thankfully."

From Stortorget they caught the route 43 bus to Kungsträdgården.

"I've been here before. I was here just yesterday," said Jose excitedly.

"Really?"

"Yes, I lost my way a little bit and came to this park to sit down for a while."

"You know your way around this town already!" Carl said. "Many Stockholmers come here to relax. This is probably their favorite park."

Jose and Carl felt good just to sit together on the park bench, watching people.

"How about a trip to Uppsala?" asked Carl.

"I will be happy to visit that historic place."

"I remember you mentioning Celsius the last time we talked about Uppsala. Several other famous scientists were also at the University of Uppsala. Ångström, Arrhenius ... and there is one more well-known scientist ... I don't remember his name but I do know he discovered the element tantalum."

"I've heard of tantalum but I don't know who discovered it," said Jose. And then pointing to the group of men a little distance away he asked, "Carl, why are people watching the men standing still in the middle? They were there yesterday too. The people in the center don't seem to be doing anything. And they are all so quiet."

"They are chessmen," said Carl.

"Chessmen? Who are they playing against?"

"The men in the middle are the chess pieces themselves! The chess board is drawn on the ground and they are standing in their respective squares," said Carl laughing. "Let's walk over and watch."

Jose was amazed by the silence and patience of the players and the onlookers. The setting appeared to be more rustic than urban. It was easy to forget that there existed a bustling modern city just outside the park.

"Did you see those two statues? This one is of King Karl XII whom the people liked and the other is of King Karl XIII whom they ridiculed. The Swedes have a saying for the two statues. 'One is a lion among pots, and the other, a pot among lions!'"

"Very funny!"

"How about an early dinner?" asked Carl.

"That would be very welcome. I only had a banana and yogurt for lunch."

"Let's hurry back. I will cook something different tonight. Something American for a change."

"I am new to Western cuisine. I can hardly tell Swedish food from American," admitted Jose and Carl laughed.

"That will soon change. Reminds me of my initial encounters with Indian food. I couldn't tell North Indian from South Indian, Rajasthani from Andhra, Bengali food from Marathi food. They were all spicy hot! My tongue burned and my eyes watered, but I still loved it."

\*\*\*

On Sunday morning, they left for Uppsala, taking the metro (T or the *tunnelbana*) to get to the Stockholm Central station and the train to Uppsala from there.

"The murals in the underground stations are beautiful," said Jose.

"Yes, they are. It was decided to let artists use the bare walls for painting instead of letting the wide spaces be just dull gray blank areas like in metro stations in other countries."

"What I really dislike is the spray painted graffiti that can be found everywhere."

"It is not pretty but there are aesthetes who claim graffiti to be innovative, ground-breaking art. An expression of the society's angst."

"How can it be art? It is ugly and repulsive. Can it not be cleaned up?"

"Very expensive. Paint removal and repainting is costly and takes time. And what is the guarantee that the graffiti will not reappear?"

"It is such a shame to see walls, buildings and public transport being desecrated by these vandals. That is what it is – vandalism," Jose said spiritedly.

"By the way, I just remembered the name of the Swedish scientist who discovered tantalum. His name is Ekeberg. But the botanist Carl Linnaeus may well be the most famous and widely known scientist who was at Uppsala University."

"I have heard of Linnaeus but not of Ekeberg. Wasn't Linnaeus the man who devised a classification system for plants?" asked Jose.

"You are absolutely right. Linnaeus' name in Swedish was Carl von Linné and Linnégatan which is just two blocks from Jungfrugatan is named after him."

"I never realized that!"

The majestic architecture, especially the three towering spires, and the green copper roof of the Cathedral impressed Jose. Inside the cathedral, the high vaulted ceiling and the massive organ awed Jose. They wandered around the side aisles of the nave looking into the twenty odd chapels.

"This is the monument in honor of Linnaeus but his grave is a little farther down," explained Carl.

Of special interest to Jose were the eight pillars around the High Altar carved with the six reliefs of the Way of Life and the six of the Way of Death.

They were just in time for the second service of Sunday morning.

"There are just seven of us in this massive Cathedral," Jose whispered to Carl.

"Religion is not big in Sweden anymore. Many churches have been converted to movie theaters, shops, or even night clubs," Carl whispered back.

"In Kerala, churches are filled to capacity every Sunday. If you are late, you have to stand outside. It is such a pity that you have such big, beautiful churches but so few worshippers."

The priest (like the violinist at the Indian music recital) seemed to be intrigued by the presence of the unmistakable alien. Jose with his Orthodox background made the sign of the cross at appropriate points in the service but he did not look forward to meeting the priest after the service. Jose nudged Carl gently and nodded towards the door and they were out of the cathedral and in the open air again.

After quick visits to the Uppsala University and to the grave of Dag Hammarskjöld at the Uppsala Gamla kyrkogård, they had lunch at a small restaurant near the town's railway station before catching the train back to Stockholm.

"Do you think Hammarskjöld's death in the plane crash in the Congo was an accident? Or was he killed by the Russians?" asked Jose.

"Difficult to tell. There is a theory that it was the opposite side that did it. There is a strong suspicion of the involvement of South African mercenaries. One may never know the truth. But it is generally accepted as an accident in Sweden."

Jose watched the beautiful landscape from the train window for a while and then began reading the brochure he had picked up at the Uppsala Cathedral. A little later he turned to Carl and said, "Carl, look at what I found in this guidebook. This has explanations about the carvings on the pillars near the altar. I found something funny. Here's what the guide tells about the twelfth relief, titled Despair. Listen. 'The Way of Life and the Way of Death both end in catastrophy. However, the Way of Life ends in a good catastrophy while the Way of Death ends in an evil one.' How can a catastrophe ever be good? And why do they spell catastrophe with a 'y'?"

"Here, let me take a look," said Carl holding out his hand.

As he read, his grin became wider.

"This is rich!" he said laughing, slapping his thigh. "Good catastrophe and bad catastrophe!"

"It is really funny. I wonder why the Cathedral allows the printing of such crazy drivel," wondered Jose.

"That is one of the reasons why I am not a Christian. The church is full of such bunkum and nonsense."

"Not my church, Carl!" said Jose. "Our Orthodox faith was founded by the apostle St. Thomas himself. It was he who brought the gospel to India. And later on, the Syrians and the Armenians strengthened the Orthodox tradition."

"Well, let's not argue about dogma and superstitions. The Soviet Russian Republic of Armenia is one of my favorite places. I am suddenly reminded of the Khor Virap monastery and the ancient church that lie just below the towering Mt. Ararat. It is believed that the pagan king imprisoned St. Gregory the Illuminator in a deep pit. When it was discovered thirteen years later that he had not died but was still alive, the cruel king and the entire kingdom converted to Christianity and Armenia became the first ever Christian nation."

"What an amazing story. I never knew that Armenia was the first Christian nation."

"This is historical and true, even for an atheist and skeptic like me. St. Gregory the Illuminator became the first bishop of Armenia."

After reaching Stockholm they watched *Cheers*. Jose found the predicament of the man whose son was dating a black classmate of the same sex hilariously funny. Carl joined in the laughter. While Carl cooked pasta for supper, Jose watched a Swedish program on the TV.

Carl called Jose over to watch the pasta being cooked and said, "Pasta, rightly cooked, has to be *al dente*."

"What does that mean?" asked Jose puzzled.

"It means firm and resilient to the bite. Italian. I will get the tomato sauce and the minced meat ready and we will be good to go."

"Where are we going? Isn't it late?" asked Jose.

Carl laughed. "We aren't going anywhere. That is just a phrase meaning we would be done. We would be ready to eat. It is an American phrase. You probably wouldn't have heard it on the BBC."

After supper, they sat and sipped Jack Daniel's. Jose's mind wandered to Inga. He wondered how her Sunday was going and what she was doing now. He couldn't wait to meet her again, hopefully on Monday. Carl studied Jose over the rim of the whiskey glass and said, "A penny for your thoughts."

"No, nothing," Jose said evasively.

BBC radio reported peace and calm in India. When the conversation wandered to war and strife, Carl appeared agitated and poured himself a double.

"War is the single most useless human invention. It is depravity at its worst. It is nothing but evil," Carl said with uncharacteristic emotion.

"Have you had any first-hand experience, Carl? Have you fought in any war?" asked Jose.

Carl did not answer but gulped down his drink and poured himself another.

"Remember my telling you about my loss of faith and of leaving America?" Carl said somberly. He paused seeming to consider whether to proceed further or not before adding, "Both had to do with my experience in the US Marines in the Second World War. I lost my best friend on a boat in the Pacific. He was sitting less than three feet away when he was hit in the chest. One moment we were chatting and the next he had crumpled to the floor of the boat dead. A shell had hit him full in the chest." Carl bit his lips before continuing. "He was gone and I cradled his body in my arms ..."

Jose did not know what to say.

Carl banged the glass down hard on the table. "The bloody war! It is stupid! Why did the shell have to hit him and not me? I was there right next to him." He paused. "His death was the end of the world for me. I loved him dearly."

Jose was moved by Carl's story and he listened riveted and wordless.

"I decided right there that there was no god. I quit the Marines as soon as I could and, for reasons you can guess, did not go back to the States. Instead, I came here to Stockholm."

"What a story! I'm sorry you had to go through such grief, Carl" Jose said consolingly.

"Thanks, Jose. It still hurts. If Charlie were alive my life would have taken a different turn." And then forcing a smile, "Then again, I have you as a friend, Jose. And another land to call my own – Kerala."

There were a thousand questions that Jose wanted to ask. "Why did Carl not go back to America?" "Did he ever marry?" "What about his relatives back home?" But Jose realized that even sharing this much had required a tremendous effort on Carl's part and the whiskey seemed to have taken its toll on both of them.

"Jose, you know what I'd really like now?" asked Carl.

"No. What?"

"A good catastrophe. Yes, a good catastrophe is what I want," said Carl winking furiously.

It took some time for Jose to get the drift. When he finally understood what Carl was getting at, he said, "As I said before, Carl, my inclinations, unfortunately, do not lie in that direction. But I am your friend."

"Thanks, Jose. I understand. Goodnight!"

Jose dreamt that night of Inga. He dreamt of her golden blonde hair streaming in the wind as they fled from a group of soldiers in hot pursuit. In his dream, they ran through fields of yellow daffodils and up a grassy knoll before huddling together in a red barn. Inga clung to him in fear as they heard the approaching footsteps of their pursuers. When the soldiers rattled the barn door trying to open it, Jose woke up in a cold sweat.

Sleep would not return and he lay peering out at the twilight, wanting the day to come so he could meet Inga again.

## Chapter 7

Carl paused a moment at the front door the next morning before leaving for work.

"I can't believe you will be leaving one week from today. How quickly has time flown!"

"Yes, I know. The last week passed like a dream."

"I'm glad. There are several more things I've planned for you. We need to do all of that this week."

"Don't worry, Carl. Being here in your company is more than enough for me. Everything else is extra."

"Jose, that's why I love you. You are easy to please and you are gracious."

"I can never hope to be the gracious host that you are, Carl!" Jose said seriously.

Carl winked, waved a goodbye and was gone.

Jose rushed to the bathroom and had a shower. Then dressed in street clothes, he waited for Inga. He strained his ears to hear her footsteps or the sound of the other apartment door opening. But there was only silence. He went several times to the door and squinted through the peephole viewer. There was no sign of Inga. He was so desperate to see her that he debated on going to the next apartment and asking if Inga was in but decided against it. He wanted to watch television but was afraid he would succumb to the temptations of strip poker. He paced the room nervously, noisily clearing his throat several times. The waiting was not doing him any good. Finally, he forced himself to sit down on the sofa in front of the TV. Nothing of what he heard or saw registered in his feverish mind. Within a few minutes, Jose dozed off.

The doorbell startled him and he leapt from the sofa disoriented. For a moment, he wasn't sure of where he was and thought he had woken up to the alarm clock in the morning. Then it struck him. It must be Inga!

He rushed to the door to open it. There stood a beaming Inga in a bright yellow T-shirt and blue jeans.

"Hej, hej!" she said chirpily.

Inga in person was even more beautiful and alluring than the dream. Jose's tongue clung to the roof of his mouth as he tried to clear his head and comprehend the angelic vision of yellow and gold at the door.

"Good morning ... good afternoon," he stuttered.

"It is still morning. I am early. My boss requested me to come in an hour early today. She is leaving for Skellefteå in the afternoon."

"OK ..." was only what Jose could come up with.

"Well, are you going to just stand in the doorway? Won't you let me in?" Inga asked with an impish grin.

"I'm sorry! Please come in," said Jose stepping aside in confusion.

"Nice apartment! Very exotic decorations! Is your friend from India?" asked Inga twirling around in the middle of the room like a ballerina.

"No! He is a Swedish citizen. I mean, he is originally from America but he has lived here for forty years. He is for all practical purposes a Swede."

"But ..." said Inga pointing to the batik from Sri Lanka and other curios.

"Ah! Carl – that is the name of my friend – loves the South Asian region, especially India."

"I have never been outside Sweden. Tell me about India," Inga said settling down on the sofa in graceful slow motion.

"What can I tell you about India?" asked Jose gesturing nervously with his hands. "It is the second largest country in terms of population ..." he began hesitantly.

"I know all that," interrupted Inga with a laugh. "Tell me what your country is *really* like."

"It is not easy. India is like Europe."

"Like *Europe*?" asked a puzzled Inga frowning.

"I mean, each state or province has its own language. The cuisine and customs vary from state to state. The states are almost like small countries. That is what I meant."

"I see. Tell me what your own state is like."

Jose walked to his room and came back with the Reader's Digest atlas of the world. He looked around hesitantly, wondering where to sit. Inga patted the space next to her and Jose sat down gingerly. He pointed out Kerala on the map of India and began explaining what his state was like.

"It is very beautiful. On one side is the Arabian Sea and on the other, the border is a mountain range. It rains a lot being close to the sea. Everything is green. Lots of trees. Green paddy fields ... backwaters ..."

"What is paddy?" interposed Inga.

"Paddy? Rice fields. Sorry! There are also coconut and areca nut palms, and fruit trees like mango, jackfruit, litchi ... and lots of vegetables."

"Sounds lovely! How cold is it in winter?"

"Cold? Winter?" laughed Jose. "There is no winter! We are so close to the equator; the temperatures are almost the same the whole year round. It is only slightly cooler in January. We have just one season!"

"No wonder your friend Carl likes your state!" exclaimed Inga.

"He loves my state. I think he secretly wishes he had been born there. He likes animals too. We have many elephants, both domesticated and wild."

"Wow! How fascinating!" gushed Inga.

Jose smiled, "Thank you."

"I hope I can visit your country someday. After I have worked for some years and saved enough money," Inga said wistfully.

"You are very welcome. I will be very happy to be your host and guide."

Inga looked at him intently, her hands clasped together in her lap.

"You have beautiful eyes. Your eyelashes are like a girl's!" she said with unabashed candidness.

"Thank you, but I don't think I look like a girl," replied Jose uneasily squirming in his seat.

"No! I didn't mean it that way. You are a very nice looking young man. Tell me are you hungry? Have you had lunch?"

"No, not yet."

"I will fix up something quickly. I am hungry too," said Inga rising.

Jose nearly swooned when Inga came in even closer proximity to him as she arose from the sofa. She herself seemed completely oblivious of the effect she was having on him.

Inga quickly found the ingredients for a salad but could not locate any salad dressing. Jose squeezed into the narrow kitchen space acutely aware of Inga's nearness and got out the Italian dressing.

"Thanks! I see the mayonnaise as well," Inga said with a smile.

Inga dished up an excellent salad with chopped chicken and vegetables. After they had had coffee, Jose said he would do the dishes later.

"Do you fancy a walk?" Inga asked.

"Of course! I was going to ask you but didn't want to seem as if I was chasing you out of the house."

Inga laughed.

As they walked down the stairs, Jose said to her, "Thank you very much for coming in. The time spent with you is wonderful."

"Likewise!" Inga said with a happy smile.

"Shall we go to Strandvägen and walk by the quay?" asked Jose.

"Sure! That is a nice spot."

The feeling of unreality could not have been greater for Jose as he walked next to the beautiful Inga on the picture-perfect Strandvägen. They found a spot by the bank to sit and watch the boats on the water and the Nordiska Museet and the Vasa Museet on the opposite shore.

"The seagulls do not seem to have a care in the world," said Jose.

"What kind of work do you do, Jose?" asked Inga.

"Me? I work as a junior manager on a tea plantation. Why do you ask?" asked Jose.

"No, no reason," said Inga looking away.

Jose was again conscious of Inga's nearness. He glanced with wonder at the golden hair streaming in the gentle breeze blowing in from the water. He felt an irresistible urge to take her in his arms and hug her. To prevent himself from doing anything rash, he gripped the bench tightly with both hands. When Inga turned to look at him, he averted his eyes guiltily.

"Did you say that you do not have a girlfriend?" asked Inga.

"Yes, that's true. It is not our custom to have girlfriends. Our parents and relatives choose our spouse for us. And we meet them before marriage only in the presence of family. Never alone. We cannot have friends of the opposite sex."

"Someone else selects your life-partner? That is crazy!" Inga said incredulously.

"It might seem crazy according to Western customs but—believe me—arranged marriages are strong and seldom fail."

"I cannot dream of allowing someone else to choose my husband. It is *weird*!" Inga said shaking her head.

"Do you have a boyfriend?" Jose found the courage to ask suddenly.

"No, not right now. My boyfriend and I broke up two months ago. He was cheating on me. We weren't compatible anyways. He had no ambition, no long-term goals."

"Are you sad?"

"No, I am not. But in some ways, I miss him. He was careless but he was funny. It is difficult being alone."

"I have been alone all my adult life. And I have to be this way till my elders find me a wife," said Jose matter-of-factly.

"Your elders? Not your parents?" asked Inga.

"My parents are no more. It is my uncle and other elders who have to do the bride selection for me."

"I'm sorry," said Inga.

"That's OK. It has been many years now."

"You are a very strange man! And very interesting as well. I am not working tomorrow. My boss will return from Skellefteå only the day after in the evening."

"You get two days off?" asked Jose.

"Yes! Two paid days off. But I will try and put in a few extra hours when she is back."

"You smell nice," blurted out Jose suddenly.

Inga laughed.

Jose impulsively continued. "When you laugh, you laugh with your blue eyes. And the dimples that form when you laugh are so cute!"

Inga almost doubled up laughing. Then raising her head, she said, "Thank you, Jose. That's the nicest thing anyone has said to me in a long time. I was not laughing at you or at what you said. You were so earnest about it, it was funny."

They looked at each other without speaking a word, eyes searching the other's eyes.

"Anyway, what are you doing tomorrow morning?" asked Inga breaking the spell.

"Nothing in particular. I might just walk around sightseeing – unless Carl my friend has some plans. But I doubt it."

"Care to go out again? Have you been to the Old Town? We call it Gamla Sta'n."

"No, I haven't been there. It will be nice to see you again," said Jose gratefully.

"I will be there by nine o'clock. Do you think you can find your way back home from here? I will take the bus. I have a class this evening."

"Yes, I know the way home. Thank you for your company. I enjoyed it."

"I enjoyed talking to you," said Inga rising.

Jose was in the process of getting up when Inga leaned over and planted a quick kiss on his cheek. Jose shrank back startled.

"Did I offend you? I am sorry," said Inga apologetically.

"No, no! I was only surprised. I told you I have not been in the company of women before!" he said lightly.

"I'll remember that! Bye for now! Hej-hej!"

And with that, she was gone, walking away in the opposite direction towards the bus stop.

If Jose had felt unreal walking with Inga to Strandvägen, walking back alone to Jungfrugatan after being in Inga's company was even more so. Jose felt as if he was floating on air. He not only had another friend in Sweden but that friend was also a young lady, beautiful beyond his wildest fantasies.

*** 

Carl returned early.

"Did you just get back?" he asked with some surprise looking at the street clothes Jose was wearing.

"No, Carl. I came back almost two hours ago. I lay down for a few minutes and didn't realize how the time passed." How could he tell Carl that he had been dreaming about Inga from the time he got back?

"I hope you are not beginning to feel homesick," said Carl with some concern.

"I am fine, Carl. Believe me."

Jose pondered if he should tell Carl about his new-found friend but decided against it. Since Carl had helped him with the travel cost, he worried that Carl would be upset if he had another friend.

"I have a small surprise for you today," Carl said mysteriously.

"What is it, Carl?" asked Jose.

Carl pulled out two tickets from his shirt pocket and waved them in the air. "I have two tickets for us to the Konserthuset this evening!"

"What kind of music? *ABBA*?" asked Jose expectantly.

"No! It is classical music but not Indian music this time. We will listen to Western classical music by two Swedish composers and a famous Russian composer."

After a quick dinner, they were off to Hötorget. In the main lobby of the Concert House Jose immediately noted how different the audience was from the last concert. Unlike the casual attire at the Indian classical soirée, almost everyone, with the exception of Carl and himself and only a few others, were formally attired. The majority of them clearly had the markings and the demeanor of the upper class. An announcement ten minutes before the scheduled start brought the stragglers to their seats and quietened the audience down. To Jose's inexperienced ears the performers seemed to be taking an interminable time to tune up. After fifteen minutes of waiting, he meant to ask Carl about it but Carl preempted the question by bringing his index finger to his lips. After another twenty minutes, there was a pause and Jose joined in the applause, although he presumed it to be the ironic response of an impatient audience. When the performers resumed after a brief respite they still did not seem to be anywhere near the start of the evening's performance. But soon they stopped and the audience clapped even more vigorously than before.

Then everyone rose and moved to the adjoining room where white-gloved waiters carried glasses of champagne on silver salvers. Carl picked up a glass and Jose followed suit taking his cue from Carl. The bubbly stuff tasted good to Jose's palate but it also induced an involuntary bout of burping, much to Jose's mortification.

Just then a snooty gentleman walked up to Jose and asked in an imperious, but heavily accented tone, with his nose in the air, "And who are you?"

Jose was nonplussed by the rudeness of the query but without taking offense pointed to Carl and said, "I'm a friend of his." The inquirer merely grunted and moved away without another word.

In a short while, the audience resumed their seats and the orchestra went back to what they were doing, except this time the dissonance was even more pronounced. Jose would have fallen asleep had it not been for the jarring assault on his senses. Much to Jose's surprise, and relief, the music abruptly stopped and the audience burst into loud applause and then slowly rose to its feet for a standing ovation. The director and the musicians lined up and bowed but, to Jose's delight, declined an encore.

"When is the real show, I mean the performance?" asked Jose when they were out on the street again. It was past nine thirty but it was still light.

"What do you mean?" asked Carl puzzled.

"Wasn't this a rehearsal? Or a meeting of the patrons or something? It sounded like they were tuning up and adjusting their instruments all the time."

"No!" Carl replied with ill-concealed amusement. "This *was* the performance! The two pieces before the interval were by Hans Eklund and Ture Rangström. The one after the interval was Stravinsky's *Rite of Spring* or *Le Sacre du Printemps*, to give its original French name."

"Really! But that did not sound like music at all!" exclaimed Jose.

"I am not surprised at your reaction, Jose. When it was performed for the very first time in 1913 in Paris it caused a riot. Many of the classical music aficionados were outraged by its strange dissonances and audacious rhythms. Maybe *Le Sacre du Printemps* is not the best introduction to Western classical music!"

"Give me *ABBA* any day!" Jose said dryly. But quickly added, "Thanks for the experience, though. If it weren't for you, would I ever get an opportunity to go to a Western classical music performance?"

"I will let you listen to some Bach or Strauss before you return to India. I have a feeling you will love Bach. But isn't it amazing that neither of us connected easily to the classical music of the other's country? You did not enjoy today's performance of Western classical music and I did not understand classical Carnatic music from India, though I desperately want to."

"But I love listening to the music of *ABBA* which is from your country and you have no difficulty relating to Bollywood film music from my country, even if you do not understand the lyrics."

"Quite true. There must be something there."

When they reached Jungfrugatan, Carl threw wide his arms and said, "Here we are – back on home turf again!"

"Carl, do you see the irony?" asked Jose.

"The irony of what? Stravinsky?"

"No! Don't you see the irony of you living on this street? Jungfrugatan – meaning the street of young women or virgins. And you yourself, you are gay!"

Jose laughed hysterically. Carl looked at him quizzically and then, shaking his head, joined in the laughter.

***

The next morning Jose was ready almost an hour before the appointed time. The thought of being with the beautiful Inga again drove him wild with expectation.

Inga came exactly at nine o'clock. To Jose's disappointment, she did not enter the house. For a moment, Jose thought of inviting her in, but then thought the better of it.

"Do you want to walk or catch the bus?" asked Inga.

"If walking is OK for you, I will walk too," answered Jose.

"It's not too far from here. And it's such a perfect summer's day. It's beautiful outside."

The fast walker that he was, he marveled at the speed and stamina of Inga as she set the pace, striding effortlessly. When they reached Riddarholms Kyrkan Jose realized that he had been in the vicinity before.

"Carl brought me to the town square where there were public executions and flogging in the past. It is somewhere near here," said Jose.

"That must be Stortorget. You are right. It is near here. But instead of going in that direction let us take the longer route via Kornhamnstorg and then walk back through Gamla Sta'n along Skeppsbron."

Jose readily agreed. He really did not care where they were going or which route they were taking. For him what was of paramount importance was being with Inga. He was willing to walk anywhere with her, and the longer it took, the better. He would gladly have walked to the moon with Inga.

When they reached the cobbled narrow lanes of Gamla Sta'n Jose was amazed at how old the Old Town really was. The copper green roofs and the ancient haphazard construction only added to the charm.

"It's like being in a fairytale ... going back in time," said Jose wide-eyed.

Inga smiled. "This is how Stockholm was at one time. If you see the stark, heartless architecture of Skärholmen you would find it hard to believe that both are parts of the same city."

"I don't think I have been there."

"It's not worth a visit. I don't think Sweden will ever build anything so cold and impersonal ever again."

Like two truant school children they wandered around Gamla Sta'n, Jose torn between the excitement of being with Inga and the wonder of the well-preserved ancient town.

"The wrought-iron street lamps and the ornate brackets above the doors are so beautiful," said Jose almost reverently.

When they reached a winding, narrow row of steps between buildings, Inga held out her hand and Jose, with obvious delight, took her hand in his. Her hand felt so soft and delicate, Jose squeezed it ever so gently and his heart missed a beat when Inga reciprocated. Emboldened, Jose tightened his hold and Inga turned to him and smiled. The sunlight caught her golden hair and the dimples on her cheeks were flushed from the exertion of walking.

"You have the most symmetrical face I have ever seen. And your skin is so translucent, light almost passes through it. You are exquisitely beautiful," said Jose.

"Stop it! You are embarrassing me!"

"Your eyes are so blue!" exclaimed Jose at the top of the steps.

"And you are a handsome, brown-eyed boy! How about a cup of coffee?"

Jose did not hesitate. They found a small café nearby. As they sat at the table opposite each other, Inga laid both her hands palm upwards on the table and Jose placed his hands in hers. They looked into each other's eyes, searching, wordlessly exchanging thoughts. Jose squeezed Inga's hands lightly, fingers softly rubbing the palm of her hand and playing with the tips of her fingernails. When Inga playfully scratched the palm of his hand it sent a shiver of excitement down his spine. The waitress in a flouncy skirt looked them over while taking their order of coffee and pastries. Jose insisted on paying though Inga suggested they go Dutch.

As they passed by a curio shop, Inga pulled Jose's arm.

"Let's go in there. There's something I am looking for."

The shop sold knick-knacks and mementos for tourists. Two racks in the front of the shop had picture postcards for every taste. While Inga spoke to the bespectacled, elderly shopkeeper, Jose looked around the shop, at the keychains, refrigerator magnets, small Swedish flags and metal figurines. The prices were way beyond Jose's budget. Inga appeared at his side and pressed a brown paper packet into his hand.

"Here, Jose. This is a small present for you – to remember this perfect day," said Inga.

"Thank you. Thank you, very much," said Jose, taken aback.

"Won't you open it to see what's inside?" asked Inga.

"Of course."

Jose gently opened the mouth of the paper bag and gingerly drew out a small gift-wrapped packet. When he carefully opened it, he found to his delight that it was a cassette tape of Swedish folk or *gamla* music.

"This is beautiful. Thank you," Jose gushed. "I will always remember you and Gamla Sta'n and Sweden whenever I play this cassette."

"You are welcome. I'm glad you like it," said Inga simply.

They walked hand in hand, fingers entwining, all the way back to Jungfrugatan, this time walking north along Österlånggatan before crossing over the Strömbron.

When they neared the apartment building Jose sensed that Inga was trying to make her mind up about something. He wasn't sure if it would be proper to invite her in.

"I think I won't come in today. I will go straight home from here," said Inga.

Jose was loath to let her go. He was reluctant to part with Inga. At the same time, he did not feel bold enough to suggest that she come up.

"I wish you didn't have to go so soon. Must you go now? Can't we spend some more time together?" asked Jose hesitantly.

"No, I think I should go. It has been a perfect day and I want to remember it like this. Tomorrow it is back to regular hours for me and I will see you when I get off from work."

Inga brought her face close to his and he gently kissed her cheek. Impulsively Inga turned her head and kissed Jose on the lips and his hands folded around her instinctively.

"You are the most beautiful girl in the world. And I love you," Jose said, surprised at his own courage.

Inga slowly separated herself.

"Thank you. But I must go now," she said almost in a whisper, lightly patting his chest with the palm of her right hand.

And with that she walked away, not looking back. Jose stood staring at her receding figure till she turned the corner. He waited another minute hoping to see her miraculously change her mind and return. When that did not happen, he turned away and entered the building and climbed the stairs slowly, the happiness of a wonderful day mixed with the ache of first love.

***

That evening Carl returned later than usual.

"I'm too tired to cook. It was non-stop work. It's like that sometimes. The heavens fall down on you. What do you want to do today?"

"We don't need to do anything. We can stay indoors and just watch TV or something," said Jose.

"That's what I would have done if I had been alone. But you are here and it's such a shame to sit cooped up indoors. I would rather take you out and flaunt you!" Carl winked.

Jose felt slightly uncomfortable. He really did not want people to think he was Carl's gay partner. But he also thought he should not care too much about other people's opinions.

"OK, if you're not tired, let us go out," agreed Jose.

"Let's have a quick cup of coffee and leave."

They walked to Karlaplan and caught the *tunnelbana* to Sergels Torg.

"This is Stockholm's biggest underground station," explained Carl.

"I wouldn't have imagined such a big stairway as the entrance to an underground station!" exclaimed Jose as they exited the station.

Jose's mouth fell open when he saw the fountains overground.

"I cannot believe this! So much water!"

"Yes, it is quite a lot. I am told it pumps up twenty-five tons of water every minute through forty-six nozzles,' Carl said.

"One minute's supply would have been enough for my town's need for a whole day," said Jose.

"Yes, I know how difficult water supply is in India. At least in Kerala, most houses have wells to draw water from. I saw mobile water trucks were the only source in the other states," said Carl.

"That's true, Carl. Even if there is a tap, water is supplied briefly only twice a day. The water you use for entertainment here can meet the daily needs of whole communities in developing countries," said Jose.

"Now you are making me feel guilty," said Carl with a wry smile. "Those buildings you see are mostly bank offices. That spire you see is the Klara church. Let's go into the shopping area."

"This shopping mall is really beautiful!" exclaimed Jose. "I love the lights strung across and the potted flower plants lining the center."

"I'm glad you like this place. This is very popular with Swedes too. You may find it hard to believe, but in winter this entire area is heated."

"Really?" Jose was surprised.

"Yes, it's true. It gets incredibly cold in winter here."

"Let's check out that camera store," suggested Jose.

After looking at all the price tags, Jose shook his head. "They are all much beyond my budget. Let us just window shop."

It was then that Carl noticed the Kodak camera on sale.

"I don't know if you can get the 110 film size for this camera in India," said Carl.

"I think it will be available," Jose said.

"In that case, I would like to buy this Kodak camera for you," said Carl.

"You don't need to do that. You have already spent a lot of money on me."

"Don't worry. This is on sale. I want you to take some pictures from here to show your friends in India."

Jose thanked Carl profusely for the camera and six rolls of film.

They then walked up Sergelgatan towards Hötorget and the Konserthuset.

"That's where we were the other night," Jose said recognizing the Concert House.

"That's right. By the way, do you know what Hötorget means?"

"No," conceded Jose.

"Hötorget is Swedish for 'hay market'."

"Isn't there a Haymarket in London?" asked Jose.

"There sure is! There is a famous theater there. Then there is the Haymarket of Chicago infamous for the labor riots of 1886."

After a dinner of *lavash* (flat bread) and *khorovats* (barbecued meat and vegetables) at a small Armenian restaurant called *Sevan*, Carl had one more surprise up his sleeve.

"We are going to take that glass-walled elevator on the outside of the building," said Carl pointing upwards.

"Carl, I have a fear of heights. And we just had dinner," said Jose hesitantly.

"Don't be such a chicken! You will be all right. Just imagine the elevator to be *inside* the building. This is the only one of its kind in Sweden."

In spite of his initial fears, Jose found the experience exhilarating. The aerial view of Stockholm, resplendent with evening lights, was simply stunning and Jose snapped a few pictures through the glass walls of the elevator.

When they got home, Carl suggested ice cream.

"What will it be? Chocolate or strawberry?"

"I don't know. Whatever you choose," said Jose.

"You need to make up your own mind!" said Carl smiling. "I cannot choose for you. Do you eat a lot of ice cream in India?" asked Carl.

"Not so much. Since there is no refrigerator at home, I have ice cream only when I eat out."

"I like the small coffee shops of Kerala with thatched coconut leaves for walls and wooden benches and tables. I love the way the bare-chested shopkeeper cools coffee by pouring it from one cup to the other with his arms swinging about. I am always amazed that no coffee gets spilled. The liquid seems to defy the laws of physics. And when he places the steel or glass tumbler in front of you, the temperature is just right."

"I'm surprised you even went to such small shops. Did you go to a toddy shop too?" asked Jose smiling.

"I did, but I did not drink the arrack. I found the stench too strong. But I sampled what they were eating – tapioca and steamed sardines with grated coconut – and I loved it."

"You have seen facets of Kerala that I haven't. Toddy shops are strictly out of bounds for me. They are considered the dens of gamblers and ne'er-do-wells."

"I think I have the perfect segue for the subject we are discussing," said Carl rising and fetching two small glasses of cognac.

"Try this," suggested Carl offering a glass to Jose and adding, "Skål!"

Jose, never having had cognac before, tipped the whole glass into his mouth, only to jump up sputtering and coughing, much to Carl's amusement.

"This is pretty strong," said Jose finally.

"It is. I thought you would take a sip first."

"May I have a second shot?"

"Of course! This is Rémy Martin. The cognac I like best – after Armenian. The best cognac in the world comes from Armenia. No one can beat them. Not even the French."

## Chapter 8

"I need to buy a few things to take back with me, Carl," said Jose the next morning over breakfast.

"What do you have in mind?" asked Carl sipping from his gigantic coffee cup.

"I don't know. I have nothing particular in mind. Anything that is useful, I guess. I love the uniquely Swedish design and innovation."

Jose reached for the sugar bowl and added sugar to his coffee, careful not to wet the spoon.

"I would recommend *Tempo* at Nybrogatan. We have passed by that store several times. You will find it quite easily. There's also the equivalent of the dollar store. That store sign would read *5an-10an-25an.*"

After Carl had left for work, Jose quickly got ready and walked towards Nybrogatan. He found both the stores easily and went on a shopping binge of sorts. He could not wait to show Carl his purchases in the evening. He hurried back to the apartment with the bags.

\*\*\*

Jose put away the shopping inside his suitcase, freshened himself up and was ready when Inga knocked on the door. As soon as she stepped in the door she spread her arms wide and gave Jose a hug.

"It is so good to see you!" she said.

"I should be saying that," responded Jose. "I am truly lucky to have you as a girlfriend ... I mean ..." Jose stammered. "No ... sorry ... I didn't mean it that way."

"You didn't say anything wrong, Jose. We *are* friends, aren't we?" Inga said with a smile.

"Thank you, Inga. Even if I had a girlfriend in India, she would never be as beautiful as you."

"Stop it! I am not beautiful. And Indian girls are way more beautiful than me."

"To me, you are the most beautiful girl in the whole wide world! The whole universe!" said Jose earnestly.

"Thank you, Jose. Nobody compliments me the way you do," said Inga touched. She took his hand in hers and softly rubbed it.

On an impulse, Jose took her head in his hands and gently pulled her close and kissed her. Inga reciprocated, her lips opening and her arms entwining round his neck. Jose had to drag his lips away after a while. He kissed her cheeks, her nose, her eyes, her hair and her neck. She writhed with pleasure in his arms.

"You are tickling me," she whispered in his ear.

She ran her hands through his hair.

"Your hair is so thick and heavy," said Inga.

"And yours is so soft, light and golden. And it smells so good," said Jose burying his nose in her hair.

Inga suddenly disengaged herself.

"If we don't stop now we will both regret it," she said looking away.

Jose did not know what to say. This was his first real kiss and he was ecstatic.

On Inga's suggestion, they left the apartment and walked to Strandvägen. Jose's fingers caressed her fingertips as they walked hand in hand. Neither said a word as they sat side-by-side looking across the water. When Inga put her right hand around him and rested her head on his shoulder, Jose's heart flushed with a happiness he had never known before.

"When do you go back to India?" asked Inga suddenly.

Jose could not see her face as she nestled her head against his chest.

"I'll go back next Monday. Today I have to go with Carl to book my train ticket to Frankfurt."

Jose felt her stiffen. Her arm wrapped itself tighter around him. But she didn't say a word.

***

That evening Jose went with Carl to the resebyrå of the Statens Järnvägar (the Swedish State Railways) on Karlavägen.

When Carl attempted to request the reservation on his behalf, the lady pointed to Jose and asked haughtily, "Is he dumb? Doesn't he have a tongue?"

Jose was reminded of the arrogant lady at the travel office in Delhi but he decided not to protest, seeing that even Carl was docilely quiet.

The ticket to Frankfurt via Hässelhom, Helsingborg, Puttgarden, Hamburg and Hannover cost seven hundred sixty-three kronor. Jose checked to confirm that the price included a sleeping berth and Carl confirmed that the 'Sovsplatsbiljett' was indeed that. He had the lower berth in a three-berth compartment from Stockholm to Hamburg.

"I just realized something but it is too late to do anything about it," said Carl rubbing his chin. "You'll miss the Midsummer's Day celebration next week."

"That will have to wait another time, Carl. My flight to Delhi from Frankfurt cannot be changed."

"All right! There's nothing we can do about it. Now that your train ticket is booked, I'm going to take you to the top of the tallest building in Sweden. Correction: the tallest building in all of Scandinavia."

"That must be the TV tower," guessed Jose correctly.

They took the elevator to the top of Kaknästornet.

"Wow! I can see forever!" exclaimed Jose staggered by the view.

"That is the Gärdet or the common," said Carl pointing to the green. "Beyond that, you can see the skerries or islands and there is central Stockholm, from a totally different perspective."

"I'm glad I have the camera with me."

"The revolving restaurant here is too expensive. Let's head on down to road level."

When they reached the apartment after fish and chips at a small restaurant, Jose showed Carl his purchases. Among other things, there was a new-design Swedish can opener, a complete set of kitchen knives (including a cleaver) in a blister pack, two sets of deep red plastic cups and saucers, two red egg cups, two engraved, circular stainless-steel salvers, and several other household things.

"I am surprised by the things you purchased. I was expecting to see touristy souvenirs. Do you know what this is?"

"I have no idea what that is for. It looks like a palette of some sort and it is beautiful."

"Well, it is a ceramic cheese board for slicing and serving cheese. You don't eat much cheese, do you?"

"No, we don't get much cheese in India. But the board is so beautiful and sturdy and it can be used for some other purpose in the house. As a cutting board?"

"Those cups and saucers are not made of ordinary plastic. The material is a new invention. They are heat resistant to near boiling temperatures."

"The sales assistant said something to that effect."

"What are the salvers for?" asked Carl.

"One of them is a present for my boss. I will keep the other as a souvenir. They were made in Sweden and the engraving is exquisite. I bought these kitchen knives because they are from Sheffield. Our family had a highly prized cutlery set made in Sheffield. But this is my best purchase," said Jose holding up the bright red can opener with the rotating handle.

"You bought a can opener to take back to India?" asked Carl with some surprise. "Who buys canned food in India?"

"You have one like this in your kitchen. I saw how cleanly it cuts cans. And I just had to have one. This is an ingenious Swedish invention. The can openers we have in India are of ancient design, requiring the strength of a Hercules to open a can of mackerel."

Carl brought out the Jack Daniel's and ice and they sat sipping whiskey.

"In four days, you will be gone," said Carl wistfully.

"I know. Time has flown by so fast. It is all a dream to me."

"You must come back again."

"I will try. Is it easy to find a job here?" asked Jose.

"I don't think I will recommend that option. Kerala is a much nicer place for you to live in," said Carl.

"You have no idea how much more attractive Sweden is to me!" exclaimed Jose in surprise.

"I can understand that. But it will mean a tough adjustment for you. You will need a thick skin."

"You are referring to racial prejudice?" asked Jose.

"Yes, but it is more than that. Look at me. I am white, have a Swedish name and speak Swedish like a native. Yet they have never let me forget that I was not born a Swede. They make that clear in so many subtle ways. They never let you forget."

Jose was disappointed. "Learning Swedish might be difficult. Maybe I will try to immigrate to America instead. At least I won't have to learn a new language!"

"Talking about languages, I did not show you my new transceiver, did I?" asked Carl.

"No, you did not. And you also did not operate on ham radio since I came here," said Jose.

Carl took a big swig of whiskey. "Jose, you are the only reason I go on the air so frequently. When you are here with me, what need do I have of talking on the radio to anyone else in some far away country?"

"Thank you, Carl. Let's a take look at your radio transceiver," Jose said.

When Carl got to his feet, Jose noticed that he was slightly unsteady. This was very unusual for Carl who could usually hold his liquor down very well. They went through the bedroom to the small study with the stamp albums. Jose could not see any sign of a ham radio station. Then Carl slid back a sliding panel that looked like a wall and there it was – a gleaming Yaesu-Musen FT1000 MP transceiver with all its accessories. On the wall above were the confirmatory QSL cards received from other stations, the centerpiece of which was Jose's VU2KKJ card.

"The Yaesu transceiver is really lovely. It looks even better than it does in the catalog," said Jose.

"If you like you can operate my station. Go ahead!" offered Carl.

"Thanks, Carl, but no. I will not operate from here. I only want to touch and see what the rig feels like."

Carl flicked on the power switch and the radio came to life through the external speaker. Jose gently twirled the knob and admired the smoothness with which it moved.

"I am really impressed with your rig, Carl. This is quite simply the best transceiver in the world today. Your station is very neat and tidy," praised Jose.

"Thank you. I have neither the time for building transmitters nor the inclination for experimenting with electronics. My goal is only to make personal contacts through radio. And I hate clutter."

Carl quietly slid the panel back in place and they retired to the living room.

"Since you have only four more days here in Stockholm, I am going to cook the remaining dinners myself. You are the best guest I have had."

"Thanks, Carl. You have been a very generous host."

"I only have one regret. I just wish you were gay," blurted out Carl.

Jose took a step back.

"That will never happen," Jose said firmly. "I have moral and religious objections to that and moreover I find homosexuality distasteful," Jose said evenly.

"That is a pity," Carl said gulping down his whiskey.

Jose decided retreat was the better part of valor and hastily excused himself. As he left, he saw Carl, longing and loneliness writ large on his face, pour himself another double whiskey.

\*\*\*

The next morning at breakfast it was all back to normalcy again. There was no hint or suggestion of what had transpired the previous night. After Carl left for work Jose waited anxiously for Inga. The minutes seemed to hang heavy and unmoving like hours and the hours seemed like days. Jose could neither read a book or magazine nor watch television. He made a vain attempt to arrange the purchases he had made for easier packing later. But he just could not concentrate. His mind was stuck on Inga and Inga alone. He had a shower at ten o'clock and changed into street clothes. Then he paced the room looking every other minute at the clock. After eleven o'clock it was almost like torture. The minutes dragged by. Five minutes past noon and there was still no sign of Inga. He opened the door and looked out, recalling his faux pas. The hall was empty. Doubts began to gnaw his mind. Had she ditched him? Did she banish him forever from her heart? Dejected and dispirited he sprawled on the sofa staring at the ceiling, heaving a long drawn out sigh. He lay unmoving as the minutes ticked by.

The light knock on the door had the effect of an electric shock on Jose who sprang from the sofa and leapt to the door like a madman. When he opened the door, and saw Inga in blue jeans and a pink shirt his heart soared. But it was quickly apparent that she was in the same desperate state as he was.

Pushing the door shut behind her and dropping her bag on the floor, she flew into his arms, clinging to him with desperate passion. Jose's surprise lasted only an instant as he reciprocated in equal measure. He smothered her face with kisses and his right hand caressed her blonde hair. She nuzzled his neck and jaw as she pressed herself against him. Emboldened his hands fondled her, gently at first and then with fierce urgency. Not to be outdone she pulled his face to hers and kissed him, her lips parted, tongue seeking his. They writhed in each other's arms like dervishes.

Then, just as suddenly as it had started, it came to an abrupt end. Inga pushed Jose away, smoothed her hair in place with her hands and stooped to pick up the bag she had dropped. Jose stood transfixed for a moment before collapsing on the sofa with his right hand on his forehead.

"Why did you stop?" he asked plaintively.

She looked at him with a wry smile.

"You very well know why," she said gently. "You wouldn't have stopped. And neither would have I."

Jose stretched out his right arm and Inga moved closer and placed her hand in his outstretched hand. He caressed her hand softly and then his hand moved up her forearm.

"You are starting again. You are tickling me! I'm getting goose pimples," Inga said in mock annoyance.

Jose pulled her gently towards him. He let go of her hand and placed both hands on her hips. As Inga looked down at the seated Jose, her golden hair hung like a curtain, gently brushing his upturned face. His eyes pleaded with hers but Inga resolutely resisted her own desire and, dropping her hands to her sides, slowly pushed his hands away and stepped back.

"No, Jose, no. I don't want to hurt you. And I don't want to hurt myself. I've been hurt before and I know what it feels like," Inga said turning away.

"I don't see how there can be more pain than what I am feeling now," Jose said despondently.

"Believe me, there is far greater pain than this. And it comes after intimacy. I was so much in love that I could not bear to be away from him – even for a moment. But then he disappeared. He didn't love me anymore. I've been there. It's painful."

"I won't leave you. I promise," pleaded Jose.

"You will be gone in three days. You cannot stay here. You don't have a job. You don't have a visa. You *must* go. You will go and marry someone from India. We have got to be practical about this."

"I can always come back."

"That's what they always say," Inga replied and she immediately realized she had said the wrong thing.

"You think I am just another foreigner who wants to seduce you and then ditch you?"

"I'm sorry, I did not mean it that way. I don't think you are like those stupid Turks. But even if you want to come back, it is not easy. I don't see a future for us, Jose. I wish there was one."

When she turned around to face him, Jose saw that Inga was on the verge of tears and realized the pain she was going through.

They looked at each other silently for a minute.

"Jose, I think I should leave."

"Please don't go. We can sit and talk."

"No, I think I should be going," Inga said firmly. "But I will see you before you return to India."

With that, Inga picked up her bag from the sofa and walk determinedly to the door. She turned to wave before slipping out.

***

Carl suggested a visit to Hötorget and Sergels Torg and a still dejected Jose readily agreed. This time they took the bus instead. The seats were all taken and there was only standing room. Jose thought about Inga while he held on to the upright support. At the next stop, more people got on board but he was impervious to his surroundings as he continued daydreaming.

He was startled out of his reverie by Carl's shout.

*"Move back, Jose!"* Carl yelled not hiding his anger. "Can't you see you are blocking the aisle?"

Jose turned around to see the empty expanse behind him and quickly stumbled to the back of the bus in confusion. He was deeply hurt that Carl had yelled at him publicly in front of strangers.

When they got off the bus, Jose apologized.

"I am sorry about blocking the way in the bus. In India, passengers stand wherever they want in buses and others simply go around them."

"Not here, they don't. You need to keep moving to the back to free up space in front for those who get on."

"But you didn't have to yell at me in public, Carl," Jose injured.

Carl turned to look Jose in the face.

"I'm sorry. I think it was culturally inappropriate. I didn't mean to be rude. I yelled only because the other passengers were getting restive and you were lost in a world of your own. I'm sorry if I upset you."

"That's all right," Jose said. But it was obvious that he was still unhappy.

To take their minds off what had happened, Carl suggested ice cream. Cones in their hands, they wandered around looking at shop windows and enjoying the summer afternoon sun.

Carl looked at his watch. "I just remembered something. I need a haircut." Looking at Jose, he added, "And you need one too."

"I think I will be fine, Carl. I will be back in India in a few days. But I didn't see any barber shops here. How much does it cost to have a haircut here?"

"A haircut costs approximately twelve dollars. You must have seen the distinctive red and white striped signs of hair salons or barbershops. You will see it when we get to my barber."

"*Twelve* dollars for a haircut?" Jose asked astounded. "I pay the equivalent of only twenty-five cents."

When they got to the *frisör* on Östermalmstorg, Carl pointed to the red and white stripes and asked, "Do you know what the colors stand for?"

"No. What?"

"The red is for blood and the white for bandages."

"Even after charging a fortune, are they that clumsy with the scissors?" Jose asked surprised.

"No!" laughed Carl. "In olden days' barbers were surgeons too and they did bloodletting. Not anymore, though."

To Jose, the barber in his short white coat looked as dignified as a doctor and the shop itself looked cleaner than some primary health centers in India. Traditional Swedish folk music, barely audible, played in the background. Carl was in luck – there were no waiting customers. While Carl had his haircut, Jose sat in the waiting area and looked around. A barber in India traditionally belonged to the lowest social class but here in Sweden, he was a distinguished professional, Jose realized.

Carl smiled at him through the mirror and Jose waved back. Out of curiosity, he looked at the Swedish magazines on the table and picked one up. It was on modern Swedish design. Jose marveled at the innovative and ergonomic designs of furniture. The bold curves, the pearl white or blood red colors, and the simplicity fascinated him. He then picked up another magazine at random from the pile and his eyes nearly fell out when he opened it. Inside were pictures of beautiful girls, totally nude. Jose could not believe his eyes. As if the frontal nudity was not shocking enough, the girls seemed to be displaying elaborate pubic designs. Jose quickly dropped the magazine on the table and picked up the furniture magazine instead. But Carl had been watching him through the mirror and he winked twice. Jose was too embarrassed to smile back. In his mind's eye he could still see the naked girls. Inga came to his mind too, adding to his confusion.

When they were outside, Carl teased him. "The visit wasn't a total waste, was it? I saw you found something interesting."

"For a moment, there I wondered if he was a barber only of the head!" Jose said with a twinkle in his eye.

Carl laughed uproariously. "Good one! You know I have a box full of gay magazines at home."

"Not interested, Carl. I will never find that sort of thing attractive. I already told you." And then he added, "The barber must be making a lot of money."

"He is. He can afford to go every year to Nepal for three weeks. He has been doing that for as long as I can remember. Maybe he even has a house there. I don't know. He likes Nepal the way I love India."

When they got home, Carl got down to cooking after a round of Jack Daniel's. Jose stood by watching as Carl julienned the vegetables, measured the ingredients and warmed the oven.

"In India cooking consists of either boiling or frying. I think only the very rich and Westernized have ovens and do any baking. I wish I could cook like you, Carl."

"I will teach you the next time you come. And maybe you could open a restaurant serving Western cuisine in India and I could open an Indian restaurant here in Stockholm." Carl stopped what he was doing and turned to look at Jose. "You know what? That is not a bad idea. You could be the chef.

That may be one way for you to move to Sweden! And we will rake in the moolah hand over fist."

"Very tempting," agreed Jose, thinking again of Inga.

The meal was delicious, topped off with lemon meringue pie. They continued drinking whiskey after dinner while watching TV.

***

At breakfast, the next morning Jose feigned a headache and went back to bed. He lay there thinking about Inga and contemplating the past eleven days. His world had been turned upside down. He had come with the intention of discovering the Western world but had no dreams of falling in love, let alone his love being reciprocated. But the unexpected had actually happened. He had fallen in love with an indescribably beautiful woman and she loved him in return.

His heartache became even more acute when he realized that today was probably the last day he would see Inga alone. Monday was a possibility but Carl was likely to take the day off to be with Jose on his last day in Stockholm.

He got out of bed with alacrity and searched through his bag till he found out what he was looking for – a small sandalwood elephant that fit the palm of his hand. He also found a cake of the fragrant Mysore Sandal soap. Then he had a shower and got dressed.

The waiting was unadulterated agony. He counted the minutes as the clock ticked slowly to noon. But he did not have to wait long. Inga arrived two minutes past the hour. As she stepped into the apartment she kissed Jose on both cheeks and gave him a light hug.

"How are you today?" she asked sitting down on the sofa next to Jose.

"I'm doing fine, thanks. But in three days I will be gone. I am going to miss you. I don't know how I will live without you."

"You will be fine. The moment you land in India you will forget you ever had a friend called Inga."

"No, don't ever say that. That will never happen. I will remember you till the day I die. I love you, Inga," Jose said solemnly.

Inga looked into his eyes for a long time without saying a word. Then, leaning over, she held his face in both hands and kissed him on the lips.

"I love you, too, Jose," Inga said.

They sat staring into each other's eyes for some time.

"Can you guess what '*Jag älskar dig!*' means?" asked Inga.

"No. What does it mean?"

"It is 'I love you!' in Swedish," Inga said smiling.

Jose remembered the gifts then. He rushed to his room and came back with the sandalwood elephant and the sandalwood soap.

Inga was delighted with the elephant. "What a lovely smell! Will the perfume wear off?" she asked.

"No, it is not a perfume added to the wood. The wood – the tree itself – smells that way. The wood is considered very valuable. It is called sandalwood."

"How nice! The whole forest must smell so good if there were many sandalwood trees," said Inga.

"I also have a soap made from the sandalwood oil extracted from the same tree. If you bathe with this soap you will smell of sandalwood the whole day long."

"Wow! Thanks, Jose, for the gifts. I'm sorry I did not bring anything for you. I am not as thoughtful as you are," she said with a grimace.

"You already gave me the *gamla* music cassette. And you have given me the far greater gift, Inga – the gift of love," Jose said gravely. "I had no idea what love was till I met you."

Inga smiled and beckoned him closer. They kissed passionately on the sofa their tongues searching, their hands stroking and fondling each other. Jose feared an abrupt end any moment but Inga gave no indication of stopping. Emboldened Jose pressed her closer to him and Inga obliged, moaning softly. But the dreaded end came, as suddenly as it had on previous occasions. Inga gently pushed him away and straightened her disheveled hair. Jose tenderly tugged on her arm as if to make her change her mind. Inga looked at him expressionlessly for a long minute. She then smiled mysteriously, pressed her forefinger to his lips and walked to the bathroom. Jose collapsed on the sofa in frustration. This was too tantalizing for him to bear. He almost wished he had never fallen in love.

He heard the water running and switched the television on. A little later the bathroom door opened and Inga stepped out. Jose sat bolt upright, as if struck by lightning. There stood Inga with only the white bath towel wrapped around her, knotted high under her right armpit and barely reaching mid-thigh. The wet strands of hair framed her fresh-scrubbed face. The fragrance of the sandalwood soap filled the room.

"It is my turn to model a towel!" she grinned.

Inga's wicked smile widened further when she saw Jose's openmouthed look. With a flick of her left thumb, she loosened the knot to send the towel slithering down her body to the floor and there stood Inga with not a stitch on her golden body. She did not stop there. She did a quick pirouette and then struck a pose throwing her arms outstretched in a flourish.

"You are blonde," Jose blurted out in a hoarse voice.

That cracked her up. She covered her face with her hands and nearly doubled up laughing.

***

Afterward, they walked again to Strandvägen, their favorite spot. Jose noticed a major change in Inga. She clung to him closer than she had ever done before.

"We know only our names and nothing else," he said.

"We know a lot more than that," Inga replied, breaking into peals of laughter. Jose could not help smiling widely.

"I mean our addresses. How do we keep in touch?"

She looked at him, eyes filled sadness. "I keep forgetting this might be the last time we will ever meet."

"Don't say that. Please! I cannot bear to think of not seeing you again. All I have been thinking of since yesterday is how can I come back again to Stockholm very soon."

Inga tore two pages from a small notebook and they exchanged their addresses. Jose stood up from the bench to put Inga's address in the back pocket of his trousers and securely buttoned it.

"I won't risk keeping your address in an open pocket and losing it," he said.

"I cannot see you tomorrow or the day after on Sunday. I could see you on Monday when I come to work. What time do you leave?"

"I am not sure when Carl and I will leave home. The train is at 5:42 p.m. Will you stop by after work? Please!" pleaded Jose.

"I would like to. But you haven't introduced me to your friend yet."

"Carl? Just come. We will play it by ear."

They held hands and leaned against each other.

They communed silently, not knowing how to put their thoughts into words.

Finally, Inga said, "It's time for me to go. I don't want to. But I must."

"I wish there was a way I could take you with me to India. I don't want to be apart from you," Jose said, fighting back tears.

"We mustn't be sad. Let us hope we will meet again. If we don't, let us just remember the good times we had, without any regrets."

"Must you go?" Jose pleaded.

Inga's answer was a kiss. Jose ran his hands through her golden hair as they kissed, savoring the feeling.

Then they walked towards Jungfrugatan before parting ways.

Jose stood watching Inga's receding figure till she turned the corner and was gone.

## Chapter 9

On Saturday and Sunday Carl took Jose for leisurely rides around Stockholm by the *tunnelbana* metro and by bus, generally soaking up the sights unhurriedly. He bought another present for Jose – a Gillette razor – and Jose bought some more souvenirs, including several miniature Swedish flags. Jose was given the choice of restaurants for lunch and he chose *Sevan*, the Armenian restaurant they had visited once before.

"Do you know where this restaurant gets its name from?" asked Carl.

"No, I have no idea. Although there is a place called Siwan in Bihar State. It definitely can't be that. It is one of the most dreadful places in the whole of India. And Bihar itself is the most lawless and uncouth of all Indian states."

"No, it does not come from Bihar. Lake Sevan is a large lake more than six thousand feet above sea level in Armenia. In fame and popularity, it is second only to Mt. Ararat. By the way, I don't know if I mentioned this. Mt. Ararat, though Armenian, is in present day Turkey. I hope someday the Turks will return Mt. Ararat to Armenia – and apologize for the genocide."

This time they had *lavash, tjvjik,* and *dolma*.

"I am beginning to love Armenian cuisine. *Lavash* is somewhat similar to the Indian flat bread, *chapati*. But *lavash* is far superior any day," said Jose.

"There is one dish on this menu that I will not order today on purpose. I will save it for our last dinner."

The highlight of Saturday was a visit to the Postmuseum at Lilla Nygatan. Jose was overawed by the vast collection of stamps, especially the two rare 1847 stamps from Mauritius.

When they got home, Jose began his preparations for the return trip by doing his laundry. The floor by now was cluttered with his purchases. Jose had accumulated quite a bit of soiled linen. He needed help with using the washing machine. Carl helped him set the controls and measure out the detergent.

"Just dump them all in," Carl said pointing to the pile of clothes on the floor. "Then come and join me for some Jack Daniel's. You don't need to watch over it."

Jose was relieved he did not have to scrub the clothes one by one or rinse them repeatedly in a bucket as he did in India. With immense relief, he chucked all his clothes into the washing machine and hurried to the living room.

"Carl, I'm going to miss these cultured evenings with you sipping Jack Daniel's. Most of all I am going to miss your company."

"I'll miss your company more than you will miss mine. You will be with your friends again. Life in India is not as insulated as it is here. I'll to go back to living alone again after you leave. Not lonely, though. Just alone."

"I will wait for your visit in the winter."

"How about another shot?"

"Need you ask?" said a smiling Jose.

It was only after the third drink that Jose remembered Inga's address in the back pocket of his trousers. He ran pell-mell to the washing machine. There was still six minutes of the cycle left to go. He switched off the washing machine but could not open it right away. When he finally got the door open and retrieved the piece of paper, it was just a soggy, pulpy mass that came apart in his hands.

Carl was all concern. "Was it money?" he asked.

"No, it wasn't money. It was something I had written down."

"It must have been something important. You look upset."

"I *am* upset. I hate making mistakes like this. But there's nothing I can do now. It's gone," said Jose rising from the floor. "Let's go back to our Jack Daniel's. I need another peg."

Later that night Jose was close to tears as he lay in bed. He could not believe how careless he had been with Inga's address. All depended now on his meeting Inga on Monday, before his departure.

The special dinner that Carl cooked the next evening was *imam bayaldi* and Jose relished it straight away.

"This is an Armenian favorite that was on the *Sevan* menu. But it curiously has a Turkish name.

You won't find an imam in Armenia. And thank God for that!"

"I like the eggplant, tomato, onions, and garlic mixed with minced beef. This is really superb!"

"The name literally means 'the imam fainted'. And it is usually vegetarian. But I like topping it with beef."

Carl then revealed the second secret.

"When you gave me the banana chips I had promised you something special made with banana. Here it is! Banana pudding!"

Jose took a bite and said, "This is delicious!"

"I'm glad you like it. It is my signature dish," said Carl with a happy smile.

"Your cooking is a labor of love," said Jose.

"That reminds me of what I found on a paper napkin at lunch one day. It read, *'Love, in the overwhelming majority of cases, is the result of a good dinner.'* That's as it may be, but I would add that a good dinner is the result of love – love for the person being served, perhaps, and certainly love for the raw materials and the art of cooking," Carl said.

"Thank you, Carl, for a truly lovely dinner."

Later, while sipping whiskey, Carl asked Jose about the piece of paper lost in the washing the previous day.

"It is nothing important. It was an address that I had copied down from somewhere."

"OK! I am glad it doesn't bother you anymore. Tell me something. Of all the food you had while you were here, what was it that you liked the best?" asked Carl.

Jose took some time to answer. "Let me think. I think it was the baked herring on the smörgåsbord cruise."

The moment the words were out of his mouth he knew he had said the wrong thing. Carl could not hide his disappointment.

\*\*\*

Carl took the day off from work on Jose's last day. Jose clung to the hope of a last meeting with Inga. It was almost inevitable that his secret would be out when Carl and Inga met, but that was a small price to pay for staying connected with Inga. He decided he would make a clean breast of it to Carl when their meeting happened. Meeting Inga one final time assumed critical importance to Jose. Even if no intimacy was possible because of Carl's presence, he longed to see her once more before he left Sweden.

He rushed out after breakfast to do some last minute shopping at *Tempo* and *5an-10an-25an*. On his return, he had one ear on the door for Inga's knock as he readied his bags. Packing was not an easy task. Initially, it looked extremely doubtful if he could get everything in. But by eleven o'clock the bags were somehow packed. Carl suggested lunch but Jose was not hungry. He watched the Swedish programming on TV desultorily as he anxiously waited for Inga's knock. Noon came and went. There was no sign of Inga. His anxiety increased in the next half hour. And after that, dejection set in. Exhausted from the waiting, he trudged to his room and lay down, staring at the ceiling. His waiting had been futile. Inga did not turn up.

Finally, he got up, had a shower, and dressed for the return journey.

***

Jose's bags were heavier than when he came. When it was time to leave, Jose looked around as if to remember every little detail of the apartment where he had lived for the past two weeks. He felt a catch in his throat as he looked at Carl. But Carl was his normal self, emotions firmly in check.

"This might sound rather formal but I must say it anyway. Thank you for coming to this country and for being my guest. I hope to see you in India on my next visit. And I also hope you will come back again to my humble abode," said Carl.

"Carl, I have no words to thank you. I could not have come to Stockholm without your help. This trip was an eye-opener and a big education for me. You have been a very generous host. If I have upset you in any way, I hope you will forgive me."

"There never was any occasion for that. You are the best guest I have had. I enjoyed your company, Jose."

Carl opened his arms for a hug and Jose hugged him without reservation.

Then they were off to the station. Jose slung the cabin bag over his shoulder and carried the suitcase in his hand. It was only when they got to Östermalmstorg that Jose began to feel the weight of the suitcase. He wondered briefly if he should suggest getting a taxi.

"Carl, can we stop for a minute. I am winded," gasped Jose.

"Of course! We have plenty of time. We don't need to rush."

A thought struck Jose.

"Carl, did anyone come to the house looking for me today?" asked Jose.

"Looking for you? Why would anyone come looking for you?" Carl appeared surprised. "No, no one came. Why do you ask?"

"No reason," replied Jose quietly.

"Wait a minute! Come to think of it, someone *did* come – a young lady. She appeared to be confused. Said she had the wrong apartment."

"Did she have blonde hair?" asked Jose.

"Yes, she did! How did you know?" Carl was surprised.

"Just a wild guess. There are far more blondes than brunettes in Sweden," said Jose with a wan smile.

He was sure he had missed his chance of meeting Inga. He felt crushed and defeated by fate.

The bags were heavy. Jose wondered if he would have the strength to make it to the station but finally, they were at the *tunnelbana* station. Once inside the metro, Jose collapsed in relief, sweating profusely.

"We made it!" beamed Carl, raising his arms in a gesture of victory.

The train to Hamburg was already on the platform when they reached the Stockholm Central station. Jose came to the door after placing his bags near his seat. Carl stood nearby on the platform and smiled but did not say a word. When it was time for the train to start, Jose was on the verge of tears.

"Goodbye, Carl!" Jose said, his voice cracking, fighting to keep his composure.

"Don't feel sad, Jose. This is not the end – it's just the beginning."

"Goodbye, Carl!"

"Bye-bye, Jose! And write when you get home."

Noiselessly the train glided out and soon Carl was only a speck in the distance as the train gathered speed. Jose went to his seat to find only one other occupant in the compartment, a well-built, athletic young man who did not bother to even look up from the German magazine he was reading. It soon became clear that the fellow traveler wanted to completely shut him out. But Jose did not mind this obvious rejection. He sat, lost in thought, looking at the beautiful scenery moving past his window. Everything he saw were poignant reminders of Inga and of Carl. The man in the opposite seat opened his bag to take out a box of crackers and several chocolates and began to munch, unmindful of Jose. "How very different from the kind lady visiting her sister at the East German border!" wondered Jose. After changing into his pajamas, he lay on his berth, staring at the berth above him, and dreaming of Inga's blonde hair and red lips. He found it hard to believe that all that he had experienced in the past two weeks, had actually happened. He slowly drifted off to sleep, with Inga on his mind.

***

The rest of the journey passed in a blur. He changed trains at Hamburg and reached Frankfurt airport a little after 6:00 p.m. the next day. His flight to Delhi was only at 10:00 a.m. the following morning. Though he had sixteen hours to while away, Jose did not even consider the expensive option of spending the night at a hotel. He decided instead to explore the airport and its vicinity and sleep in an airport chair if he really had to. But first, he had to get rid of the burden of the heavy luggage. While looking around to see if there was a cloakroom at the terminal, he was happy to see the automated self-service lockers. Thanking his lucky stars, he quickly inserted coins into the slots and locked up his two bags and was then free to wander around as he pleased.

Jose felt incredibly thirsty and walked over to the nearest McDonald's to buy a Coca-Cola. As he waited in line, he witnessed a transaction that warmed his heart. A young man was in earnest conversation with an older gentleman who appeared to be down on his luck. They were obviously strangers and, from the way they gestured to each other, Jose guessed that they did not speak a common language. To Jose, they looked like a father and son duo in spite of the obvious differences of race, nationality, and language. As Jose watched in amazement, the young man pressed the older man to accept the sandwich and soda he had just purchased ostensibly for himself. The compassion of the benefactor did not end there. Touched by the grateful response of the indigent man, he also thrust some money into the man's hands. Then, with much gentleness, the youth took leave of the other man and went back to stand in line again. Jose silently applauded the empathy and kindness he had just witnessed. The image of this disinterested expression of compassion stuck indelibly in Jose's mind.

Soda in hand, Jose sauntered out of the airport into the small garden. None of the people out there looked like air travelers to him. Just then a garishly made-up young woman in a diaphanous red dress sashayed past him into the airport. His suspicion that he might be in the wrong company was confirmed by the sound of shattering glass. Startled, Jose turned to see a bearded man throw a second empty beer bottle in the direction of two aliens on the far bench, who ducked in time to let the bottle crash on to the low wall behind them. Jose decided then and there that this was not a safe environment to be in and hurried back into the security of the airport terminal. He saw the woman in the flimsy red dress flitting around giving waiting passengers the glad eye. This was an unfamiliar world that he had only read about in books. He watched fascinated as a repulsive Turk left the airport with the woman-in-red, dragging a heavy suitcase behind him.

Jose wandered around the glittering duty-free shops window-shopping. The variety of merchandise on sale was mind-boggling. But what shocked him most was *Dr. Müller's Sex Shop.* He was amazed that there could be a shop selling sex gadgets at the airport. He walked back to McDonald's and bought a burger and a soda. It was only 10:30 p.m. and he still had a long wait ahead. He went to the lockers to check whether his bags were intact and then resumed his exploration of the airport. That was when he discovered the cinema theaters in the terminal. His amazement went up another notch when he saw that in addition to regular films there was also an adult movie on offer. He wondered how pornographic movies were screened at an international airport. As he looked at the movie posters, he recalled his colleague Asokan's taunts prior to his departure. He, who had not had the courage to even watch strip poker on television in the privacy of Carl's apartment, suddenly decided to throw caution to the winds and watch the adult movie. The ticket clerk looked at him dubiously as he paid the money. The movie had already begun when he entered. The few who were watching turned around to look at him when he entered. Jose realized that he was the only obvious alien in the room. It was an Italian movie dubbed in German with English subtitles. Jose soon discovered, both to his dismay and relief, that the film was only soft-core porn with nothing explicit. The tiredness of the journey caught up with him in the darkened room and he promptly fell asleep. He awoke briefly when the film ended and the people shuffled out. He got many curious stares but he did not care. The movie began again and Jose watched a little of the beginning and then slept again. When the movie came to an end the second time, Jose stood up to leave. He could now tell Asokan with all honesty that he had actually watched a porn film. But he definitely wasn't going to tell him anything at all about Inga.

After coming out of the theater Jose wandered around the different concourses. Sleep seemed to have fled. He watched fascinated another community come to life after the duty-free shops and the lounges shut down for the night. Diverse groups of male and female cleaners, all immigrants, began their nightly tasks, cleaning the restrooms, emptying the trashcans, and scrubbing and vacuuming the floor. From their appearance, Jose guessed that several of the workers were from the Asian subcontinent.

A group of unkempt men carrying flattened cardboard cartons came to the corner where he was sitting. They eyed him suspiciously for a while. As Jose looked around for another vacant chair on the other side of the room to move to, one of them, bristling with ill-concealed resentment walked up to him and asked, "Are you a Sri Lankan?"

"No, I am from India," replied Jose indignantly.

"Are you Tamil?" the man asked again.

"No, I am from Kerala. I am a *Malayali*," said Jose.

The man turned to his group and announced in Tamil, "He is OK. He is not our enemy. He is Indian."

"Are you traveling to India by Lufthansa tomorrow?" asked Jose.

The man laughed. "We are not going anywhere. We do not have passports. We are Tamil Tigers fighting for the liberation of Tamil Eelam. We cannot go back to Sri Lanka. We would be killed. We cannot enter West Germany because our asylum papers have not been approved yet. We have been living in this airport for more than three months now. We cannot go out. We cannot go back. Frankfurt airport is our home."

Jose did not want to get into any trouble with the West German authorities. He did not want to be seen hobnobbing with these stateless persons. On the pretext of getting a drink, he slipped away. As he walked back to the main concourse he saw persons of other ethnic groups (Slavic, he guessed) also setting up sleeping areas like the Sri Lankan Tamils had done. Obviously, the airport was also a place of refuge for stateless persons.

Jose considered himself lucky to find three adjacent vacant seats. Uncomfortable though it was, he curled up on the chairs and soon fell asleep.

\*\*\*

When he awoke, it was almost five in the morning. Frankfurt airport was coming back to life. He hurried to the nearest restroom and completed his morning ablutions and then retrieved his bags from the locker. It was a long wait before check-in commenced but that didn't bother him. When his flight to Delhi flight took off on schedule at 10:00 a.m., Jose immediately fell asleep. He woke up when the lunch service came around and then watched the movie *Educating Rita* with Michael Caine and Julie Walters.

"This whole trip has been *Educating Jose*," he thought wryly.

Then an idea struck him. If he had enough money left, he would fly to Cochin from Delhi instead of taking the train. That would get him home on the same day instead of three days later.

And that is what Jose did. After landing at Delhi in the wee hours of the morning, he waited at the international airport till daybreak before taking the free airport shuttle bus to the domestic terminal. The Indian Airlines flight to Cochin was scheduled to leave in two hours and there were seats available. When he boarded the plane, he felt as if he was back home already. The majority of the passengers were *Malayali* and he heard Malayalam being spoken for the first time in two weeks. It was a three-hop flight; first to Hyderabad, and then to Madras, before landing at Cochin. When Jose saw from the plane's window the green Kerala State next to the blue Arabian Sea, he felt indescribably happy. The bus ride to Munnar via Muvattupuzha and Kothamangalam passed in a daze. When he reached the tea estate early in the evening, his friends gawked at him.

"You have changed. You look like a white man now!" they chortled half in jest, half in envy.

Asokan whispered something in engineer Hari's ears and they both laughed.

"Want to join us for some drinks tonight?" Asokan asked with a leer.

Jose shook his head vigorously and began walking to his quarters.

Chandy came up to Jose and insisted on carrying the heavier bag. Jose protested but Chandy would have none of it.

"You have had a long journey." Then he added, "Jose, I am so glad you're back. Those two were making my life miserable. They have sold their souls to the devil."

"Was there any trouble?" asked Jose.

"No, not yet. But there soon will be. Asokan has got himself a mistress now. A young tea-picking girl. As for Hari, he is drunk most of the time. He came to the factory floor one morning with his shirt inside out and his belt all twisted."

"That is not a good sign," Jose said with concern.

"At this rate, Hari will drown himself in alcohol and Asokan will be killed by the irate workers."

Jose was silent.

"Anyway, it was not my intention to dump all the problems on you before you even set your bags down and had a cup of coffee. I actually wanted to tell you that your uncle came to see you. He seemed terribly displeased that you had gone abroad. Didn't you inform him?" asked Chandy.

Jose did not answer. He only frowned, creasing his forehead in thought. He had not told his uncle and the uncle's visit did not bode well.

\*\*\*

The next morning the *babus* and the menial staff surrounded him. They fawned on him as he handed out the trinkets he had brought. He hoped he had brought enough to go around. The golden key rings with the picture of Stockholm embedded in clear plastic were a big hit. His boss, the marketing manager, nodded his head when he entered.

"So, you are back. How was Sweden?" he asked turning back to the papers on his table.

"It was nice, sir," Jose said respectfully. "Here's a small present for you," he added, handing over the box with the steel salver. The manager received it sitting down and opened the flap to peer inside.

"Hmm. Why did you have to spend your money on presents for me?" he asked with mock concern. Then he added without looking up. "Did you bring any Johnnie Walker?"

"No, sir, I did not buy any duty-free scotch or cigarettes."

Jose saw that his boss was disappointed.

It looked as if the others had used his desk as a dumping ground in his absence. Files, loose papers, unopened envelopes, and even newspapers, had been haphazardly thrown on his desk. He spent the morning clearing the mess and distributing files and papers to desks where they rightfully belonged. Having restored some semblance of order, he dove right into the pending correspondence. There were queries about previous orders and requests for a better rate on new orders. Not all of it was within his powers but he would have to nonetheless put down his recommendations for the boss to approve. Tiers of authority, miles of red tape, that was the style of work.

When the office boy came around with the sooty aluminum tea-kettle, flitting from desk to desk, pouring tea for everyone, Jose leaned back in his uncomfortable chair and looked around the office. What a far cry from the elegant and graceful Swedish aesthetics! It all seemed like an evanescent dream. The clutter of the office, the uncouth furniture, and the bundles of bulging old files tied with rope stacked in the corners of the room and piled on the floor – they all repelled him. When he closed his eyes, he saw the blue and yellow petunias on the windowsills – and Inga.

In the evening, he turned his radio transmitter on. The winds had shifted the antenna direction in his absence. Jose went out and manually rotated the bamboo pole on which the beam antenna was fixed so that it pointed roughly in the direction of Europe.

"SM5BFE SM5BFE SM5BFE this is VU2KKJ VU2KKJ VU2KKJ" he repeated several times into the microphone but there was no answering call. Frustrated, he scanned the band for other ham stations from Scandinavia. Even the powerful Finnish stations were not to be heard.

He decided to lie down and take a nap. But when he closed his eyes all he saw was Inga. He hugged his pillow tightly. He sighed as he remembered the all too brief encounter with love and intimacy in Stockholm. He wished there was a way for him to go back, marry Inga, and raise a family in Sweden. But doubts began to creep in about their future together. He wondered if Inga would agree to marry him or if it was all just a passing summer dalliance for her. Jose sighed again. For the first time in his life, he was beginning to realize how acutely painful being in love was.

A knock on the door brought him out of his reverie. It turned out to be Kurup the errand boy bringing a summons from Asokan.

Jose pondered whether to go or not. He decided it was better to go and get it over with. After throwing some water on his face and combing his hair he locked his quarters and walked towards Asokan's. It was already dusk and the laborers were wending their way home after their evening excursion to the row of shops at the gate of the tea estate. Most of the men were bare-chested, with their white towels tied over their heads in a turban of sorts. The others had the ubiquitous towel over their left shoulder. On seeing Jose, the women giggled and pressed to the other side of the narrow lane. Jose merely nodded in their general direction.

When he opened the front door, and stepped inside, he immediately realized what he was in for. "They must have begun drinking right after work," thought Jose. From the way he waved his hand in an inebriated manner, it was clear that Hari was already high. Chandy, deferential as always, rose to pull up a chair for Jose.

"The *sayip* has arrived!" announced Asokan with gusto, using the local slang term for a white man.

"I am the same old self," said Jose self-consciously as he sat down. "I haven't changed."

"Kurup, pour Jose *sar* a double peg!" ordered Asokan.

"No need. I will pour it myself," said Jose.

"So, tell us about your adventures. How many women did you lay? Did you find yourself a white woman for a wife?" asked Asokan laughing crudely.

"I had a good time and I learned a lot. It was well worth the money. You should all go on a foreign trip. I strongly recommend it," Jose said ignoring Asokan's taunts.

"It will only be a dream for me," Chandy the tea-taster said sipping fruit squash. "I don't think I will be able to adjust to their customs and their language. I won't be able to even eat their food," said Chandy.

"What's the news here?" asked Jose.

"Nothing much," Chandy replied. "Except the labor union held a big meeting. They are demanding a twenty percent increase in wages and many other additional benefits. They want an education allowance for their children and better medical facilities for their families. The representative of the Marxist-Leninist Communist Party was the chief guest. He was very good at whipping up their emotions. He called for the violent overthrow of the bourgeois and the capitalists all over the country. He wanted the government to nationalize all tea estates."

"Nothing will happen," said Asokan cynically. "I can sign this on a stamped paper and have it notarized. The management will buy off the union leaders. And cheap arrack will take care of the rest."

"That is not how I read the situation. I think this time they are determined. They want the tea companies to share more of their profits with the workers."

"Let us forget about our small town of Munnar and the tea estates here. Tell us about the whores you met," shouted Hari, drunkenly banging his fist on the table.

Jose had guessed right. His account of the train going on the ferry, ships passing overhead, rail stations underneath the airport, glass-walled elevators on the outside of buildings, trains that ran precisely on time, ATM machines that handed out cash, door locks without keys, litter-free streets, sex shops and porn movies at the airport, the midnight sun that never set, etc. were met with skepticism and ridicule.

"Just because we are drunkards and are not rich enough to travel abroad, you think you can fool us with your tall stories?" Hari was confused and drunk.

"How were the women?" asked Asokan.

"Like everywhere else, I think," Jose started to say. Then he decided to play along. "All of them are blonde and tall and well-proportioned. Stacked, is the right word. They look like angels with their golden hair and rosy cheeks and red lips and their shapely bodies."

Asokan licked his lips lasciviously and winked.

"Was everything very costly?" Chandy asked, changing the topic to something safer.

"Yes, but not as expensive as I had imagined."

Just then Hari slumped on the table in a drunken stupor knocking his glass to the floor.

Kurup came running in as if on cue with a broom to sweep up the broken shards of glass. He then laid a torn gunny bag on the floor to soak up the spilled whiskey.

It was time to leave. At the door, Asokan put his arm around his shoulder and said conspiratorially. "I have a maid now to clean my quarters. She comes in the mornings. And she comes also at night after Kurup leaves." He leered drunkenly. "Let me know if you need a maid. I will ask her to find one for you."

Jose knew what Asokan was getting at.

"No, thanks. See you at the office tomorrow," he said and walked out with Chandy.

"Did you call your uncle?" asked Chandy.

"No. I think he will get in touch with me if it is anything important. No news is good news."

When he got home he wrote two letters, one to Carl and the other to Inga. He posted Carl's letter the next day but had no address for Inga's. He hoped her letter would arrive soon with her address.

\*\*\*

Jose's uncle came calling two days later.

As was his normal manner, his uncle came straight to the point with no pleasantries.

"I heard you went to America or England. What was the purpose of your trip? If you are looking for a foreign job that is a good thing. You will be a millionaire in no time at all," the uncle said. He sat on the wooden chair, his right arm stretched out imperiously and resting on the hooked handle of the umbrella that he had vertically planted on the floor.

"No, it was not for any job. I went for a radio conference," Jose replied.

"I have told you a thousand times to stop playing with radios. It is the hobby of rich men. Did they pay all your travel expenses?"

"No, I did." Jose decided there was no need to tell him of Carl's help. It might upset his uncle that he did not give him some of the money he had received.

"You are wasting tens of thousands of rupees. Do you have any thoughts about our ancestral home? Do you know how hard I have to work to take care of the cows and the paddy field? And you go gallivanting around the world wasting hard-earned money."

It was on the tip of his tongue to retort that it was money he had earned himself but decided to let it pass. For one thing, his uncle still held his parent's money in trust for him; and for another, Jose did not like squabbles, especially with elders.

"You know why I came to see you? We have received a marriage proposal for you. The girl is from a respected family. The father is a bank manager in Kuwait. They have the means to pay a good dowry. And if you play your cards right they might even find a job for you in the Gulf."

Jose's heart sank. He remembered Inga. "How could I betray her?" he asked himself.

"I don't think I am ready to marry right now," Jose said hesitantly to his uncle.

"Not ready to marry? Is that for you to decide? Are you trying to change our customs and traditions? You think you are wiser than our ancestors who laid down rules for our society?" His uncle fumed and the blood vessels in his neck and temples seemed on the point of bursting. "You are twenty-nine years old! Not ready to marry! Who is putting all these foolish ideas into your head? If we don't marry you off now who knows what you will do tomorrow? You might marry some foreign woman and bring dishonor and disgrace on our clan. No! You will have to marry now! If there is something wrong with this girl, we will look for another. But you cannot put it off. I am getting old. Who will find a wife for you after my death?"

Jose did not know how to respond. All this talk of customs and traditions wearied him. The only thing he cared about was the small bequest that his father had left behind. His uncle would confiscate it if he did not obey his directions. He was also certain that his uncle would pocket part of the dowry as 'expenses'. There was very little Jose could do to prevent it, as the parents of the bride would pay the dowry to his uncle. The only way to cut his uncle out was to break tradition and marry on his own. But in that case, he would almost certainly lose his small inheritance to his greedy uncle. And get no dowry either. It was a no-win situation.

"I will think about it," Jose said finally.

"Don't speak to me in that haughty manner!" shouted his uncle raising his voice. "I am your father's brother and you have to obey me. If you disobey me I will disinherit you. Make no mistake." The threat could not have been more explicit. Jose knew that there was no way out.

He sent Kurup out to the tea-shop nearby to get some snacks and coffee for his uncle.

After his uncle left, Jose returned to the office. But try as he might he could not concentrate. When it was time to go home, he stopped by the club mess to tell Kurup that he would not be coming for dinner. When he reached his quarters, he went straight to bed. In the deepening dusk, he lay on his bed thinking, staring vacantly at the ceiling. "What control have I over my own life?" he asked himself. "It is all fate. And life itself is *maya* – an illusion."

He got up and poured himself a stiff whiskey. He wished it were Jack Daniel's but it was a cheap Indian whiskey that tasted like wood spirit mixed with turpentine.

***

That Saturday as he twirled the radio dial he nearly jumped out of his skin. There he was – loud and clear – Carl with his SM5 Big Fat Elephant call.

After establishing contact, they chatted like old times again.

"I have been looking for you ever since I got back. Where were you Carl?" asked Jose.

"I was in Larnaca, Cyprus," Carl said.

"Cyprus? You didn't tell me you were going there."

"No, it came up suddenly. My travel agent informed me of a heavily discounted seat on a charter flight that was going cheap and I jumped at the opportunity."

"Cyprus is divided now, isn't it?" asked Jose.

"Yes, it is. The marauding Turks captured half the island in 1974. Both Armenia and Cyprus have suffered terrible atrocities at the hands of the Turks. The Mediterranean climate of Cyprus is wonderful. The food is great, they speak British English, and drive on the left side of road like you do in India."

"Carl, there is something I want to tell you. I think I am going to get married."

"Getting *married*? It is only a week since you left Stockholm. And you told me you didn't have a girlfriend."

"I didn't. And I still don't. I haven't even seen the girl I am going to marry. You know how it is done here. It is all arranged by the elders. I will get to see the girl formally in the presence of her family. And if I say 'yes' I will see her again on the wedding day at church."

"It must be very painful for the girl if you reject her publicly after seeing her," said Carl.

"No, no, no! Nothing is said directly. I tell my decision to my uncle and he passes it on through the marriage-brokers and the go-betweens to the girl's family."

"It all sounds very convoluted. So, what makes you so sure you will agree to this marriage?" asked Carl.

"I sensed the determination of my uncle. If I turn this one down, he will come up with another proposal. And he will keep pushing me till I finally agree."

"I cannot believe this is happening the way it is. It's all so sudden. And an arranged marriage at that! For Pete's sake, you are only twenty-nine! You are going to marry a girl you haven't even seen? Goodnight!"

"It is too difficult to explain, but I have very limited choices in the matter."

"I know it's a cultural thing. And I am sure you will do what's right for you."

***

As it turned out, Jose fell hook, line, and sinker for Leena.

When, after traveling three hours in a taxi, they arrived at the town of Chengannur to 'see the girl' (as the ritual was called), Jose, his uncle, and four other male elders of the clan were received with great respect and formality by the male elders of Leena's family. Jose felt uncomfortable when the members of the other family looked him up and downsizing him up. He answered their questions about his job and education as briefly as he could, gesticulating with his arms out of nervousness. And then Leena came out with coffee on a tray. As she placed his cup on the small table before him, their eyes met and he decided then and there that she was the one for him.

Leena had lustrous black hair that fell beyond her waist and dark expressive eyes, with the most beautiful eyelashes he had ever seen. Her black hair and dark eyes accentuated her fair skin. She looked absolutely fetching in the pink blouse and the floral sari.

After the ceremony, Jose spent the night in his uncle's house near Kottayam. The next morning, before he left for Munnar, he told his uncle of his consent to the arrangement.

That night when he was back in Munnar he hugged his pillow and wept inconsolably. He knew he was a cad for turning his back on Inga. He felt ashamed that he did not have the guts to stand up to his uncle. "Inga, I have sold you for my paternal inheritance – for my family tradition. I have taken the easy way out. Please forgive me!" he sobbed into his pillow.

He woke up early next morning and wrote a rambling, five-page letter of apology to Inga. But not having an address to mail it to, he placed it with the first letter he had written after his return from Stockholm.

***

The marriage took place two months later at Leena's Orthodox church in Chengannur. There were at least a thousand guests for the feast. Jose's uncle spared no expense and spent a good portion of the dowry on the lavish wedding.

This was also the first time that Jose met Leena's overbearing father and submissive mother. The father lost no time in insisting that Jose and Leena move to Kuwait to look for a job there. Jose did not want to be indebted to Leena's parents and could not dream of living close to them. He decided he would rather be content with the tea estate job, which he had got by his own efforts. He politely declined, much to the chagrin and barely-concealed anger of the father.

Although Jose had mailed him an invitation, Carl could not make it to the wedding owing to the shortness of the notice. He, however, promised to meet Jose and Leena when he visited Kerala later that winter.

\*\*\*

On the political front, the earth-shattering news came two months later. On October 31st, Indira Gandhi, the Indian Prime Minister, was killed by two of her Sikh bodyguards in revenge for ordering the army attack on the holy temple of the Sikhs in Amritsar. The city of Delhi erupted in a violent retaliatory attack on the large Sikh community in the capital. Businesses and houses were looted, cars and trucks burned and hundreds of Sikhs were killed on the streets of Delhi. The violence against the Sikhs in the capital, and on a smaller scale at other locations in North India, were in stark contrast to the celebrations of Indira Gandhi's killing at some places in Punjab State. For a while, there was apprehension that the country would descend into communal violence reminiscent of the Hindu-Muslim carnage on the eve of India's independence. Political leaders were anxious about how the Sikhs in the armed forces would respond to the mob fury unleashed on innocent Sikhs.

Carl hastily canceled his trip to India and instead traveled again to Cyprus.

Jose received letters regularly from Carl. But the much-awaited letter from Inga never came.

## Chapter 10

The first months of marriage were blissful. After a two-week honeymoon at the hill-station of Ooty (or Ootacamund to give its full name) in the Nilgiri Hills, the newlyweds arrived at the tea garden in Munnar to a warm reception by the staff and their families. Jose, who had led a lonely life so far, reveled in the companionship and comfort Leena offered. Her way of thinking was completely different from his and she had a knack for getting on with people that he lacked. Leena's infectious charm won her immediate acceptance into the closed society of the tea estate. In many ways, she was the perfect complement to Jose.

But marriage also brought in its wake major changes in his life. He no longer participated in the drinking parties at Asokan's house after making the disastrous mistake of taking Leena with him the first time. He, and all those present, knew right away that it was a blunder. Everyone was formal and taciturn that evening. Only after Jose and Leena left early on some pretext did Asokan and Hari relax and resume their binge drinking. Chandy, however, felt the absence of Jose at these sessions. He had found a kindred spirit in Jose but he saw no common ground with the other two. Leena took an instant dislike to Asokan and forbade Jose from ever inviting him to their quarters.

*\*\*\**

His uncle brought him his paternal inheritance. There were the gold ornaments of his mother; the small bank balance of his father; and the sale proceeds of his parental home. Jose noted that his uncle had not included any interest although he had held the money for several years. But he decided to let it pass.

"What about the dowry given by Leena's parents?" Jose asked hesitantly. "Have you brought that also?"

"Do you have any idea how much your wedding cost? Half the amount went for the wedding celebration. I will give you the balance in six months. I hope you won't grudge me the delay, considering the grand wedding I arranged for you. Can you even imagine the trouble I went through to make it a big success? Your money is safe with me. I don't want it. I will give it to you in six months," the uncle replied disdainfully.

After his uncle left, Leena consoled an angry Jose.

"We don't need the money right now, do we?"

"That is not the point. He has no business to hold on to our money. He may be my uncle but I don't trust him one bit. If your parents come to know of this there will be big trouble. As it is they are angry with me."

"They won't come to know of it from me," Leena replied matter-of-factly.

*\*\*\**

Jose told Leena about Carl as he showed her pictures taken during his visit. To Jose's immense relief, Leena took an immediate liking to Carl and encouraged their friendship. She could not wait to see Carl in person. She examined very intently the photos Jose had taken of the inside of Carl's apartment – the living room, the dining space, the bedroom with the adjacent study, and, most of all, the kitchen with the shiny cooking range and the large refrigerator.

The other thing that fascinated Leena was Jose's experiences on his trip to Germany and Sweden. As he related the stories of his visit, she watched him entranced, her hands cupping her face in an expression of wonderment.

***

Their first major quarrel came a month after Indira Gandhi's assassination and it caught Jose completely by surprise. On a Wednesday evening, he was chatting on the radio with his Japanese friends when Leena stormed into the small room that he used as a radio shack.

"How many times do I have to call you to come and have dinner?" She exploded in unrestrained fury. "The food is getting cold on the table and you are busy with your radio. If you don't stop fooling around with that stupid radio, I will throw that contraption of yours into the river! This is the third time I have called you after I served the food. Are you a man or a heartless machine?" And with that, she stormed out of the room and banged the bedroom door shut.

Jose had had the presence of mind to quickly switch the microphone off lest it transmit Leena's outburst over the airwaves. He quickly shut the whole station down and hurried after her. But no amount of cajoling and pleading had any impact on Leena. She steadfastly refused to open the bedroom door. He heard her sobs but initially after that there was only silence. Jose was crushed. He had had no inkling of the building up of any unhappiness in Leena. He put the food away in the refrigerator (bought with a part of the money returned by his uncle) and sat in the living room thinking back on all that happened that day, trying to figure out the cause of Leena's unexpected outburst. A little later he tried again to coax Leena out, but to no avail. His anxiety began to rise. "Had Leena caused herself an injury?" he wondered? He went back to the bedroom door and pleaded again, almost in tears. But there was no response. Hunger and fear combined to cause acute stomach pangs. Sometime later, exhausted physically and emotionally, he fell asleep on the sofa.

When he awoke next morning, he was relieved to find Leena, unharmed and safe, in the kitchen. She made coffee for him and continued cooking breakfast but she refused to say a word. It was like banging his head against a brick wall. Even when he came back from work in the evening she still held herself behind the wall of silence. Jose had his dinner alone. Leena did not lock the bedroom door but she had her back to him and stuck to her apparent vow of reticence.

Leena finally broke her silence the following evening. She was calm and matter of fact as she quietly set down conditions.

"You don't know how callous your behavior has been since our marriage. The whole day I am all alone at home while you are in the office with your colleagues and friends. Where is the chance for me to go out for shopping or for meeting friends in this tea estate far from the nearest town? Each day I eagerly wait for your return in the evening. But you, what do you do when you get home? After a quick cup of tea with me you go and turn on that radio of yours and leave me alone again. How long can I suffer like this? You have to choose between me and the radio. I have made up my mind. If you want the radio it is better for me to go back to my parents."

Jose tried to explain how radio had changed his life; how he had learned English by listening to the BBC; and how amateur radio had opened up new horizons.

Leena's response was, "If all that is so important to you why do you need a wife? Why did you marry me?"

Jose was stumped. If there was one thing that had brought him unalloyed happiness before his marriage to Leena, that was amateur radio. Ham radio had allowed him to connect with people in other lands from within the confines of a remote tea estate. The thought of having to give what was so precious to him was almost unthinkable. He even wondered if the marriage had been a mistake.

But he caved in ultimately. He did not see another option. Jose agreed to restrict ham radio to three hours on Saturdays when Leena went to the weekly women's club meeting.

The next day at the office, he wrote a long letter to Carl explaining the situation.

Initially, Jose found it very difficult to handle the abrupt end to his hobby. It had taken so much time and effort to get the government license and now he could only use it occasionally. Nonetheless, he realized that his marriage was the more important of the two. His whole life now depended on finding happiness with Leena. He shuddered to think of reverting to the emptiness and loneliness of living alone again. Moreover, divorce, being a rare occurrence in the Orthodox Christian community, and usually the result of infidelity or worse, would have brought shame and dishonor to his extended family. He wanted to avoid sullying the prestige and reputation of his ancestral clan at any cost.

\*\*\*

Carl switched easily from ham radio to postal communication. He was a prolific letter writer, penning at least a letter a week to Jose in his distinctive American handwriting. Sridharan, the khaki-clad postman knew how eagerly Jose awaited letters from abroad and, instead of leaving Jose's mail at the front desk with the rest of the office mail, he would come round to his desk to personally hand them over. Jose reciprocated by giving him a small tip from time to time. He hoped against hope for a letter from Inga but it never came.

Jose and Leena vicariously experienced Carl's adventures in Cyprus that winter. Carl generously included photographs with his letters, including pictures of the astounding spread at the breakfast buffet at his hotel in Larnaca.

"How can they start the day with so much meat for breakfast?" asked Leena looking at the bacon, sausages, and other meat dishes in the photo.

Jose for his part enjoyed studying the photos of ancient and new Cypriot churches. Carl's description of the Turkish invasion of Cyprus angered Jose almost as much as the Turkish genocide of over two million Armenians at the turn of the twentieth century. Jose looked intently at every photo – pelicans on the road near the harbor area in Larnaca, the old wine press from a village in the mountains, the church of St. Lazarus in Larnaca, the ancient monastery at the center of Agia Napa, the historic Larnaca shopping center ... and many more.

Behind the picture of a newly constructed church and an ancient church right next to it Carl had scrawled: "I think the old church is handsomer than the new one. Will they tear it down? Wouldn't be surprised."

***

Later that year TV came to Jose's town. He bought a black and white Philips television set and he and Leena watched the news in Hindi and English, Hindi sitcoms, and old BBC comedies. Jose's limited ham radio activity received another blow when he found out that his transmissions caused radio frequency interference in the TVs of his neighbors.

***

Carl returned to India the following winter. But instead of flying directly to Madras and from there to Cochin, Carl arrived first in Delhi from Stockholm to participate in the INDPEX (the Indian Philatelic Expo). During his ten-day stay in the capital, Carl visited the Taj Mahal for the fifth time and also Fatehpur Sikri. From Delhi, he traveled to Madras and spent a week with Kannan.

Carl finally arrived in Cochin with only a week left of his vacation. This left little time for traveling and Jose and Leena had to bear the disappointment of Carl not visiting their home at the tea estate in

Munnar. Instead, they traveled to Cochin to meet Carl there.

To Jose's great relief Carl and Leena hit it off from their very first meeting. The petite Leena, completely dwarfed by the imposing Carl, did not hide her admiration for the urbane and chivalrous white man. Carl was the first Westerner that Leena had personally come in contact with. Carl thought Leena was extraordinarily beautiful and said so. The only impediment to a free exchange of thoughts was Leena's initial hesitancy to speak in English and her difficulty in sometimes understanding Carl's accent.

While sipping coconut juice on the restaurant terrace overlooking the Arabian Sea, Carl recounted his Delhi adventure.

"My Delhi trip was an absolute disaster. The stamp expo was nothing to write home about. A total waste of time with boring speeches and a pedestrian exhibition. The worst part of the whole trip was that I was duped by a conman. I lost a thousand dollars. I may have to pay another thousand to the customs when I leave."

"Why? What happened? Two thousand dollars is a lot of money!" said a horrified Jose.

"It *is* a lot of money. In hindsight, I was really, really stupid. I should have seen it coming. Instead, I fell for it like a complete jackass," Carl said ruefully shaking his head.

"Was he a pickpocket?" asked Leena.

"No! I was tricked by a conman. It all goes back to the Independence Day celebrations at the Indian Embassy in Stockholm on August 15th. I went there for the festivities – and to sample the delectable Indian food. There I met this smooth-talking Indian businessman who said his name was Vijay Tandon. I made the mistake of telling him about my upcoming trip to India. He asked me straight out if I wanted to make some money on the side. In the beginning, I thought it was some illegal deal or even drug running. But all I had to do was buy a full set of golf clubs and take it with me to India and I would be paid the cost in Indian rupees on arrival in Delhi plus a bonus of twenty-five per cent. He said it was all legal and aboveboard with instant dividends on the investment. When I asked him why he couldn't take it himself, he said the import duty was a whopping two hundred per cent for Indians while it was zero for foreigners."

"Let me guess. The customs charged you import duty and the man paid only the basic price?" asked Jose.

"It is worse than that. What that crook Tandon told me about the customs duty was utterly false. The duty is applicable to foreigners as well. When I told the customs staff that I would take the clubs back with me to Sweden, they docketed it on my passport so I would be forced to pay the duty if the golf clubs weren't there with me at my departure. After this ordeal with the customs for more than two hours, I come out of the airport to find this guy waiting for me."

"Who? Tandon?" asked Jose.

"No. This was some other guy who had come to get the golf clubs. Never even found out his name. He was bald, mustachioed, and fat. That's all I remember of him. When I told him of the import duty he said it was no problem he would pay it. He said he would still pay me the bonus of twenty-five per cent. This sounded too good to be true. And it was!"

"What happened?" Jose could not contain his curiosity.

"He said the money was in his car and suggested we complete the transaction over whiskey at the hotel bar. By this time, I was badly in need of a drink! He said his car was in the parking lot and offered to give me a ride to the hotel. I was relieved this was turning out so well. It looked like I wasn't going to lose any money after all. Then this guy casually picks up the golf bag from the trolley and walks off towards the parking area. And that is the last I saw of him."

"He did not come back?" asked Leena deeply concerned.

"No, he did not! I waited like a fool at the curb for almost an hour before I realized I had been duped. I ultimately took a taxi – and the taxi driver cheated me as well – and got to my hotel a total wreck."

Leena clapped her hand over her mouth, her eyes filled with sadness.

"I am truly sorry. I feel ashamed of my countrymen," said Jose.

"Don't be. Every country has its share of rascals and conmen. It is my fault that I was so gullible. I fell for the bait of a twenty-five percent windfall. I was too greedy."

"It is still shameful. I feel really bad," Jose said. "Do you have enough money for the trip?"

"That I have. I carried enough in traveler's checks."

"What about the customs duty that you have to pay?"

"I think I have enough for that too. But if I ever meet that Tandon guy again I'm going to wring his neck."

"We could go to the Commissioner of Customs here in Cochin and see if something can be done about the customs duty," suggested Jose.

"There is no harm trying," agreed Carl.

***

Jose hired a tourist taxi the next day and they went sightseeing. The first stop was the old synagogue at Mattancheri dating back to the sixteenth century.

"All the Jews have emigrated to Israel. There are only eight elderly people left," Jose translated the caretaker's words.

"My guidebook tells me the oldest European church on Indian soil is also somewhere near here," said Carl.

"Yes, that is the St. Francis church built by the Portuguese at the beginning of the sixteenth century."

"What interests me as much as the old religious buildings are these warehouses," said Carl pointing to the old, tile-roofed buildings. "The heady aroma of pepper, cardamom, and tea takes my thoughts back centuries to the times of the Portuguese, the Dutch, and the British."

"It smells really nice," said Leena timidly.

"The copra trade has come down. But that used to be one of the staple exports along with pepper and other spices. Exports of nutmeg and cinnamon are also down."

Then they went to the seashore and watched black catamarans steered by swarthy boatmen skim past ocean-going freighters and oil tankers docked at the port. Carl, always interested in watching people at work, took pictures of the fishermen. But what interested Carl most were the Chinese fishing nets that dotted the water.

"It is so amazing that this town and the state of Kerala itself has been the confluence of so many cultures. And such vastly different ones! Portuguese, Dutch, Armenian, Ethiopian, British, ... I could go on. Simply amazing!"

For lunch they repaired to an old Malabar restaurant and feasted on rice, *parippu* curry, *avial, thoran*, fish *moilee,* curried beef, and *pappadam.*

"Leena, the food here is so delicious," said Carl appreciatively.

"Carl is an excellent cook. His *imam bayaldi* and banana pudding have got to be the best in the world. Those were the best dishes I had on my visit to Sweden – better than any at a restaurant."

"I thought you preferred something you had at the smörgåsbord?" asked Carl with a mischievous smile.

"That was what I liked best *outside* of your cooking. There is nothing to compare with your culinary skills, Carl! Sorry, I didn't make that clear when you asked me in Stockholm."

"Thank you, Jose. I hope someday I will get a chance to cook for *both* of you."

"We even talked about opening an Indian restaurant in Stockholm with me as the chef. Or an European restaurant in India with Carl as the chef," Jose said.

"With you as the chef?" Leena asked Jose with a laugh. "Who would come to eat at that restaurant? You are only good as a – what was the word you used at home? – a scullion!"

"He did all the dish washing for me when he was in Stockholm too," said Carl laughing.

After lunch, they drove to the office of the Commissioner of Customs. While Leena waited in the car, Jose and Carl climbed the steps to the dusty government office.

They returned after nearly an hour.

"What happened? Could you get it done?" Leena asked Carl and Jose.

Carl opened his passport and showed the cancellation of the stamp of the Delhi customs department.

"Jose has a knack for dealing with bureaucrats. He took me straight to the chambers of the big boss, the Commissioner. While I explained what happened to the top dog, Jose slipped out to meet the *babus*. By the time the Commissioner and I finished our little chat, Jose had already struck the deal with the clerks for canceling the docket on the passport."

"What deal, Jose?" asked Leena arching her eyebrows.

"Nothing much. I insinuated that Carl was in the country in connection with the Bofors arms deal. I also paid them three hundred rupees for tea and snacks. They watched me leave it under the blotter on their desk. No words were said about the money."

"I would never have been able to swing this on my own," Carl said shaking his head.

"It is not so difficult if you consider bribes to be a part of the cost of doing business."

"Many thanks for saving me a thousand bucks!"

From the customs office, they drove to a nearby Orthodox Christian church.

"This church was built by Armenian traders. The Orthodox Church in Kerala has three factions. One of them still owes allegiance to the Catholicos or Patriarch of the Armenian Orthodox Church," Jose explained.

"Really? And what about the service? Is it in Malayalam?" asked Carl.

"They still follow the same old liturgy. I am not sure which language it is in. But all of it is not in the local language."

"I will have to say goodbye to the two of you soon," said Carl looking at his watch. "I have my last oil-bath today."

"Do you go to an *Ayurvedic* clinic?" asked Leena.

"No, a *Kathakali* dancer comes to my room and does it for me. I tell you, it takes a lot of oil for a man my size!"

"*That* is the *Kathakali* secret you said you would tell me in Stockholm and did not. I forgot to remind you."

On the way back, they saw a three-story building under construction. All the work – mixing the concrete, carrying bricks, cement, and sand –

was done manually. Carl stopped the taxi and got out to take pictures.

"I shot a whole roll of film. How beautiful the workers look! All those sinewy black bodies dripping with perspiration!" Carl winked at Jose slyly without Leena noticing.

"On your next visit, you must come to our house and stay with us. I am not as good a cook as you are, but I will cook all the Malabar food you want," Leena said.

The parting was awkward. Carl wanted to hug them both but he suspected it would be culturally inappropriate in the case of Leena and to hug Jose alone would have looked odd. Jose appeared to be immobilized by the occasion. The parting turned out to be stiff and formal with only a formal shaking of hands. Leena brought her hands together in the traditional Indian sign of respect. Carl reciprocated, bowing slightly, and saying, "*Namaste! Dhanyavad!*"

***

On the political front, an upheaval was taking place in India. Rajiv Gandhi, the son of the slain prime minister, who had won a landslide election victory in December of the preceding year, led India on a different path from that of his mother and, Nehru, his grandfather. His attempts to modernize India made him the darling of business magnates, industrialists, and the rich but the steep rise in prices alienated himself and the Congress party from the general public and widened the gap between the rich and the poor.

Immediately after coming to power, Rajiv Gandhi's government also signed an agreement with the Swedish firm of Bofors for the supply of the most modern anti-aircraft guns. This would prove to be his undoing because of allegations, even from within his own party and government, of kickbacks and bribes and the involvement of shady middlemen from Italy.

Rajiv Gandhi also got India entangled in a proxy war in Sri Lanka. The Indian Peace-Keeping Force that was sent to disarm the Tamil Tiger insurgents, ended up on the Sri Lankan side fighting against the Tamil rebels. The result was the disenchantment of Tamils in India with Rajiv Gandhi and his government.

***

The work at the estate ground on inexorably. Jose's hard work earned him the reputation of being the best management trainee. Hari, on the other hand, received a formal warning to improve his performance and to desist from drunkenness. Crafty Asokan continued his nefarious activities in secret. Chandy was earnest in his work and toiled hard but, because of his rigid religious beliefs, was never part of the inner clique.

Jose's trysts with ham radio became increasingly infrequent. He did not want anything to come between him and Leena and was careful not to cause the slightest pain to her. Mercifully, the outburst of anger that had stunned him never recurred. But on several occasions, he found Leena depressed, her eyes brimming with tears. He knew what the cause of her sadness was.

"I long to have a child. Why is it that I cannot conceive?" she asked him again one night.

"I want to be a father too. But I am not desperate. We are still young. It will happen if it is

God's will. Even if we don't have children I will still love you. Children are God's gift. Don't worry," Jose consoled Leena.

"I don't want people to start talking about me. I think I heard them whispering behind my back at the last women's club meeting. I did not hear exactly what they were saying but on seeing me they stopped. You know how they look down on barren women in our society. I don't want that."

"Don't worry too much about what other people say. You will become paranoid."

"I have not been happy ever since I had the second miscarriage."

"Children are a gift from God. We cannot demand it. If we don't have our own, we can always adopt a child. Let us give it some more time," suggested Jose.

"I really wish for a child of our own – of your flesh and mine," Leena said.

She broke down then. Jose held her close to him as the tears poured down in torrents.

"I love you, Leena!" said Jose.

"You keep saying 'I love you' like a foreigner. It is not our custom to say that. Who else will I love if not you?"

"It is just a way of expressing my love for you," Jose said defensively.

"That may be needed for lovers. We are married now. We love each other. That is understood. Don't keep saying 'I love you'. It is like saying the sun is bright. It is always bright."

Jose sold his transceiver and accessories that week to a ham in Bombay. Surprisingly, the death of his once beloved hobby was not as painful as he had imagined it to be.

\*\*\*

The assassination of the internationally well-known and popular Swedish Prime Minister, Olof Palme, shocked the world. It added fuel to the Bofors fire raging in India. Though the killing remained unsolved, theories that made the rounds involved arms merchants and the apartheid regime of South Africa. If the latter were true, there was an eerie resemblance in Palme's death to Hammarskjöld's, conjectured Carl.

Carl grieved for Palme in his letters to Jose. He seemed unable to come to grips with the fact that it had happened in a land as peaceful and safe as Sweden, where elected representatives and government leaders moved around like ordinary citizens, without bodyguards. That was also the part that surprised Jose the most – that the Prime Minister of a nation would mingle with the public without being surrounded by security personnel.

## Chapter 11

The weeks and the months passed by. Jose and Leena settled into the staid routine of married life – work, home, the weekly women's club, occasional parties at the tea planters' club. Inga and Stockholm faded away as distant memories.

Carl, however, wrote faithfully, at least once a week, sometimes twice. He enclosed cartoon clippings from newspapers, funny limericks, and short humorous poems by Ogden Nash and one even by Samuel Taylor Coleridge. Leena read all the letters but she somehow could not get the humor of most of the limericks or the cartoons. She did not find some of them funny at all, like the cartoon of the man reading a girlie magazine at the beach surrounded by naked women. Or the harmless limerick about the 'dainty young thing from St. Paul' who 'wore a newspaper dress to a ball'. Leena found the limerick about the 'nymphomaniacal Alice' positively distasteful.

Leena was not much of a letter writer and it was Jose who always wrote on their behalf signing each letter, 'Affectionately yours, Leena and Jose'. Once, when Jose failed to write for two weeks, Carl enclosed a postcard with the words *'Ett brev betyder så mycket'* above the picture of an elderly lady in a rocking chair holding a letter. On the reverse Carl translated: 'A letter means so much'. And added, 'It is a hint – C'.

Tragedy struck Hari. He received a telegram from home informing him of the death of his younger brother in a drowning accident in a pond not far from their home. He was a changed man when he returned after the cremation. He withdrew into a shell and drank even more heavily than before. Not even excess alcohol could bring back the old *joie de vivre*. The only person who could make a connection with Hari was Chandy. They made a strange pair, the dissolute upper-caste Brahmin Hindu and the born-again Pentecostal Christian who considered it his duty to minister to his suffering colleague.

Meanwhile, the labor union was getting restive and militant. Maoists had infiltrated the labor unions in some neighboring tea estates. The violence and intimidation that they resorted to caused monetary loss and the flight of experienced middle-level managers who feared for their safety and the safety of their families. Jose's estate wanted to avoid the same fate at any cost. It set up cooperative fair price shops run by the workers' union and also sanctioned the recruitment of additional teachers for the elementary and middle schools for the children of the laborers. The biggest benefit the management gave the workers was the posting of a full-time nurse at the clinic.

Jose sympathized with the plight of the workers. At management meetings, he supported the legitimate demands of the unions and advocated a more benevolent approach to dealing with them. The old guard had different ideas. They believed in teaching the 'rabble' (as they called them) their place. "No concessions to the riff-raff," seemed to be their motto. The management recognized the trust the trade union leaders placed in Jose and included him in the joint discussions that took place from time to time.

***

Articles and editorials in Indian newspapers gave credence to the notion of corruption at the highest levels in the nation's arms deal with the Swedish firm, Bofors. The 'Mr. Clean' image of Rajiv Gandhi was irreparably tarnished and his popularity nose-dived. To add to his woes, the Indian forces sent to Sri Lanka were caught in a quagmire that polarized the nation.

Meanwhile, Hindu fundamentalist forces were gaining popularity. Hindu mythologies on television raced to the top of viewer ratings. The Rashtriya Swayamsevak Sangh, an extreme right-wing group, aligned themselves with the Bharatiya Janata Party and together they made the concept of a 'Hindu India' their rallying call.

The Indian economy meanwhile was slowly opening up to international trade and commerce. While the stock index soared to astronomical heights, the gulf between the rich and the poor only kept getting wider.

***

Within a month of the agreement with the labor union, came word of his uncle's unexpected demise. Jose and Leena attended the funeral the following day. The aunt narrated how he had returned home after developing chest pains while on his way to the market. He had passed away while she was fomenting his chest with warm water. She had scampered, frantic with fright, through the paddy fields to call the neighbors half a mile away. But it was too late. When they arrived at the house, the neighbor, a contemporary of Jose's uncle, confirmed what the aunt had feared.

A week after the funeral Jose returned alone to ask his aunt about the rest of the dowry. She brought out the bank passbook and other papers. Jose was dumbfounded when he added up the numbers. There was a shortage of five hundred thousand (or five *lakhs* in Indian terminology) rupees.

"Maybe uncle kept this in cash in the house?" suggested Jose to his aunt.

"No, only a few hundred rupees were found in notes and coins," she replied.

"Do you know if my uncle lent money to anyone?"

"These are all the papers I could find. He did not tell me of his business dealings," she replied.

"Do you know if my uncle bought land recently? Or paid an advance for the purchase of land?"

"He did not tell me anything. He considered me a fool who couldn't understand money and business."

Fortunately for Jose, his aunt did not contest his claim for the balance in the cooperative bank account.

"From where else could he have got that much money, if not from your dowry?" she admitted candidly.

Jose told Leena the whole story when he got home.

She was philosophical. "He was your uncle and we had to trust him. What else could we have done?"

"But he lost our money! And we will never know how. He was a crook and I shouldn't have been so naïve."

"Nothing can be done now. Get what you can from your aunt when the bank releases the money after the formalities are complete."

***

Jose and Leena were disappointed when Carl decided to skip India and visit Sarajevo that year. He sent them pictures of the bridge near which the Bosnian Serb Gavrilo Princip had assassinated the Austrian heir apparent Archduke Ferdinand and his consort Sophie.

"That started off World War I. But I am sure Palme's killing will not start any upheavals in Sweden or anywhere else in the world," wrote Carl.

Carl, the storyteller that he was, wrote about the quaint restaurant called *Inat Kuća, The House of Despite,* in Sarajevo whose owner had refused to relinquish his land to the Austro-Hungarian rulers. ("I think they meant 'spite' – not 'despite'", wrote Carl.)

On December 7th, 1988 the city of Leninakan in Carl's beloved Armenia suffered a devastating earthquake that killed over twenty-five thousand people. Carl followed the rescue and relief work closely and included detailed information in his letters to Jose. In this manner, Jose came to know that Leninakan was called Alexandropol in the past. Carl had visited Spitak some years earlier and wrote of the magic of exiting the tunnel to find himself in the midst of dense, verdant forests, in stark contrast to the arid, tree-less expanse on the Yerevan side of the tunnel. "The difference is astonishing," wrote Carl. "It is like being on two different planets."

"I also found a connection of sorts with Cyprus when I stumbled upon a group of schoolchildren doing a traditional Greek dance in the open. It turns out the whole village is Greek!" added Carl in a postscript.

Jose and Leena were not surprised when Carl decided to forego his annual vacation that year and donate the travel money he had saved up to the Red Cross for the relief of the earthquake-affected people of Armenia.

*\*\*\**

The Tiananmen Square massacre took place in June 1989. In Eastern Europe and the USSR, however, the yearning for change could no longer be quelled by brute force. A new wave of change was beginning to blow. The Berlin wall was breached in the fall of the same year. When Jose read of the dismantling of the wall, he remembered the lady whom he had met on the train who was headed to meet her sister who lived in East Germany. He hoped they were reunited now.

Jose and Leena expected Carl would come to visit them that year. Instead, Carl chose to travel to Moscow. He sent them pictures of the onion-domed St. Basil's cathedral, the mausoleum of Lenin, the Red Square, the Kremlin wall, and the bridge over Moscow River. In his letter, Carl mentioned that he got a kick out of the name—*Partizanskaya*—of the metro station nearest his hotel. From Moscow, he traveled to Armenia and visited Leninakan and Lake Sevan. Carl sent Jose and Leena photos of the ancient the 9th-century church on the shores of the picturesque Lake Sevan.

***

While Carl's letter writing waxed, Jose's waned. Carl added clippings of cartoons from the *New Yorker*, which Jose found incredibly funny. But they somehow lost their charm by the time he explained them to Leena. With one letter Carl even enclosed a paper napkin from Scandic Cater that read, *'Kärlek är I de allra flesta fall resultat av goda middagar. Chamfort.'* On the reverse, Carl had written: "Roughly translated this means - *Love, in the majority of cases, is the result of a tasty dinner.*" Jose remembered Carl telling him about this aphorism when he was in Stockholm.

Jose's correspondence became increasingly desultory. From replies once a fortnight, the frequency slowly dwindled to about once in three weeks and, occasionally, even once a month. Carl sorely missed Jose's letters and gave many oblique hints, including tiny hieroglyphic stickers depicting a pen or a pencil, but to no avail. Jose, who had the constant companionship of Leena, failed to appreciate the loneliness Carl experienced living alone in Stockholm.

***

Jose received an unexpected surprise that year. He was called into the personnel manager's chamber one fine morning.

"Good morning, sir," Jose greeted the manager but remained standing, waiting to be offered a seat.

"Good morning, Jose," replied the manager, looking at him thoughtfully, while puffing on his cheroot. That he did not immediately ask him to sit down only served to increase Jose's anxiety.

"I am being inconsiderate. Please sit down," said the manager waving his hand in the direction of the chair.

"Thank you, sir. You wished to see me?" he asked hesitantly.

"Yes, yes. With all the trouble that is brewing – good choice of word for a tea company, eh? – as I was saying, with all the trouble that is brewing in the tea estates around us, we have decided to make some changes to your responsibilities."

When the manager paused and looked down at the papers in front of him, Jose wondered if his advocacy of justice and his stance for fairness for the laborers had displeased the management so much that he was going to be punished with a transfer to some distant tea estate.

The manager studied him silently, adding to the suspense.

Finally, he said, "We have decided to promote you out of turn to the middle management cadre."

It took a moment for the import of the news to sink in. When it did, Jose relaxed visibly and his heart soared.

"Thank you. Thank you, sir," he said, half-rising from the chair and extending his hand in gratitude.

"You deserve it. Of all the management trainees, we hired, you are the only one who has shown promise of being able to shoulder higher responsibilities. Your salary will go up substantially, of course, and, in addition, you will be allotted a bigger *bungalow*. We are promoting you retrospectively from the first day of January this year. You will get a nice sum as arrears."

Jose practically ran all the way home to tell Leena.

At the end of the impromptu celebration, Leena whispered in Jose's ear, "Our joy will be complete when we have a child."

Carl rejoiced together with Jose and Leena on Jose's promotion. When he learned that the *bungalow* would be their home for as long as Jose worked at the estate, Carl sent them a check for three thousand dollars as a house-warming gift. They used it for personalizing the accommodation with additional repairs and renovations beyond what the estate did in the normal course. There was some money left over and Jose surprised Leena with a gas-electric oven and grill.

But parenthood eluded them in spite of medical tests and visits to various fertility centers, one as far away as the city of Madras. When Leena still did not conceive, she reluctantly consented to adoption.

***

Bigger changes were in the offing in the world of nations. East and West Germany officially reunited to become one nation again. Gorbachev was sowing the seeds of *glasnost* and *perestroika* which would lead ultimately to the disintegration of the Soviet Union. Lithuania was the first Baltic State to declare its independence in March 1990. The Soviet authorities responded with an iron hand.

In India, the Hindu movement, masterminded by the Bharatiya Janata Party, was gaining momentum. The arrest of its strident leader Advani resulted in the fall of the national government after it lost a vote of confidence in parliament. The unpopular Indian Peace-Keeping Force was withdrawn from Sri Lanka but the anger at Rajiv Gandhi for sending the troops to fight Tamil insurgents continued to fester.

Meanwhile, in the Middle East, Iraq invaded Kuwait and set off the short-lived Persian Gulf War. Cable and satellite television had come to Kottayam earlier that year. Jose and Leena were riveted to CNN, watching the startling images streaming in from cameras in the noses of smart bombs as Patriot missiles rained down on Iraq in Operation Desert Storm. The US and other NATO forces routed the Iraqi army in just two months.

In May 1991, while campaigning at Sriperumbudur in the state of Tamil Nadu, the former Prime Minister Rajiv Gandhi was blown up by a Tamil Tiger female suicide bomber who detonated herself. The killing sent shockwaves through India and the subcontinent.

The epoch-making year saw the collapse of the Soviet Union. First, the Baltic States, and then the other Republics, declared their independence. The Eastern Bloc nations, one after the other, had already thrown out the Communist regimes that had been oppressing them, none as dramatically as the Christmas day execution of Ceausescu in Romania.

Carl was overjoyed when Armenia gained its independence. But he grieved over the suffering the Armenian people had to undergo without power and heating during the bleak winter and the absence of any mechanized means of transport due to the lack of fuel. Carl again donated his vacation money to the

Red Cross that was spearheading relief operations in the newly independent Republic of Armenia.

***

Carl continued his almost-daily letter writing. The subject that dominated his letters was the new world order that was taking shape. "The city of Leninakan has been renamed Gyumri, its original Armenian name!" exulted Carl in one of his letters. Carl was also amazed by the quantum leap in communications around the world, especially in India.

Carl's letters came like clockwork. Jose continued to reply in an irregular manner, once in a while writing a longer letter with news about life on the tea estate.

Then in the last week of October 1992 Carl's letters abruptly stopped. It was Sridharan, the postman, who remarked one day in the first week of November: "No letter from your friend in Sweden for two weeks."

Jose realized that Sridharan was absolutely correct.

"He must be in some other country. He travels a lot."

When a letter from Carl finally arrived after yet another week of silence, its contents stunned Jose.

He put away what he was working on and immediately phoned Leena.

"Leena, I got a letter from Carl. I have some very bad news."

"What happened to Carl?" Leena asked anxiously. "Is he all right?"

"Carl is OK now but three weeks ago he had a heart attack. He nearly died."

"Oh, my God!" cried Leena. Jose heard something fall to the ground.

"You be careful there! What did you drop? Carl is all right now. He is at home in his apartment. He wrote this letter in his own hand."

Over lunch, Jose explained to Leena how Carl had had a sudden heart attack while he was alone in the house working on his stamp collection and had fallen to the floor.

"Carl could not get up. He could not shout for help. Even if he had, it is doubtful if anybody would have heard him. He tugged on the telephone cord and the phone fell to the floor. But he still could not lift the receiver to talk. The phone company presumed something was wrong because the phone was off the book and informed the emergency services. They broke the lock on the front door to get in and rushed Carl to the best hospital in Stockholm. If they had been even a few minutes late, he would have died."

"If he had a heart attack in India he would certainly have died. Our services are so slow. I don't think even Kottayam town has an ambulance," said Leena.

"They have ambulances but their response time is a few hours. We have no system here to alert emergency services merely by the phone being off the hook. We don't even have an emergency number to call!"

In the next letter, which arrived the following day, Carl wrote about the angioplasty they had performed on him immediately upon arrival at the hospital; the next three days in intensive care; and the ten days they had kept him in the hospital under observation. The most difficult part, Carl explained, was when they discharged him. He was on his own with no one to help or keep him company; no one to cook and serve him food, tidy the house, or even buy his groceries.

Leena and Jose wished there was a way for them to help their friend Carl. Jose especially felt guilty about neglecting to correspond regularly. He sat down and wrote Carl a long, ten-page letter from the heart. It was the first time ever he had done so. He suggested that Carl come and stay with them at the tea estate in Munnar and promised that he and Leena would take care of him and nurse him back to health.

\*\*\*

On the national front, dark clouds were looming on the horizon. The Bharatiya Janata Party and Hindu fundamentalists who had been vocally insisting on the construction of a Hindu temple on the site of an ancient Muslim mosque were threatening direct action. Not satisfied with pulling down a moderate government, the extremists threatened to tear apart the very fabric of a secular India, painstakingly put together after the traumatic Hindu-Muslim riots of pre-Independence days.

\*\*\*

Carl's response to Jose's offer arrived in the third week of November. He thanked Jose and Leena for the offer but regretted that he was not fit enough to travel. Instead he wondered if Jose could visit him for two weeks. Enclosed was a check for $2,000 to cover the airfare.

"How can I go alone? I would prefer to go together with you," said Jose to Leena.

"But Carl mentioned only you. How can I go uninvited?"

"Maybe the hospital expenses were too high and he cannot afford tickets for the two of us?" suggested Jose.

"I doubt if it is that. From what you told me, his apartment is small. It is probably not big enough for the three of us. As a male, you will be able to take better care of him than I can. I am not a nurse, you know."

Finally, it was agreed that Jose would travel alone to Sweden. The cheapest ticket the travel agent came up with was on Aeroflot from Calcutta via Tashkent and Moscow to Stockholm.

***

On a December day in 1992, Leena saw Jose off at the Cochin airport on the afternoon Indian Airlines flight bound for Calcutta. After landing in Calcutta in the early evening, as he rode the coach from the airport into the city, he saw hordes of people shouting slogans and marching in a long procession. Jose did not give it much thought. After all, Calcutta was the citadel of Communist trade unions and strikes and protest marches were almost a daily occurrence here.

He had barely checked into the YMCA in Chowringhee when he realized that this was no ordinary procession. While he had been in the air, Hindu chauvinists had stormed the inadequately protected Babri Masjid, the old mosque and the bone of contention, and razed it to the ground. The Muslim minority, their honor besmirched by the majority Hindus, had suddenly turned violent across the country, ransacking shops and using anything they could lay their hands on as missiles. Jose ran to the rooftop terrace where there was already a small crowd of lodgers watching the city go up in flames. The police fired in the air and an immediate curfew was imposed. Similar violence erupted spontaneously across the country. Jose went down to watch the horrible events unfold on TV.

His flight to Moscow was the following night and Jose hoped the violence would end and the curfew would be relaxed before the scheduled departure of the flight.

But the news next morning was grim. The carnage had spread like wildfire across the country. The curfew in Calcutta was not lifted. The bearer who brought the morning tea also brought the day's *Telegraph* newspaper. **'Babri Shrine Razed to the Ground'** screamed the banner headline. The residents at the YMCA were a motley crew. There was an American university professor and his wife from the Midwest, a young Japanese woman waiting for her Indian boyfriend to arrive from Tagore's university of Shantiniketan, a Bangladeshi hoping to be granted a UK visa on the fourth attempt, and an Austrian in his mid-30s who, Jose found out later, was fixated on wanting to sleep with a Hindu woman.

"Not white or mongoloid – I am not attracted to them. It has to be a beautiful, young, Hindu woman with traditional values."

"It is hardly likely that you will find a conservative Hindu girl who will jump into bed with a white man! Even if she was willing she would not be able to break away from the tight cordon of relatives she is always surrounded by," said Jose.

"You found a contradiction there! Well ... if it cannot be had the right way, I am willing to pay for it. But the filthy, pan-chewing prostitutes on Bombay's Falkland Road and Delhi's GB Road are total opposites of the 'princesses' I supposed Indian women to be."

"Good luck!" was all Jose could think of saying.

"But I hate Muslims. They are world-conquerors, destroyers, and torturers. I shifted to the YMCA when I found out that the owner of the hotel where I spent the first night was a Muslim."

"I don't think that is a fair statement. I have Muslim friends who are kind and moderate and secular."

Jose did not want to get into any trouble with the other guests at the YMCA and excused himself. He went back to his room and slept. The bearer brought tea and snacks to him secretly in his room in return for some *baksheesh*.

"We don't have enough stock in the kitchen to serve everybody," the bearer whispered conspiratorially.

The next afternoon at three o'clock the curfew was lifted for two hours to permit people to buy food and provisions. The YMCA cooks went out and bought rice and lentils to last a whole week.

Jose felt frustrated. The phones were down and because of the curfew, there was no way to send Leena a telegram from the nearest post office, which would be closed anyway. He saw on TV the news of the cancellation of flights and trains. There was no indication when normalcy would return. He had no idea whether his flight would operate that night. Getting to the airport in the middle of the night while a curfew was in place was asking for trouble. Jose decided to abort his trip to Sweden and return home at the first opportunity.

That opportunity came two days later. The moment he learned that curfew was being relaxed from the crack of dawn, he rushed to the airport with the American couple. His hunch was proved right. They were among the first passengers to get to the airport and Jose got a ticket to Cochin quite easily.

*** 

Leena was relieved to have Jose back unscathed. She did not know whether Jose had made it out to Sweden or if he had been caught up in the tumult. She was overjoyed when he called her from Cochin airport on arrival. She sent Kurup out to buy beef and fish and cooked a big meal to celebrate Jose's safe return.

In the state of Kerala itself, there was no violence; the protests were muted and generally restricted to public meetings. Being a literate and enlightened state, even Hindus condemned the highhandedness of the Hindu fundamentalists in demolishing a Muslim shrine, quite unlike the celebrations by majority Hindus in other states.

Carl, for his part, was shocked by the scale of violence that he saw on TV. In his letters, he sought more information from Jose on the situation in various parts of India. "I'm glad my heart-attack kept me from traveling to India this year," he wrote. "Had I been well I would most likely have got caught in the mayhem."

In the middle of January Carl opted to retire from his job. He sent pictures of the farewell dinner with colleagues at a restaurant of his choice. Now that he was home most of the time, Carl's letters increased in frequency. Jose replied on a weekly basis, filling Carl in on the political turmoil going on in the country.

## Chapter 12

Jose finally managed to get to Stockholm four months later in the spring of 1993. The Aeroflot flights were a far cry from the Lufthansa experience nine years earlier. There were no seat allotments at the Calcutta airport. Jose pitied the elderly and the children as the passengers made a mad dash in the dark to the aircraft parked on the tarmac. It was a free for all as the passengers grabbed the seats they wanted. After an hour's stopover at Tashkent, they landed at Sheremetyevo airport in Moscow. Things improved dramatically from there on. Jose found the duty-free shop assistants incredibly pretty. He wandered around the airport comparing it to the memories he had of Frankfurt. When he checked in for the Aeroflot flight to Stockholm, he was relieved to find that the boarding pass had a seat number. Jose also enjoyed the food served on board. "Aeroflot in Europe is not so bad after all!"' he told himself.

He phoned Carl immediately after arrival at Arlanda airport.

"You called me in the nick of time. I will explain when we meet. Take the bus to Hötorget. I will wait there for you," Carl said excitedly.

The bus was empty except for a young lady, a semi-drunk Turk, and Jose. Although Jose could not understand a word of what the man said in Swedish to the woman, it was obvious from her reactions that what he was stating so brazenly was not only acutely embarrassing but was also highly suggestive. She blushed a deep scarlet that almost matched her red hair. Jose wished she would speak up for herself and ask the man to shut up. But that did not happen. He briefly toyed with the idea of intervening but decided it would not be wise without being certain that the man was indeed making lewd or outrageous suggestions and that the woman did indeed find the man's advances unwelcome.

Carl was waiting at the bus stop and crushed Jose in a bear hug when he got off the bus.

"I am so glad to see you – at last! I was beginning to wonder if your trip was jinxed after the riots of last December."

"I am so fortunate to be able to come back for a second visit. But I wish the circumstances were different."

"Not to worry. I am well on the way to recovery. The reason I said you called in the nick of time was that I was about to take my daily dose of a diuretic. Once I take that medicine, I have to keep running to the urinal every fifteen minutes or so. I wouldn't have been able to come out here to get you."

After they got to the house by bus, Carl made a cup of coffee for Jose and acted out how his heart attack had happened.

"I'm so glad you are alive and well, Carl. I cannot tell you how much. Leena shares the same feelings."

"There is another reason you have come at the perfect time. Tomorrow's my birthday."

"This is a marvelous coincidence!" exclaimed Jose. "I had no idea when your birthday was."

\*\*\*

The gifts that Leena had personally chosen for Carl on one their rare trips to Kottayam made perfect birthday presents. Carl loved the placemats made of reeds and the spatula and large spoon carved out of wood from Meghalaya State. Jose's present was a hand-woven woolen shawl from Nagaland with a bold red and white pattern. After breakfast, Jose slept the rest of the day making up for lost sleep.

In the evening over whiskey, they reminisced about old times.

"I can no longer drink like I used to. Doctor's orders."

"After my marriage, I don't drink much either. Only socially. Leena does not like my drinking," said Jose.

"Doctor's orders or not, I still drink. Not to excess of course."

"What else is the problem, if I may ask?" asked Jose.

"I have a whole host of issues. High cholesterol, hypertension, diabetes, gout, uremia – that's what the diuretic is for – you name it, I've got it."

"You were so healthy the last time."

"I was on medication then too. But age catches up with everyone."

"If you don't mind my asking ... and I hesitate to ask this, Carl ... what about your family? Do they know?"

"I informed my brothers in the US only after I had been discharged from the hospital. They wouldn't have come in any case," Carl smiled ruefully.

"I am going to push my luck and ask you what I have been wanting to ask since our very first meeting. Were you ever married? Do you have children?"

Carl appeared not to have heard, staring wordlessly at a spot above Jose's head. Then cocking his head sideways, he looked Jose in the eye pensively.

"Since you are a close friend I will tell you. I was once married but we divorced within five years. We discovered there was no way for us to stay married. I don't need to get into details. You can guess the obvious reason. The parting wasn't amicable. She wanted everything I had."

"And children?"

"I have a son and a daughter. They live here in Stockholm somewhere. But we haven't kept in touch. Last week I bumped into the son on my way back from the chemist's. He appeared very surprised to see me. 'I thought you had died!' was what he said." Carl took another big sip of whiskey.

"That's a horrible thing to say!" exclaimed Jose.

"I didn't expect anything better. 'You wish!' was what came to my lips but I didn't say it. I think my wife and children couldn't care less if I were dead," said Carl evenly. "Needless to add, none of them will get a penny when I die."

Jose saw Carl in a new light then, realizing that behind the exterior of a suave, self-made man, there lurked a deeply lonely individual bereft of family ties and, because of social mores, without a publicly acceptable companion.

Later as he lay in bed thinking, Jose remembered the two men at Frankfurt airport and the young man's kindness to the hard up stranger. "What a contradiction!" he thought. "Cruelty to family and compassion to strangers." The irony of Leena's and his own situation was not lost on Jose. They were yearning to have children of their own while Carl who had children was estranged from them.

*\*\*\**

This second visit to Stockholm was quite unlike the first. If the aim of the first journey was to see Sweden and experience Western life, this trip was all about being with Carl and taking care of him. Jose was inwardly shocked by the changes he saw in Carl since their last meeting in India. Gone were the robust look and the sprightly walk. The new Carl, pale and gaunt, was easily out of breath even after just a few steps. The medication and the tiredness kept him indoors. Carl urged Jose to go out on his own like he had done on his first visit.

"My medicines hold me back. I don't want to walk around wearing nappies like some people do."

"I came here to see *you*. And that is my only priority. If you need to stay indoors, I will stay with you," Jose said firmly.

"In that case, let us spend the time re-arranging my stamp collection," suggested Carl.

And that was what they did, sitting on opposite sides of the dining table, carefully examining stamps under magnifying glasses, comparing them with catalogs and then gently placing them at the appropriate spot in albums. Carl suggested to Jose that he work on two identical collections of post-Independence stamps of India.

Carl still cooked but lacked the energy to make anything elaborate. Lunches were easily put together meals—bread with tomato or noodle soup one day, cream crackers and cheese with pickled artichokes the next. For two nights in a row, it was hash on bread and orange roly-poly for dinner. Jose did not mind.

He often thought about Inga, not with any desire for renewing a physical relationship (Jose was steadfastly loyal to Leena) but he longed to see how she looked now and how much her life had changed in the past nine years. Most of all, for what it was worth, he wanted to offer a personal apology for his duplicity.

\*\*\*

On the third morning, Carl delayed taking his medicines till noon and they spent the morning together in Hötorget and Sergels Torg. It was almost like old times again, except for the frequent stops for Carl to catch his breath. Carl helped Jose search for a used SLR camera. They finally found a Minolta in near mint condition for $300. Jose was overjoyed.

"What happened to the old camera? How long did it last?" asked Carl.

"The Kodak that you bought me the last time? It still works and it is the only camera I've used for the past nine years," Jose replied.

"That's amazing! It lasted this long? You must have used it very carefully."

"Yes, I believe in using things with utmost care. Remember the Gillette razor you presented me? That is still the razor I use."

"I'll be darned! If all were like you, the economy would be ruined!" Carl said jocularly.

They had lunch at a bistro, though it was a little nippy to be sitting out in April. Carl ordered quiche Lorraine. When he saw Jose struggling with the food, he apologized.

"I'm sorry, I forgot for a moment that cheese is not at the top of the charts for you."

"It is not too bad. I will probably like it on the third or fourth try."

"Cheese is an acquired taste. And I know there is no cheese to be had in Kerala!"

They hurried back to Jungfrugatan so Carl could take his medicines. After getting back to the apartment Jose had a sudden urge to go for a walk to Strandvägen. Everything looked exactly the same. The feeling was eerie. Jose thought he had gone back in time. Memories of the time spent with Inga came flooding back. On the walk back, he decided to take the bull by the horns. When he reached the hallway, he walked up to the door that Inga had waited at the first time they met and knocked softly. A primly dressed, severe looking lady opened the door and looked him up and down with disapproval.

"Hello! May I speak to Inga, please?"

"Inga *who*?" retorted the lady with a frown. She had a strong Swedish accent.

"I'm sorry! Ingrid Gustafsson. She worked here in 1984."

"*1984*? That is a long time ago. I need to know the reason why you want to see her," she said in a stern voice.

"It is not related to work. We were friends. And we lost touch because I lost her address."

"We have very strict privacy laws here. I cannot give you any information about her."

"Please! I beg of you. She will thank you for putting us in touch again," Jose pleaded.

The lady relented. "Wait right here. I will be back."

Jose felt the stirrings of hope. "If I only could see Inga again and seek her forgiveness!" he thought.

The lady returned. "I'm sorry I don't have good news for you. Ingrid resigned from her position in November 1984. She didn't tell us where she was going."

"You have no information at all?" Jose was crestfallen.

"No, nothing at all." After a brief pause, she added, "One of the workers thinks she married an older Pakistani professor and left the country with him."

"Thank you. You have been very helpful." Jose could not hide his disappointment. His shoulders drooped as he trudged back to Carl's apartment.

\*\*\*

After Jose had finished sorting the enormous pile of Indian stamps and placed surplus stamps together in envelopes, he was astounded. Of the two collections of post-independence stamps (from 1947 till 1990) that he was working on, one set was complete, with not one stamp missing, and the other had just four missing from the 70's.

"Jose, here's a surprise for you. The second set is for you. It is not complete, I know. But you will have fun searching for the four missing stamps."

"Wow! I don't know what to say. This set is very valuable. Just the album alone is worth a fortune in India, to say nothing of the stamps. We don't get this type of good quality stamp albums for love or money."

"I'll throw in a second new album for your Swedish collection as well!"

"I am touched! Many thanks, Carl! You are most kind!"

Later in the evening, over whiskey, they watched *La Cuisine des Mousquetaires* on TV5 and the BBC comedy *Jim'll Fix It*.

Jose sorely missed *Cheers*, which Carl said was not aired anymore for some reason.

***

The next morning, Jose decided to walk to Nordiska Museet to try out his new camera and returned to Jungfrugatan via Strandvägen, Artillerigatan, and Sibyllegatan.

At the bus stop on Sibyllegatan, he thought he saw Inga boarding a bus. Jose was quite a distance away but he was certain it was Inga. He raced toward the bus in desperate anticipation, clinging to his prized Minolta camera. But before he got close enough to the bus, it pulled away. He did not give up the chase, hoping to catch it at the traffic light ahead. When the light turned red, Jose's hopes rose. But, just as he was closing in on the stationary bus, to his chagrin, the lights changed. The bus made a right turn and was soon out of sight. Jose stood bent over on the sidewalk, gulping lungfuls of air. When he had recovered sufficiently, he plodded home dejected. He could not help but compare his futile pursuit of the bus to Dr. Zhivago's fatal attempt to catch up with the mirage of his beloved Lara on the tram. "The difference, is I'm still alive – and married," he reasoned.

Jose spent the rest of the day indoors. Carl was asleep on the sofa with his head slumped on his chest.

When he came back to the living room after a brief nap, he found Carl studying the obituary pages of *Dagens Nyheter* closely.

"Another of my friends has died," he announced solemnly.

"Does everyone announce their deaths?" asked Jose. Then realizing his error, he corrected himself. "I didn't say that right. Dead men cannot speak. What I meant was – are all deaths announced in the papers? Is it the law? Or maybe the custom?"

"No, it is the choice of the individual if he writes a will or leaves instructions to his successors or heirs. As for me, there will be no announcements. Not in the paper, not by mail, not by any means."

"How will your friends know of your passing?"

"I don't know. It is not my problem. As far as I am concerned, I just want to slip away quietly – unannounced."

"I am not sure if you are being fair to your friends."

Carl shrugged his shoulders in an expression of helplessness. "I don't want to make a big deal of my death. Those who love me truly will understand."

"Talking about your passing makes me uneasy. You don't know how much Leena and I worried when we heard of your heart attack."

Carl looked at Jose with great tenderness. "Thanks for telling me. And for your concern," he said quietly.

The effects of the medication wore off towards evening and Carl stepped into the kitchen with big plans. He brought out shrimps and mussels from the freezer and set about making 'pasta with seafood'. Jose watched intently as Carl cooked. The dinner turned out to be superb. Carl was happy to watch Jose eat with gusto.

After dinner, they watched *Mediterranean Cooking* on the television while having ice cream for dessert. Carl served whiskey a little later.

"Not Jack Daniel's this time. Let's have some scotch instead. This is, *Glenmorangie*, one of the best."

"Skål! This is good!" said Jose savoring the first sip.

"I felt so drowsy today. Wonder if I mixed my medicines up or something. I could barely keep my eyes open."

"Please be more careful. Accidental overdoses can have serious consequences."

"Not to worry, Jose. I'll be fine. There is a Dorothy L. Sayers mystery on TV today. Since I napped most of the day on the sofa I am going to watch it. Care to join me?"

"Of course, I enjoy watching TV with you here in Stockholm even if it is in Swedish or French or any other language."

"The episode today is *Strong Poison*. It'll be in English."

"I don't think that is a book I know. I have read *Five Red Herrings*, *Have His Carcase*, and *The Nine Tailors*. I liked *Five Red Herrings* the most. Lord Peter Wimsey is quite an interesting character!"

"If you have read Sayers and liked her books, you will love this one."

But Jose didn't. As the drama unfolded and the evil solicitor plotted to poison his cousin with arsenic to steal his inheritance, Jose felt uneasy at first and then queasy and nauseous.

"Carl, I cannot watch this any longer. This is horrible. Poisoning a relative to steal their wealth! I cannot even bear to think how one can be so heartless and greedy. I feel sick to my stomach."

Leaving his drink unfinished, Jose fled to his room, leaving a puzzled Carl to watch the drama alone.

As he lay in bed, Jose thought how easy it would be for someone unscrupulous to kill Carl by deliberately overdosing him or slipping his medicine into his drink after he had had a few. "He could be killed with his own medicines and no Lord Wimsey would ever solve that crime," he thought.

His thoughts troubled him so much that he was close to tears. He got up and walked back to the living room.

In the varying glow of the television sat Carl, bundled in the shawl that Jose had presented him, looking completely vulnerable and forlorn.

Jose rushed to Carl's side and, putting his arms around him, hugged him.

"I love you, Carl!" he cried. "You have been my best friend and support and I don't want anything bad to happen to you – ever."

Carl was taken aback by this unexpected outburst. This was the first time Jose had voluntarily hugged him. The outpouring of emotions was an even bigger surprise.

"Jose, I love you too. I always have," Carl responded.

Jose slowly let go of the seated Carl and straightened himself.

"Only today I understood the real meaning of love – of real affection," he said wiping away the tears with the palm of his hand. "Thank you for not stopping to write even when I did not reply. You did not give up on me. I am sorry for taking your love for granted. Leena and I are grateful to you for all you have done for us."

"I think you got it all wrong," said Carl with a quaver in his voice. "I am the one who has been blessed by your friendship."

"My wish for you is that you will always be healthy and happy and that you will never be lonely. Goodnight, Carl!"

"Jose, you just made my day. Or night. This is one of the happiest moments in my life. Goodnight!"

\*\*\*

When Jose came to the breakfast table the next morning he was surprised to find Carl in his bathrobe.

"Good morning, Carl! Are we going out early today?" asked Jose.

"Top of the morning to you, Jose!" said Carl jovially. "*We* are not. But *I* am."

Seeing the quizzical expression on Jose's face, he continued. "I need to go to the bank. There's an important piece of business I need to transact and it cannot wait. No, not for a single day."

"Some kind of investment?" asked Jose.

"No! You will come to know of it in good time. All I can say now is – Dorothy L. Sayers opened my eyes!"

"Sit right there, Carl. I want to take a photo of you exactly as you are now!"

Jose dashed to his room for his Minolta SLR and took several pictures of a freshly scrubbed Carl in his bathrobe.

Carl left right after breakfast, carrying a thin black folder. Jose decided to finish off the first roll of film in his new camera. He walked to Kungsträdgården and took pictures till the film ran out. "Taking photos with an SLR was so different from taking pictures with a point-and-shoot camera," he thought. He was pleased with himself that he had managed to squeeze in thirty-eight pictures on a thirty-six shot roll. On the way back, he dropped off the film for developing and printing.

Carl had not yet returned. He had cereals with milk and watched TV. With the advent of satellite television, the number of channels had multiplied since his last visit. He surfed the channels looking for the old strip poker show. It was nowhere to be found. But instead, he stumbled upon explicit adult channels that left nothing to sensibility or to the imagination. "Strip poker was absolutely tame compared to these channels," concluded Jose.

It was past 1 o'clock when Carl arrived.

"The bank took ever so long. But then that is only to be expected for documents such as these," Carl said holding up the black folder. After he changed his clothes, Carl opened the bags of groceries he had brought with him. Jose was happy to see that there was rabbit meat. And that was what they had for dinner that evening – Carl's superlative rabbit stew with rye bread.

"I don't want to be too secretive about my mission today. I went to the bank to make some important changes to my will. If you recall, the will was central to the plot in last night's murder mystery on TV. I think it is absolutely essential for everyone to have a will. That way your money won't go to undeserving folks after you have kicked the bucket. I had made mine years ago, but I decided to make a significant change."

Jose enjoyed Carl's rabbit stew even more than he had on his previous visit.

"This is a masterpiece!" he said congratulating Carl on his culinary skills.

Later in the evening, they watched *Pebble Mill* on TV.

When it was time for Jose to turn in for the night, Carl said, "Don't forget, we have a dinner invitation tomorrow!"

\*\*\*

The invitation took them, the next afternoon, by *tunnelbana* first and then by bus, to Albyvägen and to the house of Carl's ex-colleague, Nick Wagner. Jose was surprised to discover that the middle-aged Nick lived with his mother, who treated him more like a young boy than a mature man close to old age. Nick was at the beck and call of his mother and jumped to her every call. Their old, blind cat Lara stumbled around the room bumping into furniture. To Jose, the whole scene was like a Charles Addams cartoon.

After introductions, they all moved to the lakeside. Jose helped Nick carry table and chairs to the chosen spot. When the table was set, with tablecloth and place mats, they sat down to a meal of chicken salad, pickled herrings with sour cream and chives, potatoes, meatballs, and cheese. For beverages, there was beer, cardamom liqueur, and white wine.

Jose had never drunk beer from a can before and could not figure out how the can opened. He whispered a request to Carl but the reply he got was not very helpful. "I don't drink beer and I have no idea how it works. Try tugging on the tab."

That's what Jose did. The pop and fizz when he pulled open the tab took him by surprise. But before he could take a sip, Nick served wine for everyone and there was a toast. Jose did not understand a word of the toast or whom it was for. Just as he reached for his beer a second time, he was startled by his companions at the table bursting into song. This was a pattern that continued to repeat throughout the meal. A toast, followed by singing, followed by another toast, more impromptu singing and so on.

"The Swedes sing during meals at the drop of a hat," Carl said sotto voce.

Jose enjoyed the food in the idyllic setting by the bluish-green waters of the lake. The bright green of the lawn contrasted with the azure blue of the sky. When Carl went indoors to the restroom, Nick leaned over and asked Jose, "Are you in Sweden on business or pleasure?"

"Neither. I am here because my friend Carl was ill."

"That's very kind of you," Nick replied but he arched his eyebrows questioningly.

When Nick's mother retired for a nap, Nick ambled over to the hedge and chatted with a man who appeared to have been mowing his lawn on the other side for some time.

"That's Charlie. Nick's partner," whispered Carl with a conspiratorial wink.

"You mean?" asked Jose surprised.

"Yes. Nick is gay too. But his mother doesn't know. And his lover lives right next door."

When Nick returned, he showed them his daffodils and amaryllis near the gatehouse.

"Nick is an ardent gardener," Carl said.

They left a little before five. On the bus, Carl told Jose about Nick's situation in the office.

"He declared one morning he wouldn't be a doormat anymore. He said he had signed himself up for a self-assertiveness course. But, if the old Nick was likable but indecisive, the new Nick turned out to be absolutely insufferable. Nobody in the office could stand him after that."

***

The next days were spent mostly indoors. Carl was lethargic from the medication most of the time but he often had a beatific smile. Jose went on his own to *Tempo* and bought presents for his colleagues and kitchen articles for Leena. *5an-10an-25an* had apparently shut up shop. On the last day before his return, he went to Hötorget with Carl in the morning and bought another present for Leena, a digital watch. Carl purchased an electronic flash for the Minolta camera as a present for Jose and a hairdryer for Leena.

After returning home, as Jose commenced packing his bags, Carl revealed another gift for Leena – an exquisite brass cutlery set made in Thailand.

"This must be very expensive," Jose said in awe.

"Since Leena could not be here with us, she deserves a little extra," said Carl.

The next morning Carl called a taxi to take Jose to the airport. If at the end of the first trip it was Jose who was emotionally upset, this time it was Carl's turn. He could not bear to leave the apartment. When they hugged each other goodbye, Carl bit his lips to keep from breaking down.

"I will come to see you and Leena this December. I am not going to go to Armenia or Cyprus or Yugoslavia or any other place. That's a promise!" said Carl.

The flight to Moscow was short. Jose did not eat the snacks served but stuffed them in his jacket pocket for the seven-hour wait before the flight to

Calcutta. At the Sheremetyevo airport, he gazed at the Tupolev and Ilyushin aircraft parked on the tarmac. The tall, white-barked trees in the distance reminded him of the woods in *Dr. Zhivago*. But it was the rooks that roused his curiosity the most. Unlike the all-black crows in India, these were of gray plumage with only the head, wings, and tail black.

When hunger got the better of him, he surreptitiously took out the snacks he had in his pocket and nibbled at the cheese secretly. But when he noticed the curious stares of passengers waiting in line at the opposite gate, he became acutely self-conscious and put it back in his pocket.

On arrival in Calcutta, Jose transferred quickly to the Netaji Subhas Chandra Bose domestic airport and caught the first flight to Cochin. Leena was at the airport to welcome him home.

The return to office was subdued and somber. Asokan made some wisecracks about Jose being an errand boy of the middlemen of the tainted Indo-Swedish Bofors arms deal.

Leena was thrilled with the digital watch and the hairdryer and she loved the kitchen gadgets Jose had brought all the way from Stockholm. Her excitement rose to fever pitch when Jose showed her the brass cutlery set made in Thailand.

"We will use it for special occasions only. This must have cost a fortune," said Leena.

She studied all the photos intently.

"Carl looks so handsome here," Leena said holding up the photo taken in a bathrobe.

"He had just had his bath and he looked so fresh I just had to take it. Carl liked that photo too! It is one of his favorites."

## Chapter 13

Carl kept his promise and arrived in Cochin in December of the same year.

Jose and Leena together awaited him in the throng of onlookers outside the new Cochin airport. The arrival board showed that Carl's Indian Airlines flight had landed. But there was no sign of the towering six-footer in the crowd of passengers exiting the airport. Jose panicked. "Did Carl miss his connecting flight at Delhi? Or had he not left Sweden at all?" He wondered if he should go to the counter and inquire. As he was looking around, Leena tugged at his arm. "There is Carl!" she said excitedly. It took Jose a moment to recognize the frail figure hunched in the wheelchair, trailing the passengers hurrying to the exit.

"My goodness! What has become of Carl?" he whispered to Leena as he moved forward to meet Carl.

"Hello, Leena and Jose!" said Carl smiling wanly. "You didn't expect to see me in a wheelchair, did you?"

In the taxi to the hotel, Carl tried to cheer Jose and Leena.

"I am OK. It was the cramped seats on the flight from Delhi that did me in. When we got here I was just too exhausted to climb down the stairs to the tarmac and walk to the terminal on my own. I had no problems on the flight from Stockholm. There was more legroom on the SAS flight."

"You just relax for the rest of the day and don't strain yourself. Leena and I are going to stay at the same hotel as you. If you need anything just give us a tinkle."

"That sounds like a plan. I will order room service for lunch and give you a call towards evening for dinner—if I feel up to it."

Carl did not call and after waiting another hour or so Jose and Leena had dinner together at the terrace restaurant of the hotel.

Carl's call came a little past two in the morning when they were fast asleep.

"Jose, I am having a heart attack. Call the doctor quick," Carl whispered in a hoarse voice.

It took a moment for the message to register. The ringing of the phone had woken Leena. Jose rushed to the reception. The elevators were not in service and Jose ran down the stairs to the ground floor. The clerk was asleep and Jose had to shake him awake. The receptionist phoned the hotel's doctor-on-call. It was a full fifteen minutes from the time Carl had called Jose.

"Why don't you call the emergency department at the hospital?" shouted Jose angrily.

"The doctor will decide if the hospital needs to be contacted. The doctor lives next door," the clerk answered placidly.

Jose was frantic with worry. His anxiety doubled with each passing minute. There was no sign of the doctor.

Jose rushed to Carl's room. The door was locked. He knocked initially and then commenced banging hard on the door. All he heard was a low moaning. Jose ran back to the front reception and got the duplicate keys. When he opened the door, he found Carl, in boxers, kneeling on the floor, his upper torso on the bed, his chest heaving laboriously, sweat pouring down his body and neck. Jose tried to put his arms around Carl to lift him.

"Give me an injection," whispered Carl. "Tell the doctor I've had a heart attack. He will know what to do."

Just then the doctor arrived in his nightclothes along with the hotel clerk. As soon as Jose informed the doctor of Carl's condition, he placed his stethoscope on Carl's back and listened. Then, quickly taking out a syringe and a small vial from his bag, he administered the injection. The response was almost instantaneous. The heaving rapidly reduced and the breathing became quieter. Carl's body relaxed. The doctor, clerk, and Jose together managed to lift Carl on to the bed. He lay on his back, drained of all energy. Leena arrived draped in a shawl. They stood around the bed watching Carl as he lay with his eyes closed.

"He is going to sleep now," the doctor said.

"Should we call an ambulance to take him to the hospital?" asked Jose.

"No, he is going to be all right. He will be fine in the morning."

And the doctor was right. When Jose and Leena entered the restaurant for breakfast, Carl was already there, looking relaxed and refreshed.

"Good morning! Sorry about the scare last night," said Carl with a sheepish smile.

"We were worried about you!" said Leena.

"It wasn't as bad as it looked. And the doctor came quickly enough," said Carl.

"Quickly enough? He took almost half an hour to get here," Jose said indignantly.

"By Indian standards, that is pretty good. Did the doctor give a bill?"

"I paid the doctor last night," said Jose.

"Let me reimburse you the expense," Carl offered.

But Jose would have none of it.

Mid-morning, they left by taxi for Munnar. After a stop for lunch at Kothamangalam, they hit the *ghat* or hill section of the road. The driver did not seem in any mood to slow down or shift to a lower gear.

"I had forgotten how scary this road is!" Carl exclaimed, peering down into the ravine.

"Don't worry, he is an experienced driver," Jose replied.

"I will take your word for it! Probably this is what the ad writers meant by God's own country. It sure makes you feel close to God!"

Jose and Leena laughed, but the driver who did not speak a word of English was completely oblivious and did not reduce speed. The taxi careened around a switchback, barely missing a bus that seemed to be in an even greater hurry.

"It doesn't look like the road is wide enough for two-way traffic," Carl remarked.

The temperature dropped rapidly as they ascended the hills. Gone were the heat and dust and the milling crowds. Carl basked in the glorious greenery that enveloped the road. Protected forests and plantations of tea and cardamom were on either side of the climbing road. Rivers, streams, and rivulets at the bottom of the deep gorges snaked their way downhill towards the Arabian Sea. The many small waterfalls and foamy-white cascades they passed on the way fascinated Carl.

"I had clean forgotten all this existed. It's been a long time," he said quietly.

Whitewashed buildings with red clay-tiled roofs increased in frequency as they neared the town. '*Make Cardamom a Daily Habit*' proclaimed one sign. '*Garden Fresh Tea Sold at Factory Outlet*' announced another. Men in white sarongs folded up above their knees, the typical male attire of Kerala, lounged around the bus stand where overcrowded private buses stopped.

They arrived at Munnar in the early evening. For afternoon tea, they had coffee and fried plantains at the Hill Resort hotel where Carl would be staying.

"This hotel hasn't changed much since the last time I stayed here. It is nice and quiet. Far from the dust, heat, and the madding crowd of the plains. It is just that the getting here brings one's heart to one's mouth."

Jose and Leena returned to the tea estate promising to join Carl for breakfast the next morning.

"How will we send him alone from here to Madras?" asked Leena when they got home. "What if something happens to him on the way? Who will take care of him?"

"What can we do? If he requests me I could take leave from work and go with him to Madras. But you know how Westerners are. They like to be independent and self-reliant. Only if they do not have any other option will they seek help."

\*\*\*

The next day, after breakfast, they drove to Carl's hotel.

"Today's lunch will be at our house. You have done so much for Leena and me," said Jose.

"Yes, we will be blessed by your visit. Without your help, we could not have renovated the *bungalow*," Leena added.

"It was nothing. I bet you would have done the same for me," Carl replied.

It became clear when Carl stepped out of the car, that getting to Jose and Leena's house was out of the question. The gradient was too steep and the footpath that led halfway up the hillock was too narrow for Carl to be assisted up the slope.

Leena was close to tears. Jose was distraught.

"I should've anticipated this. I'm so sorry!" he said to Carl.

"There's nothing to be upset about. The important thing for me is that I am spending some quality time with the two of you. And I have seen your house with my own eyes. What more could I want? By the way, what tree is that behind the house?"

"The big one is a jackfruit tree. There are also three mango trees further behind," replied Jose.

"You have quite a few coconut trees as well," remarked Carl.

"Yes, Carl. We use coconut in almost all our cooking," Leena said.

"I think yours is the only cuisine I know of that uses coconut oil as a cooking medium. Correction: Sri Lankans use coconut oil too. It tastes quite good, even if it's not good for you, I'll admit that," said Carl.

Jose brought the Minolta out and took pictures of Carl and Leena together. He had to kneel down and slant the camera upwards to include their *bungalow* in the photo as the backdrop.

"Too bad I couldn't see the inside of your house. I bet it is nice. Your house looks much prettier than all the other houses," said Carl.

That pleased Jose and Leena who smiled broadly at the compliment.

"It's all due to your help. Without your gift, we couldn't have done it," said Jose gratefully.

"You are welcome. But I wasn't trying to remind you of that. Your house really stands out."

"Since Carl cannot come up to our house, maybe we can have a picnic in the tea garden somewhere?" suggested Leena.

"That is a good idea. But I will have to find a folding table and some chairs. Carl cannot sit cross-legged on the ground like us. I am sure I can find the furniture in the office. Let me go look."

The table and chairs were placed beneath a row of pine trees. Around them lay acres and acres of tea plants on the rolling hills. They could see the tea-pickers making their way amongst the plants with gunny bags strung on their backs for the pickings. Kurup and other servants carried the food from the house. Carl enjoyed the meal and complimented Leena on her cooking skills.

"This fish curry with the red gravy is delicious. What fish is this, if I may ask?" asked Carl.

"It is called the kingfish or the seer fish here. I'm glad you like the fish *moilee*," Leena replied, pleased.

"I like your cooking! Would love to come back on my next trip."

"Please do! You are most welcome!" chorused Leena and Jose.

"I left beef out from today's menu for your sake. Here's some roast chicken instead," offered Leena.

"Thanks, I'll have some!" said Carl. "Jose, do you know what this meal reminds me of?"

"No. What?"

"The outdoor dinner we had at Nick's place at Albyvägen."

"Of course!" laughed Jose. "There is just one difference, though. We won't be singing in the middle of the meal!"

After lunch, Carl handed out the presents he had brought for them – a new Gillette razor for Jose and Chanel perfume for Leena.

"You remembered the razor!" Jose said in surprise.

"It is probably time you retired the first one from nine years ago," said Carl smiling.

"Thank you, Carl! The perfume is wonderful!" Leena said gratefully.

They decided to restrict that afternoon's sightseeing to places in the vicinity of Munnar.

In the evening before Jose and Leena returned to their *bungalow*, Carl asked for Jose's help with his medication. Jose was extra careful. He remembered the niece who poisoned her aunt in the Dorothy L. Sayers mystery and he shuddered at the mere thought of poisoning Carl.

Chandy was waiting for them when they returned to the estate.

"How are you, *Kochamma*?" he asked Leena deferentially.

"We are fine. How are you, Chandy?" responded Leena.

"I am fine. Thank you for asking. I have an urgent message for Jose."

"What is it, Chandy? Asokan in trouble again?"

"No! He is quiet these days. This is something else. I have a message from the office. Since you are on leave your manager asked me to tell you this personally."

"Tell me, tell me," Jose said impatiently.

"It seems we have a prospective customer from Russia. The company is located at a place called Vladikavkaz. They are sending a representative to Bombay for discussions and negotiations. You will represent our company."

"That is good news!" Jose said exultantly. "We can always do with new business. We face tough competition from the new tea-growing areas of Africa."

Then a doubt struck him. He did not want to travel out of town in the middle of Carl's visit, at any cost.

"When is the trip?" he asked Chandy.

"The Russian has requested the meeting next Monday."

"Next Monday? My friend from Sweden is here ..."

"Jose, Carl is leaving on Sunday for Madras. You could go with him to Cochin in the same car and catch the Bombay flight," Leena cut in.

"You are absolutely right!" Jose exulted. "This is an answer to our prayers."

***

Carl was even more delighted when Jose and Leena told him the news the next day.

"I could do with your company on the hill roads!" said Carl with a smile.

"We won't need to hire a taxi. Since this is a business trip the company will let me use an estate car," Jose said.

"In which case, I will also come with you and see you both off at the Cochin airport," Leena chimed in.

"What a stroke of good fortune!" exclaimed Carl. "This is an unexpected extension of my time with you."

The next seven days were the happiest time Carl had had in a long while. Together the trio traveled to all the scenic spots in the vicinity by taxi, with Carl reminiscing of the previous trip he had made many years ago. They drove to Peermade, the town named after the Sufi saint Peer Mohammed who is buried there. It was the palace (now converted into a hotel) of the erstwhile rulers (the *Rajas*) of Travancore that delighted Carl the most.

"The king chose the right spot for his summer palace," remarked Carl. "Some of my most cherished stamps are from the Travancore kingdom."

"One of them Swathi Tirunal was a patron of music and a great composer of Carnatic music," said Jose.

"But the most famous of them is Raja Ravi Varma, the painter," interposed Leena. "His paintings based on Hindu epics are very famous."

"I think I have seen reproductions of them somewhere," said Carl.

In the evening, they returned to the hotel in Munnar. Carl sampled the local whiskey and nearly spat it out.

"This is terrible! It tastes like methylated spirit or varnish."

"The only other alternatives are rum and brandy. They won't have any wine. I know you don't drink beer."

"What do you recommend, Leena?" asked Carl.

"A good cup of coffee. Or freshly brewed tea grown in these hills," she suggested with a disarming smile.

"I think Carl is talking about alcoholic drinks ..." began Jose.

"I think Leena is right. This is not the best place for alcohol. I will have a cup of Munnar tea!" said Carl.

The next day they went to the Periyar wildlife sanctuary. From the boat, they watched a herd of elephants bathing and frolicking near the far shore.

"Elephants are my kith and kin, remember?" joked Carl self-deprecatingly.

Initially, Carl wanted to take the elephant ride but later decided it was too risky.

"More for the elephant's sake than mine," quipped Carl.

The bracing mountain air did wonders for Carl. No longer did he look gaunt and feeble. At times, he looked almost as strong and healthy as he had done on the preceding trip before he had had that debilitating heart attack.

Over the next few days, they traveled to Devikulam, Idukki, Kumily, Vandiperiyar, and Mundakkayam.

Carl liked to stop at roadside tea shops for coffee and snacks. He observed the antics of the shopkeepers as they deftly cooled the coffee by rapidly pouring it from one cup to the other. He even slurped like the locals as he sipped the hot coffee.

"I find it funny that in the midst of this tea-growing area, the preferred drink is coffee!" observed Carl.

Carl was a big hit wherever they went. People gaped in wonder at his height and girth. The Indian tourists they met almost always wanted their picture taken with Carl.

"We want to take a snap with you," they would say.

"I feel like a Bollywood star whenever I am in India!" remarked Carl.

"Do you find it annoying?" inquired Jose.

"Not really. I was taken aback by all the adulation the first time. Now, I kind of take it in my stride. But I don't think if I will ever get used to it. It is bad enough here but it is much worse in Tamil Nadu and in northern Indian states."

"Really?"

"Yes, much worse! Sometimes I am like the Pied Piper of all the beggars and street urchins in the town. They trail behind me wherever I go. Well-nigh impossible to shake them off. It is the other extreme in Sweden. I am just a nobody there and I don't mind that one bit!" said Carl laughing.

Carl decided he wanted to watch the elephants at the Periyar wildlife sanctuary one more time. The second trip to Thekkady was as enjoyable as the first. They spent a lot of time on the lake in the hired boat, watching the elephants by the waterside and listening to birdcalls wafting across the waters in the stillness of the sanctuary. The only loud sound was the trumpeting of the elephants, and even that seemed to blend in with the forest and the waters of the lake.

That evening Chandy brought a sealed envelope for Jose, which contained the ticket and the travel advance for the trip. Leena busied herself that night making the *appam* and curry for the journey the next day. Chandy also confirmed that the estate car would come at five in the morning.

Jose and Leena were ready well before the taxi arrived the next morning. When they arrived at the hotel in the taxi, Carl had already checked out and was seated near the front desk.

"Let's have a cup of coffee before we start," suggested Carl. "It's a little nippy outside."

"It is. We are both sorry that you are leaving today," said Jose and Leena nodded in agreement.

"You remember when you referred to me as a father figure in Stockholm?" asked Carl.

"Yes, I remember. You were not very pleased."

"Well ... I've been thinking. My position has changed a bit. Quite a bit, as a matter of fact. Last night I came to see us from a totally different perspective."

"And what is that?" asked Jose puzzled.

"I have come to the conclusion that the two of you – Jose and Leena – are the son and daughter I wish I had had," Carl said without any embarrassment.

Jose was at a loss for words and cleared his throat nervously. Leena was speechless too.

After coffee, they started on the fateful trip to Cochin that would alter their lives irrevocably.

## Chapter 14

In the Bombay hotel, Jose woke up early, as was his wont. He had not slept at all well during the night. Strange dreams had run amok in his head – dreadful nightmares filled with shrieks and wild pursuit in wooded hills and gurgling streams.

He left the hotel by nine o'clock, attired in a white, long-sleeved shirt, and dark blue, polyester trousers. He knew right away when he stepped out of the hotel into the morning sun that the tie was a mistake. The heat and the high humidity caused him to perspire profusely and fast spreading circles formed under his arms while the rivulets of sweat coursing down caused the vest and the shirt to clammily stick to his back. He decided to take a taxi instead of risking the *suburban* (as metro trains were called in Bombay) or a BEST (Bombay Electric Supply & Transport) commuter bus.

When he got to the lobby of the famed Taj Mahal Hotel at Apollo Bunder he was happy to be back in the comfort of air-conditioning. It was not too difficult to spot the Russian in the lounge. The man wore a light gray suit with a dark fedora. What surprised Jose was the fact that he was not alone. A chic young lady in an electric blue dress sat on the sofa next to him. Her straw-blond hair, highlighted eyelids, brightly rouged cheeks, oversized circular earrings, miniskirt, and knee-high black leather boots somehow reminded him of the woman-in-red at Frankfurt airport.

Jose approached and introduced himself. Only when the man stood up did Jose realize how tall he was.

"Glad to meet you, Mr. Jose! My name is Vladimir Miroshnikov of 'Import-Export Kavkaz'. You can call me Vlad. Vlad from Vladikavkaz. Ha, ha! Where shall we hold our discussions?"

Vlad spoke fluent English.

"How about the business lounge? That is a convenient place to talk," suggested Jose. "By the way, my name is pronounced slightly differently. It is pronounced j-o-s – jos. Rhymes with nose."

"My apologies, Jose! Let us move to the lounge," suggested Vladimir.

Jose bowed slightly to the young woman and said, "Glad to meet you."

"*Izvineechye! Ya ni gavaryu pa Angliski,*" she replied in Russian with a haughty smile.

"Irina is my secretary. She speaks only Russian," Vlad explained.

Then noticing the puzzled look on Jose's face, Vlad winked slyly. "She's a temporary girlfriend – not a real secretary," he whispered with a knowing look.

They found a cozy corner in the business lounge and started off by ordering coffee. Irina sat a little away from Vlad and busied herself playing with an electronic gadget while idly chewing gum. She kept crossing and uncrossing her high-booted legs much to Jose's discomfiture. Several times Jose caught her staring at him inquisitively.

The business part of the meeting went better than Jose had anticipated, due in part to the ease with which Vlad conversed in English. Jose was thrilled when the Russian importer quickly agreed to a price higher than the floor price Jose had in mind.

They celebrated the inking of the MOU with a lavish lunch late in the afternoon. Vlad insisted on ordering champagne to toast the new partnership. They dined on *tandoori* chicken, *naan, dal,* and vegetable *korma* with *jalebi* and *gulab jamun* for dessert.

The champagne must have gone to Irina's head because she kept nudging Jose's shin with her booted toe. Jose drew his feet back as far back as he could. He was afraid Irina's antics would antagonize Vlad. Jose heaved a sigh of relief when the meal finally came to a close.

*** 

Immediately after the lunch, Jose rushed back to his hotel and phoned Leena from a PCO (public call office) nearby. The response was still a busy tone like the previous night. "That is strange. Is our home phone out of order?" he wondered. He dialed the office number and got through on the first attempt. When he identified himself, there was abrupt silence at the other end. He could only hear muffled whispers as if the mouthpiece had been covered. Jose found this exasperating and raised his voice.

"Can you hear me there? This is Jose. KK Jose calling from Bombay. Why don't you answer me? Philipose, is it you? What is the matter?"

Finally, when someone came on the line, Jose was surprised to find out that it was the personnel manager.

"Jose, we have been trying to contact you since last night. What happened? Why didn't you call us after you checked in?"

Jose started to explain about the bungled hotel booking and the morning's meeting with the Russian representative, but the personnel manager cut him short.

"Jose, listen to me very carefully. You need to catch the next available flight and return to Munnar. This is very, very urgent. It is an emergency. Abandon the meeting if necessary. Come back immediately – repeat immediately. Do you hear me?"

A feeling of dread gripped Jose. His stomach knotted with anxiety. He sensed that some calamity had occurred.

"Sir, what happened? What is wrong?" asked Jose frantically.

"I am sorry, Jose. Leena is not well. She is in the hospital."

"*What?* She was all right when she saw me off at the airport yesterday. What happened? Was there a car accident?"

"No, she arrived safely from the airport. But she is now in the hospital at Kottayam. She was admitted early this morning. You catch the next flight to Cochin and take a taxi straight to the

Medical College Hospital at Kottayam. We will have our staff waiting for you there."

"Sir, please tell me what happened!" Jose pleaded.

"That's all I can tell you now. Get a plane ticket quickly and get to Leena's side." There was a click and the line went dead.

Jose, frantic with worry, was like a mad man. He caught a taxi to the city office of Indian Airlines. By the time he got there, the reservation counter had shut down for the day. When he explained his predicament the duty officer suggested that he get to the airport by 5:00 a.m. the next morning and request a seat from the emergency quota on the first flight.

Jose went back to the hotel but he didn't sleep a wink. His heart ached for Leena. He couldn't imagine how Leena could have been taken ill so suddenly. His troubled mind conjured up a myriad of horrible images. Tears flowed down his face uncontrollably. He could not wait till morning. A little past midnight, he checked out and left for the airport. When he got there the security guard would not let him in saying it was too early. After he heard Jose's story and saw how distraught he was, the guard relented. The terminal was packed with passengers who had arrived in the night on international flights, mostly from the Middle East. Many were sprawled on the floor between misshapen and unwieldy-looking luggage haphazardly strewn around. Jose walked around in a trance waiting for the ticket counters to open. Exhausted from worry, hunger, and lack of sleep he finally sat down on the floor in a corner and dozed off, leaning back against his bag.

When the counter opened the next morning, he was lucky to find a sympathetic *Malayali* from Kerala on the other side of the booking window. He canceled the previously booked ticket and got an emergency quota seat on the first flight of the day. "Leena, in a few more hours I will be with you," he said to himself.

The flight mercifully was on time. On stepping out of Cochin airport after arrival to look for a taxi to take him to the hospital at Kottayam, Jose was surprised and relieved to find Chandy.

"Chandy, what are you doing here? What happened to Leena? Is she OK?" The questions came tumbling out.

"The personnel manager told us of the telephone conversation he had with you yesterday evening. I volunteered to come here to receive you instead of waiting for you at the hospital. I thought that was the least I could do. I came here this morning in the estate car."

"Thank you, Chandy. You are always helping others. Tell me about Leena, *please*. What happened to her?"

"Jose, I am very, very sorry. I don't know how to tell you this." Tears rolled down Chandy's face as he continued, "*Kochamma* is physically all right. She is in not in any life-threatening danger."

"But why is she in the hospital then? What is the problem? Why are you not telling me?" asked Jose, shaking Chandy by his shoulders in his anxiety.

"The problem is mental. *Kochamma* has a serious psychological problem. I'm sorry, Jose. This shouldn't have happened to *Kochamma* and to you," said Chandy, breaking down again.

"*What?* What kind of mental problem? She is the most balanced person I know." Jose was flabbergasted.

"I know. It is probably the incidents of the night that caused it."

"What incidents? Why are you not telling me what happened?" screamed Jose.

"Our estate was attacked the night before last. The night you left."

"*What?*" Jose was thunderstruck. "By whom?"

"They attacked the officer's quarters. They cut the phone lines first," said Chandy.

"That's why I couldn't get through to Leena when I called. Tell me what happened. Who were they?" asked Jose.

"We suspect they were *goondas* hired by radical Maoists in the labor union. The ruffians came first to Asokan's quarters and caught him in bed with a young *Adivasi* tea picker. They thrashed the girl within an inch of her life. Then they slashed Asokan with sickles and machetes. Asokan is dead."

"Oh, my God! I cannot believe this happened in our estate," cried Jose.

"The hooligans then came to your bungalow." Chandy stopped and looked down. "I cannot go on, Jose," he added breaking down.

Jose felt as if the ground had been pulled out from under his feet. He was afraid he would pass out. He gripped Chandy by the shoulders and asked in a voice that was eerily calm. "Did they injure Leena? Did they hurt her?"

"I don't know, Jose. I don't know ... externally there is no injury. But *Kochamma* shrinks away in fear from anybody who comes near her. The doctors put her on sedatives. It was not easy giving her the injection. They had to hold *Kochamma* down. I am very, very sorry, Jose." Chandy was distraught.

"My world has come tumbling down in the most unexpected manner," Jose said with a calmness that was frightening. "Let us go. Where is the car? I must get to Leena's side right away."

Chandy tried to comfort Jose. "I will pray for you, Jose. You must believe that nothing happens to us without God's knowledge. He will protect you and guide you safely through this."

Jose did not reply.

There was very little conversation during the journey. Jose seemed to be lost in a world of his own. They did not stop anywhere for coffee or refreshments but drove straight to the Medical College Hospital at Kottayam.

As soon as the car came to a stop in front of the hospital, Jose jumped out and ran towards the building, with Chandy in hot pursuit.

"We need to see the doctor first," Chandy called from behind.

"I want to see Leena. Where is she?" Jose asked the nurse at the reception.

Chandy took Jose by the arm. "Come with me."

They ran up two flights of stairs to the psychiatric ward. Jose saw his aunt and other relatives standing in the hallway. They stepped forward to talk to him but he brushed them off.

Chandy pleaded with Jose. "They won't let you in. Come to the doctor's room first, *please!*"

The doctor was sympathetic. "I will let you see Leena. But listen to me first. She has been through some very traumatic events. I am afraid she has had a nervous breakdown. She shies away even from people she knows. She did not recognize her cousins or her uncle and aunt. She may not recognize you. Be prepared for that. But do not let it upset you. Time is a great healer. With the appropriate treatment and medicines, she is likely to recover. But be prepared for rejection today. That is almost a certainty."

They walked to the door of Leena's room.

"You will go in alone. A crowd of people will scare her."

The relatives stood in a group behind them as the doctor opened the door. Jose stepped into the darkened room and saw Leena lying huddled in a corner of the bed in a fetal curl. Her eyes were closed but her face was contorted in fear.

Jose moved towards the bed and whispered, "Leena!"

Leena opened her eyes. "Jose!" she cried, throwing her arms out. Jose ran to the bed and they clasped each other in a tight embrace.

The doctor gently pulled the door curtain closed and shooed the relatives away.

"There are things science cannot explain. Love is one of them," he said.

The women dabbed their eyes with the ends of their saris. Chandy, his own eyes brimming with tears, saw the doctor's glasses mist over.

"Do not disturb them. Love is the best healer," the doctor said gruffly as he walked away with Chandy to his chambers.

***

Jose stayed with Leena in the hospital. The doctor made an exception and permitted an extra bed to be placed in Leena's room. Jose never left Leena's side.

Leena's parents arrived from Kuwait. She sat on the bed with averted eyes, clinging tightly to Jose's hand, not saying a word. Her parents were only able to coax monosyllabic replies from her after repeating the same question several times.

When they stepped out of the room, Leena's father was livid with anger.

Poking Jose in the chest with his finger, he shouted, "If you had listened to my advice and come to Kuwait nothing would have happened to Leena. Nothing! You are directly responsible! You and your fascination for tea estates! Any sensible man would have chosen a foreign job. But you? You prefer the forest!"

With that, he stalked away in anger pulling Leena's mother by the arm.

***

Leena improved rapidly. Her initial interactions were restricted only to Jose but she extended that first to include the nurses who brought her medication and then to the other patients in the ward. In the evenings when it was cool, Jose and

Leena would go down to the lawns and walk around the enclosed garden.

Jose forgot about the rest of the world. Nothing else – his job, their friends, their relatives – nothing else mattered. Jose and Leena found love on a higher plane. The small hospital room became their world. Eating bland hospital meals together brought greater joy than any expensive restaurant dinner could have.

But they never talked about what happened that fateful night. Leena never broached the subject and Jose never asked.

"How is Carl? Did you hear from him?" asked Leena.

"No. He must be busy. Or he may have called the estate," Jose replied.

That evening Jose wrote a brief letter to Carl explaining the situation and mailed it to Kannan's address, which he had saved on a small slip of paper in his wallet. Jose wished he had a phone number to call. He could somehow have got in touch with Carl through Kannan. If there was anyone in the world Jose wanted to talk to in his hour of distress, it was Carl.

***

Chandy came to the hospital every night to see Jose and Leena. He ignored Jose's suggestion that the long bus ride every day after work was too tiring. He brought home-cooked food and news from the tea estate.

Chandy told Jose about what he knew about the incident. The police were still conducting their investigation. They had taken into custody the union leaders and mercilessly beaten them. All evidence pointed to the attackers being hit-men from out-of-state who had fled back across the border. The police had been unable so far to prove that the union leaders had hired the mercenaries.

"Right now, I cannot trust anyone – except you, Chandy. I cannot believe that our labor leaders would resort to violence after all that we did for them. They were happy with the concessions we made. Of course, they made no secret of their hatred of Asokan. But we would have taken action against Asokan if there had been even one complaint. Why didn't they complain? Why did they kill?"

"I agree. I met the leaders in jail where they were remanded to custody. My guess is that the violence was externally instigated. Maybe from the Maoist elements in their central trade union office," replied Chandy as they sat under a tree in the front yard of the hospital.

"If they were outsiders how could they have picked Asokan as the target? Why did they attack Leena? The union leaders consider me the most sympathetic of the management. It just doesn't make any sense," said Jose.

"The police pursued the same angle. They now believe that the union headquarters in Andhra Pradesh could have dispatched the hit squad. But they still think there is some inside involvement from our labor leaders. Someone must have given them directions to Asokan's house. These are the only people they have in custody anyway."

"I detest police brutality. I hope they don't use harsh third-degree methods against innocents."

"The police theory is that the attack on Kochamma was not pre-planned. The thugs must have seen Kochamma arrive alone. Or they may have wanted to avenge the dishonor of their women by attacking an upper-class woman. I don't know."

"I wish I had been at the estate and had not gone to Bombay. This tragedy would not have happened in our lives. My heart grieves for Leena. I don't know what they did to her ..." Jose's voice faltered.

"Don't punish yourself. You could not have known all this was going to happen. We cannot see the future. Only God can," replied Chandy.

"I am struggling with my faith right now. Not that I had much to start with after the death of my parents. Where did they cremate Asokan?"

"His relatives came and took his body away in a van from the mortuary at Kottayam. The police had sent the body for post-mortem. The company made an ex gratia payment to Asokan's parents while the provident fund and insurance claims are being processed. The parents were disgraced by the stories in the papers about Asokan's womanizing."

"What a horrible way to die! Chopped to pieces with grass cutting sickles. I wish he had not ignored our advice," said Jose.

"Yes, I agree. May I tell you something? Jose, you need to forgive them. You will cause yourself harm otherwise," suggested Chandy.

"How can I forgive, Chandy? Leena would not hurt a fly. And they attacked her in the middle of the night like animals. A whole gang of them wielding blood-stained machetes and sickles. Can you imagine the terror she must have felt? God only knows what they did to her. And you want me to forgive?"

"It may sound stupid. But forgiving will release you. It will take the weight off you. Let it go."

"No, I cannot think straight right now. I can only think of Leena. I must take care of her."

***

Jose was pleasantly surprised when the doctor cleared Leena's release from the hospital the following week.

"Leena has made an astonishing recovery. But she will need to be on medication for quite some time. Maybe for the rest of her life. But what she will need most is love and support. You are the best – and I think only – one to provide that. It is because of your love for each other that she recovered so quickly. But she cannot go back to the estate in Munnar. Under no circumstances! She will almost certainly suffer a serious relapse. Never make any references to the night of the incident. She will talk about it when she is ready – if she wants to. But do not ask her about what happened that night," the doctor advised Jose.

"One other thing," the doctor added. "Never leave her alone at night – at least for some time."

There seemed to be no other option for Jose than to resign from his job at the tea estate and look for a new one elsewhere. But since it would have been impossible to find another job in Kerala, the reasonable thing to do seemed to be to join the horde of educated unemployed headed to the 'Gulf'. Leena's parents repeated their appeals in their phone calls to come to Kuwait. Jose was willing to do anything for Leena's sake.

When there seemed to be no means of escape, the company threw him an unexpected lifeline. The personnel manager came to see Leena and delivered the offer in person to Jose.

"The company recognizes your talents and your loyalty, Jose. You have done an outstanding job so far and we are confident you will continue in the same manner and climb up the corporate ladder. What happened was most unfortunate. It was fate. You had no control over it. We had no control over it. We have been considering how to retain you and we have come up with a solution which we hope you will accept. We have a marketing manager's position at our head office in Kottayam. It is equivalent to your current position and in the same grade so you will receive the same salary. The only difficulty is that we do not have any quarters in the town. You will have to rent your own accommodation."

Jose, with Leena's concurrence, readily accepted the offer. He wondered if the company had made the offer as compensation for its failure to provide security on its premises.

The administration department at the head office had no difficulty in locating rented accommodation the same afternoon and the furniture and personal goods from the estate quarters were transported by truck to the rented house the next day at Jose's request. Leena was released from the hospital once the rented house was ready for occupation. The following Monday Jose was at his new desk at the head office.

Leena never went back to the estate. Jose made a business visit to the estate months later but he could not bring himself to even look at their old dwelling, let alone enter it.

When they were out of the hospital and alone together in their new home, the events of the preceding two weeks seemed like a bad dream. Jose and Leena missed the comfort of their large bungalow on the estate that they had renovated with Carl's help and made their own. The crotchety old landlady of their rented house, who lived in a small house in the same compound, did not make the transition easier.

"Carl must have returned to Stockholm by now," said Leena.

"Yes, you are right. We can expect to get a letter from him next week. I am surprised we didn't get any letter from Carl from Madras. He has never done that before," replied Jose.

"Did you tell him about our move to Kottayam?"

"No, but I sent him a short letter from the hospital. That was before we accepted the transfer. I sent that letter to Kannan's address in Madras."

***

Jose was overjoyed to find an envelope with Carl's handwriting the next day in the small bundle of personal mail that had been forwarded from the Munnar office. Carl's letter was postmarked the day after his arrival in Madras. The brief note scribbled on hotel stationery mentioned his safe arrival and thanked Jose and Leena for the wonderful time he had in their company in Kerala. The note ended, as Carl's letters always did, *'Love, Carl'*. Jose realized that this was obviously written before Carl received the letter he had written about Leena's condition and the incident. Assuming that Carl would not have received his previous letter before he returned to Stockholm, Jose wrote a longer letter explaining all that had happened since they had parted at Cochin airport and also included details of their rented house and the new phone numbers at work and at home in Kottayam. He mailed the letter to Carl's Jungfrugatan address.

***

Jose threw himself into the new role and settled quickly into the routine of the new office. He made sure he phoned Leena every other hour to be certain that she was all right and he went home for lunch every day to spend an hour with her. He liked the new office and the new colleagues but at times he missed the bucolic life on the estate. Leena, for her part, enjoyed the comforts that living in town offered. But what she did not like one bit was the constant interference from the landlady.

Jose had good news when he came home that evening. "We got a big order today and I got a small bonus," he told Leena. He was about to add that this order was from Russia and that it was the result of his Bombay trip but he kept that to himself.

Leena was happy with the news of Jose's success and she quickly prepared special snacks for their evening tea.

"I wish we had a house of our own," she said wistfully while sipping tea.

Jose wanted more than anything else to bring back stability and normalcy in Leena's life.

"I will make inquiries, Leena," he promised. "If there is a house we can afford, we will buy it."

"And then when we have our own house, we will adopt a child. No, let us adopt two. The first one will be a girl. And the second one, a boy," said Leena with a serene smile.

"I love you, Leena" Jose said.

"You and your foreign ways!" she said making a face.

*** 

The postman delivered the mail every morning and the inter-office dispatch from the estate arrived in the afternoon. Jose would eagerly search both for any communication from Carl. After two weeks in the Kottayam office, Jose began to worry about the lack of letters from Carl. He was certain that Carl would not hesitate to call from Stockholm to inquire about Leena's condition. Jose phoned the estate office in Munnar every morning to make sure that there were no letters lying overlooked and to also confirm that there had been no calls for him.

Finally, Jose decided to call Carl in Stockholm. He had never used the new direct dialing system for international calls and was pleasantly surprised when the call went through on the first attempt. But his happiness was short-lived. Nobody answered the call. The phone just kept on ringing. Jose tried a second time to make sure he had not dialed a wrong number, but met with the same result.

That afternoon when he saw the yellow postcard with the unfamiliar handwriting he didn't give it another thought. He had received many such postcards in the past from unfamiliar ham radio operators. The writing looked more Tamil than English. When he turned over the card to read what was scribbled on the other side, he almost fell out of his chair in shock. He read and re-read the card in stunned disbelief.

*Dear Mr. Jose,*

*My name is Kannan. I am Carl's friend in Madras.*

*I am sorry to inform you that Carl died three days ago. I informed the Sweden Embassy in Delhi. Their honorary consul in Madras was present for the cremation. The cremation was last Sunday.*

*Your friend,*

*Kannan*

Jose turned the card over to look at the postmark. The card had taken four days to reach Kottayam from Madras. This meant that his friend Carl had died a full week earlier and he had not known.

Jose was crushed. This blow, coming as it did after the dastardly attack on Leena and the forced relocation and job change, seemed too heavy to bear. The finality of death, the fact that he would never again talk with his friend, the near certainty that Carl died a lonely death, made Jose feel completely powerless. For the first time in his life, he felt defeated. Circumstances had overwhelmed him. He had lost.

He wondered how Leena would take the news. For a while, he toyed with the idea of hiding this news from her. But he decided that there was enough deception in his life already. He decided to let Leena know of Carl's passing right away. Jose took the rest of the day off pleading a headache and went home.

When Jose told Leena the news of Carl's passing, she hugged him as she wept. There was no wailing, no words. Just the tears that seemed to flow unending. Jose held Leena close till the tears stopped.

"Carl was a good man," she said quietly as she wiped her face with the end of her sari.

A thousand questions haunted Jose. How did Carl die? Was it a heart attack? Was it an accident? Was it foul play? What were Carl's last moments like? Did he die peacefully? Were his relatives informed?

Jose could not rest till be found the answers to these questions.

He sent a reply-paid telegram to Kannan asking for a contact number.

Although he waited all night for the reply it only came next morning while he was in the office. Jose immediately dialed the Madras number in the reply telegram. It was a government office and it took a while for Kannan to come on the line. When he did, Jose plied him with all the questions he could think of. Their conversation was in broken English interspersed with Tamil and Malayalam words.

Jose related what he had pieced together to Leena over lunch.

"Carl was in an accident. Kannan had hired an *autorickshaw* for Carl for the duration of his stay. It appears the driver was known to Carl from a previous trip."

"Was it a collision?" interrupted Leena.

"No, it seems the driver tried to get out of a traffic jam by cutting a corner. It appears the three-wheeler toppled over and fell on its side when one of its rear wheels climbed over the edge of the sidewalk. Carl must have been sitting off-center for the vehicle to tip over. I'm just guessing. Anyway, Carl had a deep gash in his left leg and was in shock. The driver of the *autorickshaw* had more severe injuries. His arm was broken is two places and several ribs were broken as well. They were both moved to the nearest government hospital in a passing private car. By the time the police arrived, Carl's money, watch, and pen had been stolen. The police found the passport and the hotel keys and they got in touch with the hotel. The hotel, in turn, contacted Kannan who had made the booking on Carl's behalf."

"A government hospital is the worst place to be in. It is a death-trap!" Leena despondently.

"Kannan had the good sense to move Carl to a small private hospital. By then Carl had lost a lot of blood. At Carl's request Kannan also called up the Swedish Embassy in New Delhi and informed them of Carl's accident."

"Then what happened?" Leena asked impatiently.

"It seems Carl's condition stabilized during the night. In the morning, the doctors discovered that the wound on his leg had some complications because of his diabetes. They gave him some injections and his condition worsened thereafter. Meanwhile on the instructions of the Swedish Embassy in Delhi, their honorary consul in Madras came to check on Carl's condition. It seems the plan was to move to him to a better hospital in Madras or airlift to Delhi or even back to Sweden. But Carl's condition had deteriorated by then. It worsened further and he moved in and out of consciousness. He had a massive heart attack and died before midnight."

"What a terrible way to die – in a foreign country, surrounded by strangers and so-called doctors who are no better than quacks." The tears were flowing as Leena mourned for Carl.

Jose rose and went to her side. "Don't cry. We cannot change the past. We helped Carl when he was with us. Let us just remember the good times we had with him. He is gone now and there is nothing we can do."

But Jose was not completely satisfied with Kannan's story. When he got back to the office he typed out a letter to the Swedish Embassy in New Delhi identifying himself as Carl's friend and asking for information on Carl's passing.

***

A few days later, one of the employees at Jose's office received a tip-off from a land agent. There was a house for sale on the edge of town, past the Thirunakkara temple and on the way to the boat jetty where the boats that plied the backwaters docked.

Leena took an immediate liking to the old house. She loved the pebbled courtyard and the small *verandahs* on the front and two sides of the house. The tall jackfruit tree in the corner of the compound reminded her of the jackfruit tree behind their bungalow in the Munnar estate. There were also five coconut trees along the perimeter of the yard.

"There is enough space for a small vegetable garden also," whispered Leena.

The house had a dilapidated look. The rose bushes had not been pruned in a long while and the jasmine vines hung in disarray from the eaves of the house. The house had lain uninhabited for almost two years. The parents had died and the children who were overseas had no intention of returning.

On their way home in the car, Jose said what he thought of the house.

"It will need a lot of work. All the walls need plastering. Even the roof tiles will have to be changed."

"You need to look beyond the present condition. Look at the renovation as an opportunity. We can make it just the way we want. If the house were in good condition, we would not have had that freedom."

"You always surprise me with your wisdom," Jose replied with a happy smile. He was secretly pleased that Leena's enthusiasm was back and she was thinking logically.

Later at night, after they had finished their dinner, Jose hugged Leena and told her, "If we have enough money to meet the asking price we will take it."

Leena's happiness was evident when she gave a spontaneous shout of glee and threw her arms around Jose.

\*\*\*

The next day Jose sent the peon out to get the bank passbooks updated. He then called the employee who had brought word of the house and told him that if the price was right he would buy it. When the peon brought the updated bank passbooks back, Jose added up the bank balances and the fixed deposits. The total added up to a little under seven hundred thousand rupees or seven *lakhs,* in Indian parlance. All he had to do now was wait with fingers crossed for the selling price.

He then immersed himself in the work that had piled up. At lunch, he told Leena of the money that they had available and added, "Let's hope the sellers will ask for a price within the money we have."

Leena was downcast. "I wish your uncle hadn't stolen our money. I don't think the price will be so low. Even if it were, where is the money for the renovation?"

Jose had forgotten about the repairs that were needed. "How did I overlook that?" he asked aloud in disbelief.

Word of the price demanded by the heirs living in England came in the afternoon. The agent had called the eldest son of the deceased owner in Bristol to confirm the price. The price demanded was fifteen *lakhs* or one and a half million rupees. When Jose heard the price, he lost all hope.

Despondently, he called Leena to convey the news. "We cannot afford the house. The owner is asking for eight *lakhs* or eight hundred thousand rupees more than what we have. And, as you rightly pointed out at lunch, we need a good sum of money for the repairs and renovation. Let us give up this dream. What other option do we have?"

"This is very discouraging," Leena said disconsolately. "My heart was set on that run-down house. I am tired of the meddling landlady."

"We will find a suitable house soon. Let us not give up. We will keep looking."

To take her mind off the disappointment, Jose took her out to watch a re-run of *The Sound of Music* that evening.

The next morning at breakfast Leena said, "If Carl were alive he would have helped us. I don't mean as a gift. How much are we short? Eight *lakhs* rupees? Carl would have given us the money as a loan."

"Yes, Carl was a good and generous man," agreed Jose. "But eight *lakhs* is around twenty-five thousand dollars. *That* is a lot of money – even as a loan."

***

Jose was glad to see Chandy when he came to the Kottayam office.

"It is good to see you in person, although we talk on the phone every day," said Chandy.

"Leena will be happier than me! You must come home for lunch with me today. Nothing special – just whatever Leena has cooked."

"I will be happy to do that. I am really glad that Kochamma is all right now and you are working harder than ever. Sorry about the death of your friend in Madras."

"We are both lucky that Leena recovered miraculously fast and I still have a job with the same company. But Carl's death almost shattered us. He was very close to us. We could not do as much for him as he did for us. I will never understand life," Jose said quietly.

"Yes, it is very difficult. But you have overcome all the setbacks."

"It is not easy, Chandy. When I think about all the unexpected things that happened, I feel like Job."

"Jose, I understand. But I came to tell you something in person. We will talk in the car on the way home."

"OK. I hope it is not news of another job change for me," laughed Jose.

"No! Nothing of the sort."

Jose phoned Leena to tell her that Chandy would be joining them for lunch. She was delighted.

When they were in the car at lunchtime, Chandy touched Jose's arm.

"Let us talk here in the car. Not while you are driving. What I have to tell you, is not official. It is just between you and me—and the Lord above. You remember Lonappan, the assist trade union leader?"

"Yes, of course. He was the youngest of the group and the most promising," said Jose.

"They will all be released from jail this weekend. The police could not provide any evidence so far and the judge did not allow further custody. Lonappan wants to meet you," said Chandy looking steadily at Jose.

Jose froze.

"Jose, listen to me. Please. If you saw Lonappan and the others now you will pity them. The police are ruthless. I am certain they had nothing directly to do with the attack on Kochamma. Lonappan wanted me to tell you that he is deeply sorry for all that happened. He wants you to forgive him. He almost cried," Chandy said.

"It is difficult. I have no idea what happened that night. And probably will never know. And what is more, I don't want to know! It's *over*! It's behind me! I don't want to remember that day anymore," Jose was visibly agitated.

"There is still a lot of anger in you, Jose. You are like my brother. I admire you. I want you to succeed in life. Don't let this incident become a stumbling block. I am asking you to forgive them for your sake – not theirs."

Jose sat motionless. When he spoke after a long pause, his voice quavered.

"I have nothing against our labor leaders. I don't think they were part of the gang that attacked. But nonetheless, they must bear moral responsibility for what happened. My feelings are neutral. I have no feelings of revenge against the actual perpetrators. But I see no reason to forgive them either. Let the law take its on course. Why must I forgive them?"

"I am glad you do not have feelings of revenge. That is good. But also, look at it from their side. They have been victimized for generations. They have been treated like dirt. Look at what Asokan did to their young girls. Is it any wonder then that they see this as a class struggle? They also have families like us," pleaded Chandy earnestly.

"My sympathies are with them. Have always been. You know that."

"Then forgive them in your heart. Forgive the criminals too. Let God deal with them."

Jose was quiet. He stared straight ahead through the windshield, hands gripping the steering. Then he covered his face with his hands and his body heaved. When Chandy gently patted his shoulder, Jose pressed his eyes with the balls of his palms and looked up.

"Chandy, I don't know what to say. You are forcing me to confront my own fears. It is probably good for me but right now I don't feel like it. It is too fresh."

"All the more reason to let go. To forgive. Don't punish yourself and Kochamma for the sins and crimes of others," Chandy urged, unwilling to give up.

Jose looked at Chandy for a long minute.

"You just said something very significant."

"I did?" Chandy asked puzzled.

"You just told me not to punish Leena myself for the sins of others. That is very profound."

"That is what the good book says. Revenge is not yours. It is the Lord's," Chandy said.

Jose smiled for the first time since they got into the car. "What you said is really very profound. You opened my eyes. I just realized that the victim unwittingly bears a part of the oppressor's punishment if the victim does not forgive. If I bear a grudge or nurse feelings of revenge, I am punishing myself."

"You have stated it much better than I did," said Chandy.

"You know what? Leena has not talked about that night. I don't know if she ever will. Why should I hold on to it? If I did, it might hurt Leena and me at some point in the future. You are right. I am going to let go. I am going to forgive our leaders. I will meet Lonappan and the others too." Jose's lips quivered as he strove to hold his emotions in check. "I forgive the attackers also," he added with some effort.

Jose started the car. Neither of them said a word for some time.

When they are halfway to the house, Chandy turned to look at Jose with a glint in his eye.

"Did you realize the significance of what just happened? An Orthodox and a Pentecostal came to an agreement on a vexing theological issue!"

They both laughed.

The lunch was a simple meal of rice, *moru, avial,* and pepper-fried mackerel. Leena did not sit down with them for the meal but bustled about serving Chandy and Jose.

Leena appeared to have forgotten about the disappointment of the house deal as she chatted away happily with Chandy. Jose was happy just watching Leena talk animatedly with Chandy.

*** 

The reply from the Embassy of Sweden in New Delhi arrived faster than Jose had expected.

The letter was polite and matter of fact. The signatory stated that she was providing the information only because Jose's name was on the list of friends to whom information concerning Carl's passing could be released. The official confirmed that Carl had died of a heart attack. She confirmed that the honorary consul was present at the cremation and that Carl's possessions of any value had been sent to the sole executors of Carl's will in Sweden. Clothes and toilet articles, the letter said, had been given to Kannan who had made arrangements for the cremation.

*** 

Jose and Leena viewed other houses put up for sale but the prices were even higher. It looked as if they would have to settle for a house far out of town.

"We will have to look at smaller towns around Kottayam. Or, since there are no flats here in our town, we will have to settle for a flat in a bigger city like Cochin," Jose suggested.

"I hate living in a flat. Not even a small garden of our own! And all those neighbors uncomfortably close! No! We cannot have a house too far from this town. I would be scared to live alone if you are working late or traveling. Renting is our only option," Leena said resignedly.

Jose sighed. "If only that crooked uncle of mine had not stolen our money we could have bought a small house right here in Kottayam."

At the office, though, Jose went from strength to strength. He was clever enough to figure out that the firm in Vladikavkaz was reselling the tea in the former Soviet republics in the region. Through trade channels, Jose collected information of tea merchants in Armenia, Georgia, Azerbaijan, Kazakhstan, and Uzbekistan. The new orders he secured got him a big bonus and a further rise in salary.

"I think we should go on a vacation," suggested Jose.

"I would love to do that but no. We need to save as much money as we can for a house of our own. We will not adopt a child as long as we live in a rented house," Leena was adamant.

***

Ten days later, on a Saturday morning, Jose was at home watching the cricket test match between India and England on the television when the phone rang. It was the guard from the office.

"Sir, the postman is here with an express foreign letter for you. He says it requires your signature and it has to be delivered immediately," the guard said.

"Ask the relief guard to fetch an *autorickshaw* and send the postman to my house. I will pay the driver when he gets here."

About fifteen minutes later the postman was at their door. Jose paid the *autorickshaw* driver first and then signed the postal receipt and gave the postman a small tip for his troubles. He looked at the thick envelope in his hands. On the front of the airmail envelope, to the left of the row of Swedish stamps, the words '*Rekommandé*' was stamped in bold letters. The sender was P.E. Banken, Stockholm.

Unable to restrain his curiosity, Jose tore open the envelope to find a letter, a legal-looking document, and a smaller sealed envelope. He read the letter:

*"We, the undersigned bank, are appointed as executor of the Will of the estate of Alain Carlson, who died on ...*

*For your information, we herewith send you a copy of the Will left by the deceased as well as a translation of the document into English ..."*

Instead of opening the smaller sealed envelope, Jose chose to look at the will first. After the customary preface the will stated:

*"On my decease, no announcement of my death shall appear in the newspapers, nor shall a specific funeral ceremony be held. My remains shall be cremated and my ashes be spread by the wind in a garden of remembrance ..."*

As Jose's eyes wandered further down the document he let out an involuntary gasp of surprise when he saw his name under the section titled 'Inheritors'. Carl had left him and Leena twenty-five per cent of his estate; the same share as three other Indians, one of whom was Kannan.

Hearing Jose's exclamation of surprise, Leena came to the front room asking, "What is it Jose? Who is the letter from?"

When Jose held out Carl's will and wordlessly pointed to their names, it was Leena's turn to be astonished. She covered her mouth to muffle her shriek of astonishment and disbelief.

Jose turned to the last page of the will. He could not hide his astonishment when he looked at the date.

"What is it, Jose?" asked Leena tugging at his arm.

"I think I know when Carl revised his will. It is all falling into place now. He amended the will when I was with him in Stockholm on my second visit last year. I still remember the morning he went to the bank. It took him almost the entire day. I have no doubt that he added our names as beneficiaries then," said Jose. He remembered the Dorothy L. Sayers' mystery, and the realization of how much he loved Carl, and his telling him so.

"It is a long story. I will tell you later. He didn't tell me he was going to add us to his will. It never even crossed my mind. He has two children of his own and relatives in America. Who would have thought he would leave us a quarter of his estate?"

While Leena continued to read the will, Jose opened the second envelope. It contained another letter from the bank.

*'In compliance with the directions of Alain Carlson (the deceased) contained in the Will and Last Testament to provide to all the beneficiaries a minimum of $25,000 as advance immediately on his demise, we the Administrators of the deceased's estate and the Executors of the deceased's Last Will and Testament, enclose herewith a cheque for $25,000.- as an advance payment against your share of the estate of the deceased ...'*

With Leena watching, Jose turned the letter over to find the attached check for twenty-five thousand dollars.

"How much will this be in our money, Jose?" asked Leena in a small voice.

"Approximately eight *lakhs* in Indian rupees give or take a few thousand," replied Jose.

Realization struck them both at the same time.

"That is the exact amount we need to buy the house!" Leena shouted, her eyes widening in astonishment.

Jose was completely bewildered. The letter and the check fell from his hands.

Leena hugged him tight. "We can have our own house! We can adopt children! It is almost as if Carl is still alive and is helping us," she whispered in his ear ecstatically.

Jose stooped to pick up the fallen letter and check.

"Leena, I met Carl only four times in my life. And he leaves me a fourth of his estate. This is unbelievable! What does this mean? How can this be? What is the meaning of love?" asked a bewildered Jose.

Leena held Jose by his shoulders and looked him straight in the eye.

"I think I now know what love is." She pulled him into her arms and held him tight. "I have never said this to anyone before. And I have mocked you for saying it. But I am going to say it now." She put her lips close to his ear and whispered, "I love you."

"I love you too, Leena," Jose whispered back. Then he added, "Carl, if you can hear me ... wherever you may be now ... I will gladly forego the inheritance you left me and all the earthly possessions I have, for the joy of having you back with us alive and well."

And then the dam broke.

The tears flowed unchecked down Jose's face and his chest heaved with sobs as he hugged Leena for dear life.

# Glossary

| | |
|---|---|
| Adivasi | generic name for aboriginal people of India |
| appam | a South Indian breakfast food made of rice |
| autorickshaw | three-wheeled motorized transport for hire |
| avial | a green vegetable curry of Kerala, India |
| Ayurveda | the traditional Indian system of medicine |
| beedi | cheap cigarette of tobacco rolled in leaves |
| biryani | seasoned rice with meat or vegetables |
| bungalow | single-story house (Indian subcontinent) |
| chapati | flat, unleavened bread cooked on a skillet |
| dal | a curry of lentils; part of most Indian meals |
| dhanyavad | 'thank you' in several North Indian languages |
| dolma | grape-leaf rolls with meat or vegetables |
| ghat | hilly or mountainous terrain (India) |
| goonda | thug or hoodlum |
| gulab jamun | a dessert of flour, milk, and sugar syrup |
| idli | fluffy, steamed rice-cakes of South India |
| imam bayaldi | eggplant with onion, garlic, and tomato |
| jalebi | a syrupy Indian dessert of fried batter |
| khorovats | barbecued meat or vegetables (Armenia) |
| kleftiko | lamb baked in a pit oven (Greece/Cyprus) |
| kochamma | a term of respect for a lady in Malayalam |
| korma | a spicy Indian curry of meat or vegetables |
| kurta | men's collarless, long-sleeved top |
| lakh | 1 lakh = 100,000 / 1 million = 10 lakhs |
| lavash | oven-baked, thin, flat bread of Armenia |
| Malayali | a native of Kerala Malayalam language |
| maya | the illusion of the real world (Hindu) |

| | |
|---|---|
| mridangam | a double-headed South Indian drum |
| moilee | fish curry with coconut milk (Kerala) |
| moru | a thin curry from buttermilk (South India) |
| mundu | men's white sarong (South India) |
| namaste | A greeting of welcome in Indian languages |
| naan | Indian flat bread baked in a *tandoor* oven |
| pappadam | a deep-fried crispy cracker eaten with rice |
| parippu curry | a South Indian dish of lentils |
| sambar | a spicy, red vegetable curry with lentils |
| sar | the native equivalent of 'Sir' |
| sayip | the deferential reference to a white man |
| stifado | meat stew (Greece/Cyprus) |
| tandoori | an adjective for food cooked in a clay oven |
| tjvjik | an Armenian dish of chicken gizzards |
| thoran | steamed vegetables with grated coconut |
| verandah | a covered patio of a house at ground level |

The author welcomes comments at:
*aa-books@outlook.com*

For more information about the author's books:
*www.abiealexander.com*